The Truth According to Blue

The Truth According to Blue

EVE YOHALEM

LITTLE, BROWN AND COMPANY
New York Boston

Little, Brown and Company
Hachette Book Group
1290 Avenue of the Americas, New York, NY 10104
Visit us at LBYR.com

First Edition: May 2020

Little, Brown and Company is a division of Hachette Book Group, Inc. The Little, Brown name and logo are trademarks of Hachette Book Group, Inc.

The publisher is not responsible for websites (or their content) that are not owned by the publisher.

Library of Congress Cataloging-in-Publication Data
Names: Yohalem, Eve, author.
Title: The truth according to Blue / Eve Yohalem.
Description: First edition. | New York : Little, Brown and Company, 2020. | Audience: Ages 8–12. | Summary: "Thirteen-year-old Blue Broen teams up with her diabetic-alert dog and the spoiled daughter of a vacationing movie star on a treasure hunt to find her family's ancestral fortune."—Provided by publisher.
Identifiers: LCCN 2019030782 | ISBN 9780316424370 (hardcover) | ISBN 9780316424400 (ebook) | ISBN 9780316424394
Subjects: CYAC: Buried treasure—Fiction. | Diabetes—Fiction. | Celebrities—Fiction. | Working dogs—Fiction. | German shepherd dog—Fiction. | Dogs—Fiction.
Classification: LCC PZ7.Y7585 Tru 2020 | DDC [Fic]—dc23
LC record available at https://lccn.loc.gov/2019030782

ISBNs: 978-0-316-42437-0 (hardcover), 978-0-316-42440-0 (ebook)

Printed in the United States of America

LSC-C

10 9 8 7 6 5 4 3 2 1

For Jen

CHAPTER ONE

True Fact: Hundreds of years ago, a wooden ship
with square sails and a cargo of gold sank near a
tiny island off New York. It's still there today.
(From <u>True Facts</u>, a journal by Blue Broen)

A long tongue licked my cheek. I smooshed my face into
my pillow, simultaneously drying the slime and hiding
from another lick. *Foiled.* The long tongue swiped my ear.

"Go away, Otis. School's out."

But Otis didn't go away. I knew because I could feel
him panting on my neck.

I rolled over and patted the blanket, which is my way
of hitting the snooze button, and eighty pounds of German
shepherd catapulted onto the bed. Otis draped his entire self
across me, his chin strategically positioned on my shoulder
so I could scratch behind his ears with both hands.

"Five more minutes...," I mumbled.

I finger-combed Otis's super-soft ear fur, lost in the orange glow of the insides of my eyelids and the dream I'd been having about an octopus that couldn't hide because its ink was gold instead of black and—

Poof! Morning brain fog evaporated. I bolted upright and four hairy dog limbs scrambled to the floor.

"The hunt, Otis! The hunt begins today!"

Otis barked.

"Breakfast!"

Wake-up mission accomplished, Otis retrieved the little pouch of diabetes supplies from my desk and dropped it on my lap before trotting out of the room. By the time I finished testing my blood sugar and entering the number of carbs I was about to eat into my pump so it would know how much insulin to give me, Otis was back, carrying a low-carb bagel with cream cheese and a mini milk carton in the basket that my mom leaves for us in the mornings. Otis and I are big fans of breakfast in bed.

I unscrewed the bagel top and offered Otis a piece, which he refused.

"Go on," I said. "You love bagels."

Otis waited.

"Fine."

I scooped a big glob of cream cheese off my side and spread it on his so he'd have double. He gulped it down whole.

2

"Get excited, Oats Magoats. We're about to change the course of history, you and me."

Otis was already excited. I could tell by the thwack of his tail and the lift of his nose. And it wasn't just because today was the first day of vacation. This summer we had big plans.

This summer, we were going treasure hunting.

I scarfed down the rest of the bagel as fast as I could.

"Clothes, please, Otis. Underwear, T-shirt, shorts."

Otis went to my closet, pulled what I was going to wear today off the shelves, and brought the whole clump back to me. Yes, my dog picks my outfits for me. It's not that I'm lazy or anything; it's that Otis loves having a job to do. Plus, okay, I'm kind of lazy, especially in the mornings. But as long as I don't care about always having to wear whichever clothes are on top of the stacks, the system works for both of us.

Dressed, bagel scarfed, and ready to go, we headed downstairs. I could smell peonies—Mom's second-favorite flower—before I got to the kitchen. While they're in season she puts vases of them everywhere: on the counter, the table, even on top of the fridge. I grabbed the supplies I needed from various drawers and stuffed them into a backpack: water bottle for me, water dish for Otis, phone for me, bone for Otis, notebook, pen, sunscreen, diabetes kit, underwater-view bucket.

3

"Towel, Otis."

Otis loped off to the laundry / Mom's gardening supply / Dad's tool / my old baby gear room.

"Why do you need a towel?" Mom said, coming in while I was emptying a box of individually wrapped packs of cashews into my bag. She opened the freezer and took out a chilled water bottle, her "outdoor AC."

"Science project. Why are you still home?"

Summer is my parents' busy season, and they're usually out of the house by seven in the morning, seven days a week. My dad builds houses, and my mom is a gardener. But because we live in Sag Harbor, which is part of the Hamptons (yes, *those* Hamptons, the New York beach resorts where rich people and celebrities go for summer vacations but also where regular families like mine live and have jobs and go to school), my dad is a "general contractor" and my mom is a "landscape designer."

The reason I had homework even though it was summer was because I got an Incomplete in school this year and had to do a makeup project. Turns out when you read *The Treasure Hunter's Bible* and *Scouring the Seas* instead of filling out Blah Blah Weather Data worksheets, it's hard to pass Earth Science. My project involved collecting water samples all around the harbor to show how the ocean affects the weather. Or possibly how the weather affects the ocean, I couldn't remember which. My parents knew about the makeup project, which worked as an excellent cover-up, because they *didn't* know about the treasure hunt. Nobody—*especially* my parents— knew about the hunt except Otis and my best friend, Nora.

Nora. Who was leaving tomorrow for seven weeks at theater camp. Which I was trying very hard not to think about.

Mom grabbed an apple from a bowl on the counter and stuck it in her tote bag. "We're going to Edward Buttersby's house, remember? For the planning meeting?"

Aha. Now I understood the floaty tunic-y thing Mom had on over her faded work jeans and T-shirt and why she had sent Otis to wake me up when I didn't have school. And, yes, she meant *that* Edward Buttersby, the movie star, a.k.a. Command Pilot Jasper Jones from *Space Voyager*. He also happened to be this year's host for the annual Cure Juvenile Diabetes Foundation fund-raiser. Since I was the poster child (literally) for the local CJDF chapter, I had to go to the party and give a speech.

You might think it would be super exciting to hang out with someone like Edward Buttersby at his house, but I've been doing these fund-raisers for a long time, and I've learned otherwise.

"That meeting's not for another week," I insisted, willing it to be true.

Otis dropped a beach towel at my feet, and I started cramming it into the backpack.

"It's this morning." Mom sighed. "I told you about it a week ago."

It's possible she was right about that. I crammed faster so I could make my escape.

"I'm sorry. I can't go. I have plans."

Mom checked her watch. "Get in the truck, Blue."

"You don't need me there anyway. Why do I have to go?"

"You're thirteen. Thirteen is plenty old enough to get more involved in community service, which is what this is."

I gave up on the towel and swung the backpack over my shoulder. "Mom, my science project is important. It's *homework*."

"Get in the truck, Blue." Mom put her hand on the small of my back and gently steered me toward the front door.

"Otis hates boring meetings. He'll throw up."

"Get in the truck, Blue." She grabbed her floppy sun hat from the hall table.

"But—"

"Come, Otis...," Mom said.

We got in the truck.

CHAPTER TWO

True Fact: Famous people, when you meet them in person, turn out one of two ways: Either they're completely normal, like they could be someone's mom or dad, or they're completely weird and full of themselves, and you're glad they can't remember your name and you'll never see them again after the party.

Edward Buttersby had rented a house in East Hampton for the summer. Or more like he'd rented an entire estate. From the road all we could see was a mile-high hedge (privet, according to Mom) that stretched across a property at least three times as wide as any other property on the street, and a driveway so long you couldn't see the end of it.

"Three biscuits says he's a weirdo," I whispered into Otis's ear. I was sitting in the passenger seat, and Otis was in his favorite spot in the middle of the back seat, where he could see out the front and breathe on my neck at the same time.

"I heard that," Mom said.

Her pickup truck crunched along the driveway, trailing mud on the pearly white pebbles.

"Dramatic dogwoods," she said.

"Astounding azaleas," I said.

"*Hex*cellent hydrangeas."

"Such an elegant English plane," I said.

"You knew that was an English plane tree?"

"Mom, please. I'm your daughter."

And then we were there. At the circular part of the driveway in front of what looked more like a beach club than a private house. It had gray shingles and white shutters and was huge. Humongously so. Ancient weeping willows drooped across the front lawn, making shaggy-dog shadows on weed-free grass.

Mom rang the bell, and the three of us waited for someone to answer it.

"Please don't do anything embarrassing," I said.

"What are you talking about?" Mom said.

"When you meet Edward Buttersby. Please don't do that thing where your voice gets really high."

Before *Space Voyager*, Edward Buttersby starred in a miniseries based on one of those nineteenth-century

English romance novels, which Mom may have watched two or ten or a hundred times.

"I have no idea what you mean," Mom said, smoothing her hair in the reflection of the window next to the front door. "Just make sure *you* don't do anything embarrassing either."

"When have *I* ever done anything embarrassing?" I protested.

Mom smiled and smoothed my hair. "Never," she said.

The door swung open. Instead of Edward Buttersby, it was my friend Robin's mom, wearing a white chef's uniform.

"Hey, Mrs. Alvarado, how are you?" I said.

Mom and Mrs. Alvarado kissed hello. Over their shoulders I could see a white floor with a white rug, white walls, and white furniture. I looked down at my fuzzy black dog and pointed to the mat.

"Wipe, Otis," I said.

Otis wiped his paws, and we went inside.

World-famous actor Edward Buttersby emerged from the whiteness. His feet were bare; he had on jeans that were frayed at the bottom and a denim shirt that had one more button undone than any dad I know would wear.

"I'm Ed. You must be Emily and Blue." He stuck out a hand for Mom and then me to shake. "And who's this?"

It felt wrong seeing Command Pilot Jasper Jones out of uniform and wearing a leather necklace with a bead on it. I couldn't decide whether to thank him for saving humanity from mutant alien fungus or tell him that Nora got the same necklace at the surf shop in town.

"Blue?" my mother said.

"Sorry," I said, praying I hadn't been staring, or if I had that no one had noticed. "Otis, meet Mr. Buttersby."

Otis stuck out a paw, which Edward Buttersby shook. Otis has excellent manners.

"He's a diabetic-alert dog," Mom explained in a Minnie Mouse squeak. "He can smell blood sugar that's too high or too low. I hope you don't mind him inside the house. We can always leave him out—"

"No, no," Ed said, leading us into a snowy-white living room with a wall of windows and a view of what everyone calls the most beautiful beach in America. "Jules and I love animals, right, Jules?"

I turned away from the ocean and buried all thoughts of boats and treasure. Lounging on the couch was a supermodel, scrolling on her phone with a piece of long gummy candy hanging out of her mouth. She was so into her phone she didn't hear the question.

"How old are you, Blue?" Ed asked.

"She just finished seventh grade," Mom said.

"My daughter, Jules, just finished seventh grade too," Ed

said. "We got here a couple of days ago, and she doesn't know a soul. This is perfect. Isn't it perfect, Jules?"

Jules, who I guess wasn't a supermodel after all—or maybe she was, if it's possible for middle schoolers to be supermodels—dragged her eyes up from her phone. "Perfect." She held out a fresh piece of dangly candy. "Worm?"

"Jules!" Ed said. "Blue has diabetes, remember? She doesn't eat candy."

Actually, I eat candy every day, but I didn't think Mom would want me to give Ed a blood sugar management lesson two minutes after saying hello.

"Sorry," Jules said, twisting the worm around her finger.

"Hey, why don't you two go hang out while Emily and I work on the boring party stuff," Ed said, like he'd just been struck by the most brilliant idea ever.

There was a long awkward pause while Jules went back to scrolling and I sent my mom a look of misery and she gave me back a look of helplessness and Otis licked the fluffy white rug.

"Jules?" said Ed.

"What? Oh. You wanna go outside or something?" Jules asked me.

I pictured grabbing Otis and making a run for it out the door, down the driveway—and then nine miles home, where I'd collapse from exhaustion and low blood sugar.

"Sure," I said to Jules. "Let's go outside. Come, Otis."

Jules and Otis and I went through one of many sets of sliding doors to a giant deck with an infinity pool that looked out over the ocean. We sat on white lounge chairs under white umbrellas for another long, awkward pause.

This one was even longer and more awkward than the first. It went on and on and on and on and—

"Aren't you supposed to be fat?"

"What?" I said.

"You know. Because you have diabetes. Isn't diabetes a thing that happens to fat people?"

Deep breath.

I get this all the time. Lots of people think you get diabetes because you eat too much sugar or you don't exercise, and if you just lose weight and choke down a bottle of cinnamon every day, it'll go away. Lots of people are wrong.

"It's not like that," I said.

"Oh. Cool." Jules flung her sheet of shiny blond hair over one shoulder. "It's hot. You wanna go swimming?"

It *was* really hot, but I'd have to test and deal with my blood sugar if I wanted to swim. Exercise would bring my sugar down, which would be fine if my blood sugar was already high, but if it was normal or low I'd have to eat something to get my sugar up, and then wait fifteen minutes and check it again to make sure it was in a good range, and then if it wasn't I'd have to eat some more, wait fifteen *more* minutes, and test *again*, which would mean we'd stay here even longer, which would mean waiting even longer to start the hunt. So...

"No thanks. But you go ahead."

I looked down at Otis, who was using my foot as a chin pillow. *Save me*, I mouthed. But Otis just snorted.

Otis and I proceeded to have a totally fantastic and not at all awkward time. He lay under a glass table pretending to be a rug, and I watched Jules do laps in the pool like she was training for the Olympics instead of killing time while her dad made her hang out with me. When Mom and Ed finally came out, it was past noon and I was ready to explode. By the time we got home and had lunch, it'd be too late to take the boat out and do any real work. First day of the treasure hunt, totally wasted.

"How's the water?" Ed said.

"Cold," Jules said, even though she'd been in it by choice for almost an hour. "You forgot to turn on the heat."

"Sorry, kiddo. Blue, you didn't want to swim?"

"I didn't bring my suit."

"Well, you'll have to bring it next time. Or borrow one of Jules's. She's got tons, right, Jules?"

Jules dove down and breaststroked to the deep end without answering. Mom's eyes got big for a split second. Let's just say if I ever ignored my parents like that, they'd

13

never let me go swimming again. Plus, we don't have a pool. Plus, if we did, it wouldn't have heat.

But Ed didn't seem to notice any of it. I guessed this was normal for them, because he was watching Jules swim with a grin so wide it belonged on a World's Proudest Dad mug.

"Hey, Blue, it's really great the way you and Jules have hit it off. Like I said, she doesn't know anyone here, and I bet you've got millions of friends. You wouldn't mind taking Jules with you to the beach or something tomorrow, would you?"

I opened my mouth to tell Ed that I was really sorry but I wasn't going to the beach tomorrow—and probably not any other day—because I had a school project to do and there was no possible way Jules could come with me because it had to be done completely alone (except for Otis, of course).

But before I could get a word out, Mom cut in and said, "What a great idea, Ed. Blue would love to take Jules to the beach tomorrow."

Blue would not *love to take Jules to the beach tomorrow! I need to start treasure hunting tomorrow!* But I couldn't say that to Mom, even if Ed and Jules hadn't been standing in front of us.

Back in the truck, Mom turned up the volume on "I Feel the Earth Move" by Carole King, which she calls her "jam."

"How could you do that to me!" I yelled over the music. "Jules is totally obnoxious—Otis, get your tongue out of my ear; you owe me three biscuits! I one hundred percent refuse to take her to the beach. I've already wasted a whole morning of my life; I'm not wasting another minute on some rich movie star's spoiled kid."

Mom looked over at me while she was driving. I hate it when she does that.

"Ed pledged half a million dollars to the Cure Juvenile Diabetes Foundation, and he's inviting two hundred people to the party and bringing in a camera crew to film the event."

Game over. Nothing I could say would change Mom's mind, not when all that money and all those people could maybe possibly help find a cure for diabetes. Which I understood, and even agreed with. But it does feel sometimes like diabetes sucks the fun out of every single thing I ever want to do.

I looked away from Mom and stared out the window. "Fine. I'll go with Jules tomorrow, but that's it. I'm not babysitting her the whole summer."

"Deal," Mom said.

CHAPTER THREE

True Fact: Best friends are called "best" for a reason.
(TF supplied by a throw pillow in the sale bin at Kmart.)

As if the morning hadn't been bad enough, that night was
Nora's last night home before leaving for theater camp.
This would be our first summer apart since we met in
kindergarten. No biking to the wildlife sanctuary, no
bonfires and s'mores on the beach, no epic rainy-day TV
marathons. We decided to go to our happy place.

Island Bowl has been around forever. My grandparents
bowled there, my parents bowled there, my friends and
I bowl there. Outside, the green, yellow, and orange ISLAND
BOWL sign was missing its *B*. Inside wafted the sounds of
pop hits from the fifties and the aroma of sixty years of foot
odor and onion rings.

Nora, Otis, and I were in lane twelve, which has been
Otis's favorite ever since he spotted a mouse running

along the wall. That was two years ago, but Otis is an optimist—he's still on the alert for another. Island Bowl doesn't allow animals, but since Otis is a service dog, he gets to go everywhere I go.

Nora eyed the four pins standing at the end of the lane, blew on her lucky green ball, and—

"Inspiration break!" She spun around to face me and Otis at the scoring desk. "What if we just take however many points we need depending on how we're *feeling* instead of how many pins we knock down?"

Nora is a big believer in finding new ways to express herself. But sadness-based scoring wasn't going to make me feel any better about us being apart for seven weeks. I forced a smile. "Go for it," I said. "But I think I'll stick to the usual methods."

"As you wish." She swung the ball between her legs granny-style and let it go. *Spare.*

Back in elementary school, Nora and I used to play for the Gutter Girls, the Island Bowl youth league team that won the state championship three years straight. Let's just say granny-style wasn't always Nora's bowling technique.

She stepped carefully over Otis, who was at his mouse-duty station on the floor between the desk and the wall, to slide in next to me. "I'm feeling pretty good right now, so I don't need the whole ten points. Just give me three."

I marked Nora's score on the score sheet and went to the ball return for my yellow nine-pounder. Lined it up, released, and...

"Another strike for Blue!" Nora cheered.

She swiveled to face Otis and picked up his paws to make him dance with her. Otis tolerated the indignity because he loves Nora. "Phoebe and Sophia asked if we wanted to hang out tonight, but I told them we were having Special Blue and Nora Time," she said to me.

Last fall Nora got a part in the middle school musical and "discovered the theater." For three months she had rehearsals every day after school and sometimes even on weekends. When it's just us, we're still as close as ever, but now Nora has a bunch of new friends to hang out with too. She invites me to do things with them, but whenever I go, I feel weird and awkward, like I'm standing in the wings watching them put on a show. It's been even worse since February, when my grandfather Pop Pop died.

I took my seat at the desk again. "You didn't have to do that," I said, even though I was relieved that she had. "They could have come."

"Well, I *did* want to have Special Blue and Nora Time."

I did too.

We played through the end of the game, both of us

getting sadder and sadder, until Nora finally rolled a gutter ball and said, "Give me a thousand."

She plopped down on the chair next to me. Otis whined softly and put his head in her lap. "What if everyone hates me and I don't make a single friend and then I catch tuberculosis and no one visits me in the infirmary?" she said.

"Not possible," I said. "Anyone who hates you is a moron and you wouldn't want to be friends with them anyway. And if you get tuberculosis, Otis and I will hitchhike to camp and visit you."

Nora kneaded one of Otis's super-soft ears between two fingers. "What if I'm so bad that I don't get cast in a single show and I have to spend the whole time sweeping the floors and shining all the actors' shoes instead?"

"Also not possible. I've seen you act and you're incredible. And I've seen you clean..." I bumped her shoulder with mine. "And you're terrible."

Nora planted her forehead on the desktop, smooshing Otis's head in her lap. Not that he cared. "What if Jules becomes your new best friend, and you forget I ever existed and move to LA and star in a reality TV show?"

I fake-gagged. "*Definitely* not possible. I'm not even going to see her again after tomorrow."

Nora sighed and sat up. "Is she really that bad?"

I pictured Jules ignoring me while she swam laps, Jules ignoring her dad when he tried to talk to her, Jules ignoring *Otis*. "Put it this way," I said, outrage building. "She didn't say a single word to Otis the entire time we were there. She didn't even try to pet him."

Nora's eyes narrowed. *"A dog-hater,"* she said. "The lowest form of life."

Her phone chirped. Nora checked it. "My mom's on her way. She said to meet her in the parking lot."

But we didn't move. Even Otis stayed perfectly still, like he wanted to freeze time as much as Nora and I did.

Suddenly, Nora said, "Wait, I almost forgot!"

"What?"

"I have a going-away present for you." She lifted Otis's head from her lap and slid out from behind the desk. "Hang on, I know it's here somewhere." She rummaged through her bag, taking out a knotted ball of rainbow yarn (Nora was learning to knit), a half-eaten roll of cherry Life Savers (for me, when my blood sugar gets low), black socks (no clue), and, finally, a decrepit copy of her favorite book, *Whitman's Jolly Limericks*.

Nora flipped through the pages. "It's right...here." She pulled out an envelope. "A new True Fact for your journal."

I've been keeping a True Facts journal since I was nine, which was around the same time I started understanding diabetes. I don't mean understanding all the day-to-day stuff—I'd been dealing with the highs and lows and everything that went with them since I got diagnosed when I was two. I mean the other stuff. Like how I was the only kid I knew who had to have her parents come on every school field trip, or who had to miss the third-grade triathlon to prick her finger and drink juice in the nurse's office, or who had never been on a sleepover at someone else's house.

I'd stay awake half the night worrying about how there was no cure for diabetes, which meant that I was going to have this disease for the rest of my life. My parents tried to help, but nothing made any difference until one day Mom finally said, "Blue, feelings and facts are both important, but they're not the same thing. You feel sad because you *may* go blind one day, but the *fact* is, you're not blind today. Try to stick to the facts."

After that, instead of worrying about what was going to happen in the future, I'd stay up making lists in my head of all the facts that were true today: *True Fact: I've never had a stroke. True Fact: My kidneys work. True Fact: I don't have any sores on my body that won't heal.* Then I started writing down my True Facts, and after that I started sleeping better.

I got up and took the envelope from Nora. Inside was a square of pale blue paper that Nora had illustrated with

21

musical notes, a boat, a quill, and a rabbit poking out of a top hat. In the center of the paper, Nora's loopy, swirly handwriting said:

> True Fact: Matthias Buchinger was an artist, a magician, a cardsharp, a musician, and a sharpshooter, and he liked to build ships in bottles. Also, he was twenty-nine inches tall and was born without hands or feet.

"He reminds me of you," Nora said, reading over my shoulder.

"Because...I'm twenty-nine inches tall?"

"Because no matter what you're born with, you can do anything."

My eyes welled up, and I threw my arms around Nora. Otis sandwiched himself between us because he was going to miss her as much as I was.

"I'm sorry I don't have a going-away present for you," I said, my voice muffled by her shoulder.

"I'm sorry my rabbit looks like a snowman," Nora said into my neck.

And then, because we couldn't actually freeze time no matter how much we wanted to, the three of us headed out to the parking lot to wait for Nora's mom to pick us up.

"Are you still not telling your parents about the treasure hunt?" Nora said.

"You know I can't. If I tell them, they'll never let me do it. Or they'll make so many rules the search won't be mine anymore."

"Well, I need to know everything that happens. Swear you'll write to me." Nora held out a hand and we hooked pinkies.

"I already put a card in the mail this morning," I said. A happy anniversary card, because Nora and I choose cards based on their covers, and this one had a fuzzy picture of two striped kittens touching noses on a bed of clouds. "And I need to know everything that happens with all those plays you'll be starring in. Swear you'll write to me?"

"I swear." We crossed pinkies again. "Three times a day, at least."

Nora's mom pulled into the parking lot. Before getting in, Nora turned for one last look at the ISLAND BOWL sign with its missing *B*.

"Farewell, owl, our faithful friend!" she sang, flapping her arms like a bird and swerving around the parking lot. She looked over her shoulder at me. "Well?"

I did a couple of noodly flaps. Nora gave me another look. I picked up steam and flapped like I meant it.

"Farewell, Island owl!" I called.

We flapped and spun and hooted. Even Otis joined in, chasing us in circles, until finally Nora's mom called out the window, "I'm getting old here waiting for you! Enough craziness! It's only seven weeks."

For Nora and me, there could never be enough craziness. And seven weeks felt like a lifetime.

CHAPTER FOUR

The next morning, I made Jules get to the beach at nine thirty. I figured nobody would be there that early except moms and toddlers, and Jules would get bored and want to leave, so I'd get to dump her and start the hunt.

No such luck.

After her dad dropped us off ("Stay as long as you like, kiddos! Here's forty dollars for snacks." *Forty dollars?*), Jules and Otis and I set up our things right behind the tide line, where the dry sand started. She spread her towel while I dug a hole for the umbrella.

"Don't you like to lay out?" she asked. "Umbrellas are for old people."

"It's for Otis," I said. "He likes shade." Although, at that particular moment, Otis was lying a few feet away, directly in the sun, happily devouring an old sandy hot dog.

"Leave it, Otis. Don't be a cannibal."

Otis dropped the hot dog and gave me his big-eyed *Why have you robbed me of all joy?* look. I tossed him his chew toy as a peace offering.

Jules kneeled on her towel and started putting on sunscreen. Otis lay down under the umbrella, and I sat in the shade between him and Jules.

"So what's it like living here?" she asked.

"It's okay, I guess," I said. "Most of the year it's pretty quiet, and then in the summer it gets crazy when all the tourists come." *Tourists like you, who clog the movie theaters and shove people like me out of line at the Five & Dime.*

"But what do you do here? Like, for fun?"

Jules actually looked interested, so I decided to tell her the truth. "Mostly I go out on our boat."

"You mean with your parents?"

"Nope. By myself."

"Cool," Jules said.

I didn't add that I'd been boating alone for only the last bunch of months. Before that, I always used to go with Pop Pop. Everything I know about the water, I learned from him.

"What do you do for fun in Hollywood?" I asked.

"The Palisades," she corrected. "Not Hollywood. And

26

not a lot. Before my parents split up, I mostly just went to my friends' houses and watched movies in somebody's screening room or whatever. Now I'm just not that into it." Jules put on a big pair of black sunglasses that hid half her face. Then out of nowhere, she said, "Want to see a picture of my mom?"

"Um...sure," I said, even though I was not at all sure why she offered.

Jules scrolled through her phone and passed it to me. I cupped my hand around the screen so I could see a picture of a smiling mom-ish-looking woman with brown hair who had her arm wrapped around Jules. Jules was smiling too, with her head leaning on her mom's shoulder. She almost looked like a different person, like a regular, happy person instead of an angry supermodel from Hollywood.

Excuse me, the *Palisades*.

"She looks nice," I said.

"She is," Jules said.

Over Jules's shoulder, I spotted three boys from my grade heading our way. Douglas, Wilder Douglas, and Fritjof play together on the soccer team in the fall, the basketball team in the winter, and the lacrosse team in the spring. They all wore hair gel, even though it was ten in the morning and they were at the beach. Also, Wilder isn't an adjective; it's a first name. I'm not sure why

27

everybody uses his last name too. They just do. And Fritjof is called Fritjof because his dad is Norwegian.

"Heyyyy! Otis, buddy! How's it going, dude?" Douglas said.

Fritjof and Wilder Douglas pounced on Otis, who was totally thrilled to pounce right back.

It's possible that some people like my dog more than they like me.

"Hey, Blue. Who's your friend?" Douglas asked, noticing Jules.

"This is Jules," I said.

There isn't a single girl at my school who looks like Jules. Which might be why Douglas was squeezing his eyes shut really hard and then rubbing his nose.

"You wanna go swimming?" Jules said.

"Oh. Yeah. Totally." Douglas yanked off his T-shirt and flung it down without looking, so it landed on my leg.

You'd never have known that Douglas, Nora, and I used to hang out when we were little. It was like all those playdates when we dressed up in superhero capes and jumped on the bed had never happened.

Jules stood up. "You coming, Blue?"

I love swimming in the ocean. I wakeboard, boogie board, bodysurf, and scuba dive. But no matter how much I like the water, I wasn't about to get into the whole insulin pump thing with Jules.

I could only imagine what she'd say when I took out the raisin-box-sized machine from my pocket and unplugged the skinny plastic tube that's part of a catheter that's buried in the skin next to my belly button, which was currently hidden by my baggy shirt and elastic-waist shorts. Words like "android" and "freak" and "ewwww" were not outside the realm of possibility. And then, of course, there's my bathing suit—a plain brown tankini— which I wear so I can cover the infusion set but still have access to the tube, and which isn't exactly what anyone on the planet would call fashionable.

Nope. Not gonna go there with Jules.

"I have to stay with Otis."

Douglas, who knew that Otis would be fine watching me from the shore if I wanted to swim, did me the small favor of saying nothing.

"Whatever. Watch my stuff, okay?"

While Jules and my former friend and his two new friends went swimming, Otis drank water from his portable dish, and I tested and took insulin so I could eat an apple and peanut butter.

I didn't used to care about people seeing me deal with diabetes. My parents made a point of treating it like it was normal—scrunching down my shorts to give me a shot in my hip at the pizzeria when I was little or telling me to go ahead and test in the middle of the bookstore—and kids at school had always known about my diabetes and were used to it. But all that changed when I got to middle school.

On the first day of sixth grade, our homeroom teacher, Ms. Gorman, made us push the desks to the sides of the room and told everyone to sit in a circle on the floor like it was kindergarten again.

"We're going to play a get-to-know-you game," Ms. Gorman said. "Everybody think of a fun fact about yourself that you can share with the class. Something unique and interesting that's special about you."

I was racking my brain for my fun fact—my thumbs are double-jointed? I once kept a pet spider for three days until it dried up and died?—when Eliza Jackson, who had gone to the same elementary school as me, said from all the way across the circle in a really loud voice:

"You're so lucky, Blue. You have diabetes."

Turns out I did have a fun fact. Something unique and interesting that was special about me. And it was a disease.

Kids I didn't know started asking questions, and other kids I *did* know started answering them.

"Diabetes? Is that the thing with the needles?"

"Yeah, Blue gives herself shots all the time. Like every hour." Which wasn't true.

"One time she passed out in gym." Which *was* true.

I got lighter and lighter and lighter until I floated from the floor to the ceiling. My body became paper-thin and see-through, and the only thing that kept me from evaporating altogether was Otis. He crawled half into my lap, anchoring me down so I wouldn't turn to dust particles and drift away.

The next summer—last summer—at the CJDF gala, my picture was everywhere—on the invitations, on the programs at every seat, on bigger-than-life-sized posters. Not my name, just my face:

CURE TYPE 1 DIABETES!
GIANT PICTURE OF BLUE'S HEAD

There were hundreds of people at that party. Hundreds more at school and even more around town. And every single one of those people knew me as Diabetes Girl. If I wanted a unique and interesting thing about me that wasn't a disease, it had to be more than having extra-bendy thumbs. My fun fact had to be something big. Something huge.

Something like finding a 350-year-old ship of gold.

CHAPTER FIVE

True Fact: If you don't know what to think of a person, ask your dog.

After Jules and the boys came back, we all went to the Shark Pit, a food truck in the parking lot with a picture on its side of sharks dancing in a swimming pool. If the boys weren't totally in love with Jules before, they definitely were after she bought them fish tacos. The whole time, Jules was Super Jules. Googolplex Jules. Ultimate Jules. She took selfies with the boys and then made a big point of erasing them because her phone was full. She knuckle-punched Douglas after he made a stupid joke and then stopped him with a stare when he tried to do it back. Half of what Jules talked about was so cool we'd never heard of it (do people really put charcoal in their lemonade?). She twisted her hair up in a knot, then shook it down, tossed it all over one shoulder, then the other, then back up again, then down but pushed off her face with her sunglasses. I think she got to hairstyle 157 just counting from our time at the Shark Pit.

For the record, my hair is black and curly. Most of the time, I wear it in a ponytail.

Otis and I were so not into this. Otis because he's not allowed to eat spicy food from the Shark Pit, and me because all I wanted to do was ditch Jules and go treasure hunting. Which, judging by the fact that we hadn't even been at the beach for two hours, wasn't going to happen anytime soon.

I was putting nylon dog booties on Otis's paws (black, to match his fur) so he wouldn't burn them on the asphalt when a little red convertible with the hood emblem of a horse rearing up on its hind legs zoomed into the parking lot. Even I knew it was a Ferrari. Ferraris aren't exactly uncommon in the Hamptons, especially in the summer, but a Ferrari with Anna Bowdin driving it? Now that's something you don't see here every day.

Everyone on the planet knows that Anna Bowdin is probably the hugest movie star in existence. And that even though she's only twenty-three, she's already been a superhero, a Revolutionary War spy, a Disney princess, and a coal miner with lung disease.

The parking lot, which had been noisy with moms reeling in their screaming kids, went silent. Even the sun hid behind a cloud, like it knew its light wasn't needed anymore now that Anna Bowdin was here.

Anna parked her Ferrari a few cars away from us and waved a big wave. "Hey, Julie Jules!"

The mouths of Douglas, Wilder Douglas, and Fritjof dropped open even wider than they already were. Douglas may actually have had drool in the corner of his. I made sure my own mouth was shut, but, really, I couldn't believe I was about to meet the world's biggest movie star.

"You *know* her?" Douglas said.

Jules gripped my upper arm like a claw and whispered in my ear, "We're leaving."

"Jules, you *know* Anna Bowdin?" Douglas said again.

"We *have* to go," Jules said, ignoring Douglas and squeezing my arm even tighter. "Now. To your house. Call your mom."

No way. If Jules came to my house, I'd lose another whole day of treasure hunting. "I can't," I said back. "I have stuff I'm supposed to do. Besides, why do you want to go to my house all of a sudden? And how do you know Anna Bowdin?"

"Don't you ever go on the Internet?" Jules was practically shouting. Then she dropped her voice to a whisper again. "Anna Bowdin is my dad's girlfriend. She's the reason he walked out on my mom. So can we *please* go to your house? *Right. Now?*"

No wonder Jules was frantic. I called Mom—even though every cell in my body was screaming at me not to. She was with a client, installing four hundred wisteria vines on the side of their pool house.

"Can you come pick us up?" I asked.

"Are you having a blood sugar reaction?" she said, instantly on the alert.

Just to be sure, I did an automatic body scan for symptoms. Nothing. Plus, Otis would have told me if there was a problem, and he was currently sitting on my foot and scratching his rump with his teeth, the only person in the parking lot who couldn't care less about Anna Bowdin.

"I'm fine," I said. "But Jules isn't. I'll explain later."

"I'll be there in ten minutes," Mom said, and hung up.

Ten minutes was forever to Jules, though, especially after we got our stuff and had to stand around watching Anna Bowdin sign autographs. After she finished, she peeled a pair of twin six-year-olds off her legs and came over to us.

"Hi, sweetie." She kissed Jules on both cheeks. "You know your dad hates the sun, and I couldn't take being at the house another second. I mean, this weather! Oh wow, who are your friends? They're adorable."

The guys just stared. Finally, Fritjof said something, except he said it in Norwegian.

Jules put her hand on Otis's head and said, "This is Otis. He's half-wolf, so you better not get too close."

Which is absolutely not true—even though Otis looks like a wolf, he's 100 percent dog—but I decided not to tell Anna Bowdin that.

Otis stood between Jules and me, looking powerful and majestic, even in his nylon booties. Whatever Anna Bowdin had been about to say, she didn't say it. She took one look at Otis the wolf-dog and got very quiet. And kind of smaller, like she was a regular person instead of a MOVIE STAR.

A horn tooted.

"That's Blue's mom," Jules said. "We gotta go. Sorry."

Otis jumped into the bed of Mom's pickup truck, and Jules and I climbed into the back seat of the cab.

"Is that Anna Bowdin?" Mom asked, sticking her head out the window for a better look.

"She's my dad's girlfriend." Jules practically spit the word "girlfriend."

"I take it you two aren't very close?" Mom said, pulling out of the parking lot.

"About as close as Earth and Neptune," Jules said.

"Neptune is the farthest planet from Earth," I helpfully explained to Mom, a fact I know because even though I got an Incomplete, I did pay attention in Earth Science every now and then.

"Thank you for rescuing me, Mrs. Broen," Jules said with none of her usual snark. "I really appreciate it."

"I'm glad I could help," Mom said, looking at Jules in the rearview mirror instead of at the road the way I hate. "You know what they say, girls: 'When the going gets tough, the tough go to sea.' Why don't you two have some fun and go boating?"

For the record, nobody says, "When the going gets tough, the tough go to sea." That's not a thing; it's Mom-code for *Why don't you get some homework done, Blue?* And while there was nothing I'd rather do than go secretly hunt for treasure while pretending to do my homework, there was nothing I'd rather do less than take Jules Buttersby with me.

CHAPTER SIX

True Fact: For most of human history, ruling the seas meant ruling the world.

I like our house. It's on a cove that leads to the harbor that leads to the Long Island Sound that leads to the Atlantic Ocean, so if I want to I can sail from my backyard all the way to France.

But now I was seeing it through Jules's eyes, and I noticed the peeling paint on some of the shutters, the crooked screen door, the wobbly handrail. Dad makes jokes about how he's like the cobbler whose children have no shoes, but I know business for both my parents has been rough recently, and diabetes isn't cheap.

Our house has three bedrooms, which always seemed like enough, but now it seemed small. And old. Which, to be fair, it is. About two hundred years old, in fact. Dad's great-something-grandfather built it, and before he did, there was another house here that his ancestors built back in the 1600s. There's still an old family graveyard across the street. Turns out a lot of my female relatives were named Lucretia in the early 1800s.

Mom dropped us off with a friendly "There's tuna salad in the fridge if you're hungry!" Which was code for *Don't forget to eat, Blue, and remember to check your blood sugar before and after.* What was especially annoying was that she was right: Just as her truck turned out of the driveway, Otis headbutted my leg.

"High or low?" I asked.

Otis bowed.

I saw Jules watching Otis and me, so I knew what was coming next:

"What's that about?" she asked.

I hesitated. Otis had just alerted—he'd told me my blood sugar was too low. Everybody loves hearing about diabetic-alert dogs and all the things they can do—how they can smell blood sugar across two campsites through a haze of barbecues, how they're on duty even when they're asleep. But if I told Jules about Otis, would she start grilling me all about what it's like to have diabetes?

"Nothing," I said. "Just a game we play."

We went inside, and Otis and I stopped in the bathroom to make sure he was right, even though Otis is never wrong about highs or lows. And he almost never misses an alert—just when he's sick or when something incredible happens to distract him, like the time an entire flock of geese made a pit stop in our backyard at dawn and he barked the whole house awake until Dad let him out so he could have the joy of chasing every last goose into the neighbor's yard.

I pricked my finger with a tiny lancet and then squeezed a drop of blood onto a test strip in my glucometer so I could check my sugar level. Otis stared at the meter with the tip of his tail wagging. He knew that if he was right, he'd get a treat.

Five...four...three...two...one...

"Good low, Oats Magoats." He gobbled down a square of turkey jerky, which I carry in a treat baggie in my pocket.

My deal with my parents is that they check the numbers stored on my pump at the end of each day, but I have to let them know in real-time if I get too high or too low. I texted them:

Me: BS 68. About to have lunch (30g carbs).
Will take 1 unit insulin after I eat
Dad: Sounds right
Mom: How are you feeling?
Me: Ok
Dad: Headache?

Me: Not too bad
Mom: Dizzy?
Me: No
Dad: Sweaty?
Me: I'm FINE

This is how it goes with us, ever since my last birthday when I convinced my parents—with a lot of help from Dr. Basch, my diabetes doctor—that they needed to start letting me be the one to deal with my diabetes instead of them making all the decisions. Every single day of my life, my parents have known every bite of food I've eaten, every place I've gone, everything I've done, every hour I've slept. For the record, there's nothing quite like the special joy a girl feels when her dad says, "You've been low for the last two days, sweetie. Period starting?"

My parents have been pressuring me to get a continuous glucose monitor—a machine that would automatically check my blood sugar every few minutes. But a CGM would mean another port in my body, and one was more than enough. Plus, I really didn't want Mom and Dad getting my blood sugar updates texted to their phones all day. Plus, CGMs are expensive. Plus, I had Otis. So...no.

I found Jules in the kitchen and prayed she wouldn't say anything about the piles and boxes near the basement door that make the hall look like a yard sale. Mom and I can be messy, but Dad, according to her, is "two psycho-logical wrong turns away from being a hoarder."

Dad hates throwing anything away, so our house just gets messier and messier and messier until finally Mom has a meltdown. "I can't take it anymore!" she'll yell. "Living in all this clutter makes me feel like I'm wearing a hair shirt." Dad will do a minor cleanup, and then the cycle repeats itself.

Last winter, though, Dad's piles grew bigger than ever, until one night at dinner Mom announced, "IT'S TIME TO CLEAN THE BASEMENT."

Otis's hind leg, which he'd been using to scratch behind his ear, froze in midair. Dad dropped his pork chop. "Oh, Em, no—" he begged.

"We need space, Hal. It's the only way."

Dad deflated. "Next year—"

"Now."

Dad put in a few weekends, but then his busy season started, and now everything he'd brought up from the basement to get rid of was piled in the hall. There was enough space to walk from the front door to the kitchen, but just barely.

Jules was looking out the kitchen window at the back-yard. Otis let himself out the door and went to pee on the wood chips that Mom had laid down for him to use as a toilet so he wouldn't poison the grass. Otis figured out how to work a lever-type door handle when he was a puppy just by watching. He also knows how to flip a light switch and when to cross at a traffic stop. He thinks he can dance too, but it's really more of a rump bop. Turns out dogs don't have much rhythm, but then again, neither do plenty of people.

I got the tuna salad from the fridge and made myself a sandwich.

"Want one?" I asked.

"No thanks," Jules said. "Your house is cool. You have so many flowers in your garden. Those are peonies, right?"

"Uh-huh," I said between bites.

"What are those?" She pointed at the flowers that covered the shady part of the yard next to the fence.

"Bluebells," I said, hoping she wouldn't ask more about them. My mom named me Bluebell for her favorite flower. Since I'm not a dairy cow, I go by Blue.

I wondered whether I should say something about Jules's dad and Anna Bowdin. I mean, what was there to say? *I'm sorry your dad dumped your nice, normal mom so he could date an actress who's young enough to be your sister?*

Luckily, Jules didn't seem to want to talk about it. Instead, she snapped, "So are we gonna go out on your boat or what?"

Obviously, I wanted to go out on the boat more than

43

anything, but I didn't want to do it with Jules. Was there a way to take Jules treasure hunting without letting her know we were treasure hunting? Maybe what I needed was a decoy. Something that would distract Jules from the seemingly dull and boring but actually super-exciting treasure hunt that I didn't want her to know about.

"Do you like tubing?" I asked.

"You mean where you lie on a raft and a boat pulls you really fast and you fall off and get rope burn and water up your nose?"

"Exactly."

Jules grinned. "What's not to like?"

Decoy activated!

"Ahoy, Otis! To the boats!"

Otis woofed with joy. German shepherds aren't usually big water dogs—not like Newfies or Labs—but Otis was raised at sea and loves the feel of spray on his muzzle. He's not a fan of actual swimming ever since he tried to eat a jellyfish, but he'll go in if I go with him.

Before heading outside, I went to the bathroom to take insulin. I'd have to recheck my blood sugar on the boat without Jules seeing, but I had a plan for that.

Otis led the way to our dock at the end of the yard, where the inner tube was leaning against the fence that separates our property from our next-door neighbor's. The tube looks like a giant rubber doughnut with a thin bottom in the hole. You can sit in the hole or lie across the whole doughnut while somebody else drives the boat. It's actually really fun—not that I had any intention of tubing today myself.

"Tube, Otis."

Otis took the rope in his mouth and dragged the tube to the dock.

"Will he do anything you tell him to?" Jules asked.

"Well, he can't open a jar of pickles," I said.

"He must be really smart," Jules said with a look of admiration. *Maybe she's not a dog-hater after all.* "I see the way he watches you and does everything you say."

Otis knows what I'm feeling as soon as I feel it, and I can read his every ear tilt, every eyebrow crinkle, every wag and thump.

"It's not just one-way," I said. "We take care of each other."

"That must be nice for you." Jules jammed on her giant sunglasses.

Was she being sarcastic? I couldn't tell.

Otis left the tube in front of the long, skinny ramp to the dock and rolled around with his tongue hanging out, scratching his back on the prickly seagrass. I gave his belly a quick rub, and then he jumped up and followed me while I dragged the tube the rest of the way.

Our boat's a twenty-two-foot Mako with an outboard

motor and a little sunshade over the wheel. It's old and not super comfortable, but it's also fast and reliable. Otis climbed on after me and settled into his usual spot in the well at the front while I tied on the tube with a bowline knot.

Jules got on after Otis, grabbing the handrail to steady herself. "You sure you know how to drive this thing?"

"Definitely. My grandfather taught me." I could steer the Mako through a harbor full of paddleboarders in a dense fog and not clip a single oar. Well, maybe not quite, but Pop Pop made sure I knew how to handle a boat.

After I finished with the tube, I rigged a sun awning for Otis by tying four lengths of rope around the corners of a beach blanket and then attaching the ropes to stanchion posts on the sides of the boat with clove hitch knots.

I lowered the motor into the water and turned the key in the ignition. The water was calm, and we'd be in a bay, not the ocean, so I didn't bother with life vests for me and Otis, but I gave Jules a vest for tubing.

"We have to get to open water first," I said, over the noise of the engine.

There was open water a few minutes from our cove, but my plan was to go all the way to Gardiner's Island, because that's where the treasure was.

At least, that's where I *thought* the treasure was.

CHAPTER SEVEN

True Fact: Cleft chins and folding tongues aren't the only things people inherit from their ancestors.

When Pop Pop first told me about the treasure, I was so little that we didn't even have Otis yet. He called me into the living room, and I climbed up next to him on the couch. On the coffee table was a mess of a book with a cracked cover and warped pages, some of which were sticking out of the binding. Pop Pop ran his fingertips over the stained leather. The wrinkled, blotchy cover looked a lot like the back of his hand. The book had to be old. *Super* old.

Pop Pop leaned in close to me, so I leaned in close to him. I could smell his smell, which I now know was a combination of mentholated shaving cream and diesel fuel.

"You see this book, BB?" he said. "Inside is the name of *every single person* in our family."

"*Whoa,*" I said in a church-library-ghost-story voice.

Pop Pop nodded, slow and serious. Then he opened the book and showed me the newest page, the one with my name on it. Next he showed me Dad's name and his own and his parents', all the way back to page one, to the very first names: Petra De Winter and Abraham Broen, my great-great-great-great-great-great-great-great-great-great-great-great-grandparents. Black ink long faded to brown said that Petra was born in 1651 in Amsterdam, and Abraham was born the same year in Java. He was a carpenter, and she was a healer.

Then Pop Pop dropped an even bigger whoa: "In 1665 Petra and Abraham sailed right here to Sag Harbor"—he paused—"*on a ship of gold.*"

I was so amazed that my eyes quadrupled in size. Or at least that's how I picture myself when I look back now.

"For really real, Pop Pop?"

"Yup. I've even got proof." He pulled a gold coin from his pocket, about the size of a half-dollar. "This coin came from their ship. See these letters? *V-O-C.* That means the ship was owned by the Dutch East India Company," he said. "My grandpa gave me this coin. One day I'll give it to you."

Pop Pop placed the coin, still warm from his pocket, in my palm.

"Where's the ship now?" I asked, tracing the raised letters with my index finger.

"Good question," he said. "It sank, and Petra and Abraham had to swim the rest of the way to land. But the gold was too heavy to bring with them. It's still out there somewhere." Pop Pop rested his hand on the book like he was taking an oath. *"In view of paradise, watched over for eternity by a sorrowful hound."*

I looked up at him. "What does *that* mean?"

"That's what we have to figure out, BB." He leaned in again, even closer this time. I loved the way the insides of his wrinkles didn't get as dark as the rest of his face. It gave him tiger stripes around his eyes. "For three hundred and fifty years, people in our family have been looking for that ship. *And you and I are going to find it.*"

From the first warm day in spring to the last warm day in fall, Pop Pop took me on his treasure hunts. "We're partners, BB," he used to say. "Shipmates." When Pop Pop got sick last October, he promised he'd be better in time to hunt for treasure again this spring. But by the time the doctors found his cancer, it was already too late.

After Pop Pop died in February, Dad sold his gold VOC coin, the one Pop Pop had always promised me. He wouldn't tell me why. I was so angry that I didn't speak to Dad for days. Now I have nothing left of my grandfather except our hunt.

49

Finding the treasure for Pop Pop became my secret life mission. All winter and spring, I schemed and researched, but I had no idea where to look until one day in May when Nora and I were out on the boat playing that game where you pick a cloud and describe it.

"I see a cloud that looks like soft-serve vanilla ice cream," I said, peering through a pair of binoculars.

"You think all clouds look like soft-serve vanilla ice cream," Nora said. "Try again."

Unlike me, Nora always saw exciting things in the clouds: roller coasters, fettuccini alfredo, Kermit the Frog.

I scanned the sky. Ice cream, ice cream, melted ice cream...

My eyes drifted lower. To the houses along the coast, to the gulls swooping over the water, to a boulder on the southwest shore of Gardiner's Island with two lumps sticking out of it that looked exactly like a dog's head.

I stood up and refocused the binoculars.

"Well?" Nora asked.

"Not ice cream," I whispered.

Goose bumps popped up on my arms. Suddenly, all the pieces clicked into place:

In view of paradise, watched over for eternity by a sorrowful hound.

Paradise = Garden of Eden = Gardiner's Island

Hound = Dog

Sorrowful = No idea

About twenty minutes after Jules, Otis, and I left our cove, we got to Gardiner's Bay, a big protected circle of open water with Sag Harbor and Shelter Island at our backs and Gardiner's Island ahead.

Picture a T-bone steak with a pointy hat on top. That's Gardiner's Island.

I steered us to the southern end of the island—the left corner of the bottom tip of the steak bone—and shifted the boat to idle, my heart racing like an open balloon when you let go of the neck. Because there it was: a boulder with a long chunk sticking out of the side in a snoutish fashion and a smaller chunk sticking up from the top in an ear-ish fashion.

The sorrowful hound.

Otis woofed. My oh-so-casual lean against the rail didn't fool him.

"Are we there yet?" Jules asked.

"We're there," I whispered. *"Finally."*

CHAPTER EIGHT

True Fact: Technically speaking, you have to tell the whole truth and nothing but the truth only when you're under oath in a court of law.

I'd pictured the first day of the hunt a million times since this winter, and none of those pictures had included Jules Buttersby. I knew what Pop Pop would have said if he'd been here: *Avast ye whining, BB. Bear down and carry on.*

I want to carry on, Pop Pop, but first I have to drag Jules around the water on a rubber doughnut until she gets bored. My plan was to swerve as much as possible at high speed, to fling Jules off the tube again and again so she'd hate it, give up, and go home. My plan also included testing my blood sugar while Jules was underwater.

My plan took fifteen minutes.

"Tubing was never this lame on Maui or Saint Lucia." Jules spit a chunk of hair out of her mouth. "Or in the Seychelles."

"Sorry," I lied. "My friends and I like to go fast."

Otis wasn't happy either. He looked seasick, curled up as small as he could make himself with his front paws over his nose. Also, he was groaning. I offered him a treat and he didn't take it. Definitely seasick. *Sorry, Otis.*

"Whatever." Jules flicked her hair off her shoulder. "Okay, it's your turn."

"I can't," I said. "Legally you're not allowed to drive unless you're fourteen or you've taken a safety class."

Jules raised her eyebrows at me, which I took to mean, "Who cares?"

I tried again. "Plus, you don't know how to drive the boat."

"How hard can it be? I watched you do it. You push the handle up to go faster and turn the wheel to steer."

"It's not that simple," I said, even though it kind of is that simple.

"So, what, you just want to go back? Already?"

No, I don't want to go back. I want to load you into a cannon and shoot you home to Hollywood—excuse me, the Palisades—so I can come here every day until I find my family's legacy that's probably buried in the sand twenty feet under us right this very second.

That's what I wanted to say. Instead, I said, "It's a really nice day. Let's hang out for a while."

I reached into my gear bag and pulled out a five-gallon

plastic yellow pail with a clear Plexiglas bottom. I'd made it myself. It took half the night, but it was totally worth the D I got on my social studies essay that was due the next day.

"What's that?" Jules asked.

"A view bucket. You use it to look at stuff underwater." I demonstrated by sticking my face in the top and leaning over the edge of the boat. "I like to look at fish this way. It's easier than snorkeling—way less gear and you can stay dry. We can take turns if you want."

Jules crossed her arms and eyed me over the top of her sunglasses. "Do you think I'm a total idiot?"

"What? Of course I don't think you're an idiot. What makes you say that?" I sputtered, trying not to look like a person with a giant secret.

Jules glared at me. "You've been trying to get rid of me the whole day. You don't want to go tubing. You made sure I didn't want to go tubing. And now you expect me to believe that your idea of fun is looking at fish through a bucket? I mean, seriously. *What. Is. Up?*"

So much for my decoy plan. I was going to have to tell Jules the truth. Well, not *the* truth. *The* truth is I got the Incomplete on purpose so I could have an excuse to be alone on the water all summer.

A truth is: "Fine. You're right. I got an Incomplete in science this year, and I have to do a water project to pass the class."

"You failed seventh-grade science? What are you, stupid?"

I could feel my face burning, and it wasn't because of the sun. "It was an Incomplete, not an F, and no, I'm not stupid! I just have better things to do. And I suppose you get straight As in every class?"

Jules picked her cover-up off the floor of the boat and shook it out. "As a matter of fact, I do. School's our job, and jobs are things you work hard at. So unless you have a serious learning disability or a personal hardship or something, or you really are stupid—which plenty of people are and it's not their fault because that's how they were born—there's no excuse for failing seventh-grade science. Or failing anything."

I was pretty sure Jules was for real. Jules, who thinks diabetes is "a thing that happens to fat people," was making me feel like an idiot.

To make things worse, after she finished her speech, Jules offered Otis the treat. *And he ate it.*

"Well, I got an Incomplete in science, and now I have to do this project. But you don't have to sit here while I do it. I can take you back." *Say yes, say yes, say yes!*

"What? And stay in my room all day while Anna Bobana bounces around our cabana? No thanks. I'd rather watch you stick your head in a bucket."

Shih tzu.

55

I killed the engine.

"Keep an eye out for boat traffic," I ordered Jules. "Fist bump, Otis."

Otis raised a paw and I tapped it. Then I whispered in his ear, "I'm mad at her, not you," and gave him a kiss on the nose for good luck.

I slid onto the tube with the view bucket and let out the rope so I'd have some distance from the boat. Otis watched me with his head hanging over the side.

"I'm not going anywhere, I promise," I said. "Stay."

I could tell Otis wanted in on the action, but he stayed.

The weather was perfect: no wind, almost no current. The water was as close to glass as it gets, and even without the bucket I could see almost to the bottom, which was about twenty feet away.

"What are you looking for?" Jules asked, leaning over the rail next to Otis.

My goal was to find the ballast pile. Ballast is heavy stuff that people stow in the bottom storage area of boats to balance cargo so boats don't tip. In the old days, they used things like bricks or rocks or lead bars. Since ballast is heavy, when a ship sinks, the ballast sits on the ocean floor, and the good stuff sits on top of it. Usually, if you find the ballast pile, you've found the ship and everything in it. *Find the ballast, find the ship.*

My problem was that this particular ship sank 350

years ago, so whatever was left of it was probably buried under sand and mud. But sand and mud shift all the time, and you never know what will surface. My plan was to search the whole area around the sorrowful hound, bit by bit in a grid pattern, until I found anything that looked like something that might be something. Not that I could tell any of that to Jules.

"Um, you know, just stuff."

"What kind of stuff?" she asked.

"Stuff that's in the water," I said.

"Like?"

Why was Jules so interested in my boring summer project? It was a good thing I hadn't told her the real reason I was out here. If she thought I was doing something exciting like looking for treasure, she'd probably duct-tape herself to the boat so she'd never have to leave, and I'd have to deal with her all summer instead of just today.

"Stuff that people leave behind. You know, litter," I said. "It's an environmental project."

I lay belly-down on the tube, every cell in my body tingling. *It could be right under me. Right here. Right now. A brick or a cup or a coin. A spoon that my great-times-twelve-grandma Petra used to eat salt peas 350 years ago.*

I squinted up at the clouds—*This is for you, Pop Pop*—then gazed out at the boulder: *Okay, sorrowful hound. Fetch.*

CHAPTER NINE

True Fact: Although it's traditional to kill rival treasure hunters, it's not required.

Looking through the view bucket was like snorkeling with super-wide-angle goggles. The sunlight was strong and the Plexi magnified rocks and seaweed on the uneven sand. Everything was light and shadow, crisp and wavy.

Professional treasure hunters use things like electric blowers and magnetometers. But a MAD (that's short for "magnetic anomaly detector") costs around $50,000, so I was using a bucket.

Which was not as hopeless as it sounded. Low-tech was how every sunken treasure in history was found up until about a hundred years ago, when fancy salvaging machines started getting invented. Pirates got rich for centuries by plundering sunken ships with no MADs or sonar. It helped to know where to look (which I did), and to search in an organized way (which I would do), and to kill other treasure hunters who tried to get there first (which I would try not to do).

Besides, I did have one high-tech skill: I knew how to scuba dive. Pop Pop told me how he used to dive for treasure when he was younger, and I decided that if we ever found the ship of gold, I would want to dive down with him to get it. After months of begging, pleading, fighting, and guilt-tripping, I made a deal with my parents that if Dr. Basch said yes, then they would let me get certified when I turned twelve. Dr. Basch said yes.

Jules listened to music and scrolled on her phone while I covered a ten-foot section of the bay. Each time I finished going over a square, I hand-paddled to another. I spotted plenty of shells and rocks, and even somebody's lost laptop, but nothing that looked like it maybe came from a ship 350 years ago. I also saw a ton of jellyfish—I couldn't believe Jules hadn't gotten stung all those times she'd fallen off the tube.

After about twenty minutes, Jules got bored. "You done?" she called out.

"Not yet," I called back.

Fifteen minutes later. "How about now?"

"Nope."

Ten more minutes. *"Seriously?"*

I wasn't finished, not even close, but it *was* getting late. I pulled the tube up to the boat, and Otis did a little happy dance when I climbed aboard. I kneeled so I could scratch his cheeks and he could lick my face.

Jules cringed. *"Ew.* Are you one of those people who lets their dog lick their mouth?"

Yes. "No."

"Good, because that's disgusting."

I got out my chart book to mark the area I'd covered. It wasn't much, but I'd get way more done the next day without Jules. And the day after and the day after that.

"I can do that for you tomorrow," Jules said.

"What do you mean?" I asked.

"You've got this whole big project," Jules said. "You didn't finish it today, did you?"

My brain slowed down like a bicycle chugging through a field of molasses. Maybe it was the heat. Or the sun. It wasn't my blood sugar because Otis would have noticed. But for some reason my mind couldn't compute what Jules was saying to me, which seemed to be—but couldn't possibly be—that she was expecting to come out here again. With me and Otis. Tomorrow.

Jules must have read my face because she said, "Look, there's no way I'm staying home with the Wicked Witch

60

of West Hollywood, and you're the only person I know here. Besides, I can help you. We've already established I'm a way better student than you are. You can teach me to drive the boat, and then I can move it from place to place so you don't have to get off the tube."

Mom's head suddenly appeared in the sky like a huge rain cloud: *Film crew. Two hundred people. Half a million dollars.*

My heart dropped straight from my chest to my stomach like one of those death-drop carnival rides. *Whooosh... boom!*

Mission accomplished, the Mom-head cloud evaporated.

I sighed. "Fine," I said to Jules. "How early can you get to my house?"

Jules said nine o'clock—which, even after only knowing her a day, I figured meant ten o'clock—and we motored north around the island, eating cashews. Jules talked about some kid at her school who was a big DJ in LA, but the whole time, I was thinking, *Why why why why why why whyyyyyy?* Until we rounded the big bend in the island and could see beyond the top of the T-bone, and Jules said, "What's that weird boat over there?"

It looked like a miniature ocean liner, which wouldn't be weird in the Hamptons. There are always at least a few privately owned boats around that sleep fifty people. But those boats gleam with fancy paintwork and are tricked

61

out with helicopters and Jacuzzis or even motorcycles (for when you go on land). This was a working boat. Nothing fancy about it except its gigantic size, the antennae farm on the flybridge, and some—

"Otis, binoculars." I shifted to idle. Otis rooted around in the gear bag and then pulled out the binocular case by its strap. "Good boy," I said, taking it from him.

I adjusted the dials and a big gray-and-white blob came into focus: an old military boat that had been cleaned up and refitted. It had a giant crane and even a submarine drone. On the deck, four people—one of them in a wet suit, another with a professional-looking video camera—were gathered around a laptop. They kept pointing at the screen and then pointing at the water. I felt a tickle in my stomach, like little frogs hopping up and down.

"What is it?" Jules asked, coming around the wheel to stand next to me. "Coast Guard? Some kind of Homeland Security thing? Drug dealers?"

Otis's ears were on high alert.

"Give me a second," I said.

I adjusted the binocular dials again. The ship went out of and then back into focus. Every detail perfectly clear, like it was ten feet away instead of a hundred. By now, the frogs were trying to jump their way out through my throat.

"What?" said Jules again.

Those guys weren't the Coast Guard or Homeland Security or drug dealers. They were worse. Way worse.

I swallowed hard. "Just a random barge."

They were treasure hunters.

CHAPTER TEN

True Fact: According to William of Ockham, a friar from the 1300s, if there's more than one explanation for something, the simplest reason is usually true. (TF supplied by Jules Buttersby.)

"Okay, Otis, but just because they're treasure hunters doesn't necessarily mean they're hunting *our* treasure, right? Long Island is loaded with wrecks. Hundreds, maybe even thousands!"

Otis looked up from his breakfast bowl in the kitchen the next morning and tilted his head at me, which I took to mean *Absolutely. Chances are they're hunting for something else.* Or possibly *What do I know? I'm a dog.*

"It's true. I read it in *Scouring the Seas.*"

I explained to Otis all the reasons why it was too soon to panic until Jules's dad's personal assistant dropped her at my house at 8:54, and Jules shoved the front page of the *East Hampton Star* in my face.

BILLIONAIRE SEARCHES FOR LOST TREASURE IN GARDINER'S BAY

Famed investor-entrepreneur William "Fitz" Fitzgibbons came clean yesterday about what his trawler, *Windfall*, is doing in Gardiner's Bay. "We're looking for the holy grail!" he announced, standing on the deck of his boat with his team, including award-winning filmmaker Sonia Jacobs, who is filming the entire hunt for a documentary. "The payroll of the *Golden Lion* is one of the most famous missing treasures of all time. And I have reason to believe it's right here in these waters."

In 1663, the Dutch ship *Golden Lion* sailed from Amsterdam to Java with the payroll of the East India Company. A week from their destination, a crew of mutineers escaped from the ship with the whole payroll, six trunks filled with three million florins of gold, silver, and copper. Soon after the *Golden Lion* reached Java, she burned to ashes in a mysterious fire. The payroll was never seen again.

Fitzgibbons wouldn't explain why he believed the payroll was here in the waters off Long Island, just that he had "a key piece of evidence and a strong hunch. I've hired the best marine salvage team in the world, and we won't rest until I've got every last gold coin in my pockets!"

Fitzgibbons is known throughout the world for anticipating the great black pepper shortage of 1998, a move that netted him his first hundred million dollars. He has since parlayed that fortune into a media franchise, his own airline, and sole ownership of the Pimientos, Puerto Rico's first professional hockey team. "Hockey," he likes to say, "is the only sport where great heroes get to beat the living daylights out of each other on ice."

Next to the article was a picture of Fitzgibbons on the bridge of his boat, his hand on the wheel and a Pimientos cap on his head.

"So?" I said, even though my head felt like it was doing quadruple axels on my neck.

Jules tossed the newspaper in the air, and Otis pounced on the falling pages.

"A: We've already established I'm not an idiot. B: Did you really think I believed you about a dumb science project? And C: When were you going to tell me?" she said.

"Actually, I really did get an Incomplete in science," I said, my brain somersaulting.

Of course Pop Pop and I had read about the *Golden Lion*'s famous missing payroll, and we even had a hunch that our family's treasure was connected to it somehow. After all, we had a VOC coin from the payroll, and we knew that Great-Times-Twelve-Grandma Petra was from Amsterdam and Great-Times-Twelve-Grandpa Abraham was from Java, which was the exact route of the *Golden Lion*. But we had no proof they were on the ship. Our family stories don't say when or how the Great-Times-Twelves met or when they came to this country. Plus, we knew they were both born in 1651, which meant they were only *twelve years old* during the mutiny.

"Okay, listen up, because this is how it's going to go," Jules said, pacing back and forth in my kitchen. "You're looking for the *Golden Lion* payroll and I'm going to look with you. We'll go out every morning and stay out all day until we find it. I overnighted one of those bucket things on Amazon. Today, we'll just take turns with yours."

For the record, an underwater-view bucket is about sixty dollars on Amazon. You can get one at a marine supply store for twenty-five. I made mine for seven. But that was beside the point, a distraction from the newspaper headlines that were flashing before my eyes, which were:

PROFESSIONAL TREASURE HUNTERS
ARE IN MY WATER!

and

JULES IS GOING TO RUIN EVERYTHING!

and

WHAT "KEY PIECE OF EVIDENCE" DOES
FITZ FITZGIBBONS HAVE THAT MAKES
HIM THINK THE *GOLDEN LION* PAYROLL
IS IN SAG HARBOR?

The *Golden Lion* burned to ashes without the payroll on it. How the payroll ended up across the globe with my ancestors was a question I couldn't begin to answer. The pieces from Pop Pop's puzzle floated in the air around me—a Dutch girl, a Javanese boy, a square-sailed wooden ship laden with gold—swirling, rearranging, coming together in a bigger, eye-crossing, dizzying picture:

The Great-Times-Twelves sailed to America with one of the most famous missing treasures in history, which they may possibly have stolen as part of a mutiny when they were twelve years old!

"Okay, fine," I said to Jules, who had stopped pacing

and was glaring at me with her hands on her hips. "I'm looking for the *Golden Lion* payroll. But you can't help me."

"Why not?"

"You don't know anything about sailing or looking for wrecks." Which was my nice way of saying *You'll get in my way and take all the credit.*

"I learn fast."

I could tell Jules wasn't going to give in, but I held back from telling her about Pop Pop and the real reason I didn't want her with me. It felt too private. "Why do you even want to come, anyway? It's just lying on a rubber doughnut with your face in a bucket in the same patch of water, day after day after day."

Jules crossed her arms in front of her chest. "Well, I'm obviously not here because of your thrilling company. Do I have to spell it out? You're the only person I know, and even being with you is better than being with *her.*"

Which, when you think about it, could have been a gigantic compliment—being with me was better than being with Anna Bowdin, a famous movie star. Except that since Jules hated Anna with the molten blaze of a thousand volcanos, it was actually a gigantic insult.

"No," I said. "You can't come with me."

Jules raised her eyebrows. "You *really* want me to tell my dad you refuse to hang out with me anymore?"

We were still standing in the kitchen. Over Jules's

shoulder I could see our family portrait on the wall, a photograph of me, Otis, Mom, and Dad together on the beach. All of a sudden, the picture came to life. Dad reached into his shirt pocket and pulled out a vial of insulin, which he held in front of him in his open palm, like Oliver Twist. *Please, sir...*

You know how people make wishes on birthday candles and stray eyelashes and shooting stars? My wishes are always for stuff I want, like no line at the movie theater or a pimple to go away or maybe a Category 4 hurricane so school will be closed for two weeks, like it was last year. One day I asked my dad what he wished for.

"I always wish for the same thing," he said.

"What's that?" I asked.

"A cure for diabetes."

UGH.

I tried Jules one last time. "No offense, but I want to do this alone."

"No offense, but I don't care."

Which was how I found myself motoring back to paradise with Jules again. Jules, whose three biggest interests were her hair, her phone, and her hair, had suddenly morphed into Jules Buttersby, investigative reporter.

"How did you know about the treasure?"

I told her the story about the Great-Times-Twelves.

"What makes you think it's here? I mean, those guys

think it's over there on the other side of the bay and they're professionals."

I showed her the sorrowful hound.

"That's not a dog head. It's a boot. Like the platform snowshoes Prada did last year except upside down."

"It's not a boot. Look at it from the side."

Jules leaned over the rail and squinted. "Nope. Still a boot."

"Otis, point."

Otis stood at attention like a hound scenting prey. "See?" I said. "Look at the angle of his nose."

Jules shook her head. "I still think we should move over to where the professional searchers are. They've got all that equipment and we've got a bucket. They must know something we don't."

"Well, I think we should stay here," I said, pronouncing each word slowly and carefully so there could be no possible misunderstanding. "And, besides, we can't go near those guys. We can't let them know we're looking for the treasure or they'll chase us off."

Jules thought about that while I hooked the bucket on my arm and tied a bandana over my head to keep the sun off my neck.

"You're right," she said. "They can't know about us. We'll stay here."

I slammed down the bucket. "Excuse me? Let's get

something straight. This is my project and my plan. You don't get to decide where we look. *I* do."

Otis came around to stand with his flank pressed against my leg, to show Jules that he and I were a team and we always would be, no matter what. Jules looked kind of awkward and un-Jules-like for a few seconds, which made me feel a little guilty—but just a little.

Then she tossed her hair over her shoulder and grabbed her tote bag. "I brought some supplies." She emptied the bag onto the deck and pointed at an orange-and-white box in the pile of stuff. "This is the French kind of sunscreen with the microspheres. It's way better than anything on the market here. That's my dad's underwater camera. It's good down to fifty feet. This is for Otis." The thing for Otis unfolded into an awning with red and white stripes. Somebody needed to call Coney Island in the 1920s and tell them they found one of their cabanas. "And I brought lunch. Brown rice veggie sushi and turkey wraps. Our chef made them."

I looked at the pile. "Thanks, but I've got sunscreen, we don't need a camera, and that umbrella thing is basically a billboard announcing to the world, 'Hey! We're here! Come check us out while we hunt for the treasure!'" I paused. "But tell Mrs. Alvarado thanks for lunch. It looks really good."

Jules glared at me. "Fine. Everything I brought is total

garbage. So tell me, Lara Croft: Tomb Raider, what do you need?"

I threw my arms up. "Nothing! That's the point. I can do this whole thing by myself. I don't need you!"

And I don't want you. I just want Otis and Pop Pop.

Jules opened her mouth and shut it. Then her face morphed from angry to smug. "Yeah, you do."

"I know, I know. Your dad, the party, the money. You've played those cards already, Jules."

"Not that," she said, stuffing things back into her tote bag. "Something else. It's not enough for you to stay out of their way. You need to know what the pros are doing. What they're finding. You need to throw them off the trail if they get close. And you need *me* to do it."

CHAPTER ELEVEN

True Fact: Real life smells way worse than it looks
in the movies.

"This is a terrible idea," I said.

"It's a fantastic idea," Jules said.

The next morning, Jules and I were at the fuel dock, the place at the Sag Harbor marina where everybody brings their boats to refuel. Everybody including Fitz Fitzgibbons and the *Windfall*.

I'd left Otis with Nora's dad, Dr. Joshi, who happens to be the town dentist. Eloise, the hygienist there, is also the dog trainer who trained Otis for us, and Otis likes to hang out with her while she cleans people's teeth. Eloise says Otis makes an excellent antianxiety dog.

Needless to say, the terrible idea was Jules's. I had told her that we could keep tabs on the *Windfall* by talking to

Fritjof's mom, Laurie. She's the harbormaster and knows everyone and everything that happens in these waters.

But Jules said that Fitz was a media mogul and therefore a master of spreading fake news. Plus, she was sure he'd made everyone on his boat sign an NDA (nondisclosure agreement—I had to ask).

It's possible Jules had a point.

Which was why we were now at the gas dock about to break the law. Or, rather, *I* was about to break the law, since I knew more about boats, while Jules got to be the lookout.

I was boiling in my sweatshirt, which I was wearing to hide the plastic bag that contained the spy camera I was supposed to install on the bridge of the *Windfall* when nobody was looking. Just to be clear, the bridge is where the captain spends most of their time steering the boat, and therefore where you might expect any important information to be shared. It's also inside the boat. As in, I had to climb onto the deck and then go inside and install a piece of spy equipment. I had to break and then I had to enter. Well, hopefully not break, but definitely enter and install.

Which was not only the first illegal thing I'd ever done, it was also the most dangerous thing I'd ever done, including the time I licked a flagpole in January on a dare from Douglas, and Nora had to run back into school for a bowl of hot water to douse me with so I wouldn't rip my tongue off. How was it that I'd known Nora practically my whole life and we'd never broken the law, but I'd known Jules all of four days, and here I was, embarking on a life of crime?

The *Windfall* was there getting her tank filled, which I estimated would take about two or three hours. But Fitz had gone to the Breakfast Buoy to get an egg sandwich, which I estimated would take about ten or fifteen minutes. The crew was also gone, and I had no idea when they'd be back.

The dock was crowded with every kind of boat—from little dinghies to comfy lobster boats to glitzy motor yachts. Which meant that tons of people were coming and going.

"Clock's ticking. Now or never." Jules shoved me toward the *Windfall* and headed for the grass in the other direction to avoid suspicion.

"Thanks for the pep talk," I said to the air.

I tried to transform myself into a completely different human being, one who was brave and daring and could kill an enemy with a single karate chop. Basically, Lara Croft. While I channeled my inner superhero, Jules lay on the grass pretending to sunbathe. At least I hoped she was just pretending, since my future freedom depended on her. She waved at me. Not a friendly *Hey, how's it going?* wave, but an urgent *Get moving* now*!* wave.

I climbed over the rail.

The door to the bridge was unlocked. Inside were more electronic instruments than I'd ever seen in one place, including the West Marine supply catalog. No wonder Fitz needed a ridiculously big boat. Knobs and monitors were spread out over a dashboard that took up the whole front and sides of the cabin. I could have been on a nuclear submarine.

Mounted on the wall over the door to the main inner cabin was a camera that sent audio and video to a website. I knew what it was because Jules had spotted it in the picture of Fitz in the *East Hampton Star* and found a small version online, which she then overnighted ("What? It's only a hundred and fifty dollars. The accountant won't see the bill for a month, and when he does he'll figure my dad bought it"). I was supposed to glue our camera under the *Windfall*'s and hope that no one would notice it was there—and also hope that no one happened to be watching the livestream while I was installing it. But the *Windfall*'s camera was screwed to the wall high up, where I couldn't reach. And the chairs on the bridge were bolted to the floor, so I had nothing to drag over and stand on. Not a step stool, not a bucket, not even a pencil cup.

Bear down and carry on, BB. That's what Pop Pop would

have said, assuming he approved of what I was doing. He definitely would have understood *why* I was doing it. Mom and Dad, on the other hand, most definitely would not have approved or understood. Which I was trying very hard not to think about.

Maybe, just maybe, if I stand on the counter along the wall, I can reach the camera from there.

I glanced out the window. Jules was safe on dry land, chatting with one of the guys who worked at the gas dock, but also, I was relieved to see, glancing around in a lookout-y kind of way. Still no sign of Fitz or his crew.

I pulled the bag out from under my sweatshirt and emptied my supplies on the counter. I'd come prepared with marine glue that I'd scooped into an old jelly jar from home. The glue was waterproof, sunproof, leakproof, and saltproof. It smelled like burnt tires, but at least I knew that once I stuck the camera to the wall it would stay there forever. Literally.

I smeared some glue on the base of the new camera with the back of a plastic spoon. Then I climbed onto the counter and eyed the old camera and wished that arms could do things like grow really long just because you wanted them to. And then, since this was real life and I wasn't Elastigirl, I leaned.

You know that game trust, where you fall backward into the waiting arms of a friend and hope they catch you? This was like that except I fell forward, and I had to stop my own fall against the opposite wall one-handed without breaking my nose or dropping the new camera.

Victory!

Behold Blue Broen, a.k.a. Lara Croft! Feet on counter, hands on wall, body in midair, bag in mouth, hair in eyes, sweat all over, really bad itch in the middle of my back.

Keeping one hand on the wall, I positioned the new camera in place. And held it there for sixty seconds that felt like sixty years.

Waiting, waiting, waiting.

Noticing, noticing, noticing.

Noticing the piece of hair that was stuck to the side of my face that I couldn't brush off. Noticing that the people I could see on the dock through the window of the bridge could see me too if they happened to look my way. Noticing the plastic spoon that was now glued to the fingers of my left hand forever.

I counted to sixty and was just starting to feel really good about my Lara Croft-y act of bravery and stealth when I heard three short blasts from a referee whistle— Jules's warning signal. Seconds later a voice boomed, "Best egg sandwich in town!"

Fitz! And possibly his crew too.

Get out get out get out get out get out!

I jumped down from the counter. My heart beat like a

woodpecker—which could have been because I was terrified but also could have been because being terrified makes my blood sugar spike, and I had no way of knowing which it was because my kit was in Jules's bag.

Fitz stood on the dock between me and freedom and insulin. Jules was good, but even she didn't have any tricks that would stop him from seeing some kid he didn't know on his boat. Somehow I had to get off the *Windfall*. Now.

I crawled out of the bridge onto the deck, trying not to picture my face on a WANTED DEAD OR ALIVE poster. I inched to the far side of the *Windfall*, which faced the water, away from the dock. Fitz couldn't see me from here, but plenty of other people could if they bothered to look this way. The marina was like a parking lot for boats, all lined up one after another. People inside those boats, people walking by—any one of them might wonder what I was doing crouched on the deck of the *Windfall* with a plastic bag in my mouth and a spoon glued to my hand.

There was only one path to safety. I peered over the edge of the deck.

Bits of seaweed, twigs, and duck feathers bobbed around blobs of engine oil that oozed on top of the water. GROSS. *Really* gross. But probably not as gross as living in a jail cell.

Holding my breath to keep out the smell, I slithered down the ladder on the side of the boat and eased feet-first into June-freezing water. *Bonfires, pizza ovens, tea kettles, Nora's attic.* I thought the hottest thoughts I possibly could while I dog-paddled through slime, grunting, straining to keep my chin above water under the weight of my wet sweatshirt. The bag hanging from my mouth splashed duck muck on my cheeks and hair. I paddled harder and *some drops sloshed into my mouth.* Normally I'm not hyper about germs—after all, I let my dog lick my lips—but *engine oil and duck waste had just infiltrated my body.* I clamped my lips tighter and paddled faster.

Finally, I made it to the boat next to the *Windfall*. Now I just had to circle that boat and climb onto the dock on its far side. Which would have been totally doable if the owner hadn't chosen that exact moment to climb up from the cabin onto the deck. Which meant I couldn't paddle. I had to put my head under the oil-duck-twig water...and swim.

Let's just say the water was even more disgusting than it looked, and I'll never eat fowl again.

I was climbing up the slimy algae-covered ladder to the dock when Jules's shadow fell over me.

"That was *so hard*. You have no idea. I had to keep those idiots busy forever. Where were you?"

I flung the bag onto the dock and spit out a feather

81

that was stuck to my lip. Mucky water streamed from my sweatshirt onto the dock. "Inside the—"

"Whatever," Jules snapped. "We have a problem."

"What?"

I found my kit in Jules's bag, then turned my back so I could test without her watching.

"The camera needs to be connected to the *Windfall*'s Wi-Fi, but their network is password protected."

I whipped around. "Are you serious? I broke the law and swam through garbage and made my blood sugar go up to two hundred and ten all to hook up a camera we can't use because we don't have the password?" I stabbed at the buttons on my insulin pump like they were eyes I could poke out and sent a quick text to Mom and Dad.

"It doesn't matter. I'll deal with it," Jules said. "Just like I have to deal with everything annoying while you get to go off on adventures."

Jules stomped toward the *Windfall*, and I stomped after her, dripping and smelly. "What are you so mad about? You're the one who waited on shore, while I was the one who risked my life!" I said.

Jules whirled around. "Exactly. Do you think I got the fun part?"

"Gosh, I don't know. I just drank garbage! Do you think *I* got the fun part?"

Jules and I death-stared each other for maybe a solid

minute until the *Windfall* crew came back. Then Jules broke away—*first*, let the record show—marched up to one of them, and plastered a fake smile on her face.

"Excuse me? I'm Jules Buttersby. My dad is Edward Buttersby, the actor? Listen, my dad just sent me a rough cut of his new movie, and I really want to watch it here outside where my friend can dry out, but I need Wi-Fi. You people are going to be here for a while getting your gas or whatever, right? Do you mind if I log on to your network?"

The crew guy's eyes got big at "Buttersby" and bigger at "new movie."

"Sure!" he said.

"Great." Jules pulled an iPad out of her tote bag. "What's your password?"

"B-I-L-L-I-O-N," he said.

"Seriously?" Jules said.

The crew guy shrugged. Jules typed and we waited.

Success. From this moment on, everything that happened on the *Windfall*'s bridge would be beamed to the cloud for us to hear and see.

Jules snapped the iPad case shut and we turned to go.

"Hey, wait a second, Julia," the crew guy said.

We stopped short.

I had a sick heavy feeling that was only partly caused by the smell wafting from my sweatshirt. The crew

83

guy looked serious. As in, there was a serious matter he wanted to discuss with us. Trespassing, for instance.

I glanced at Jules. She gave me a *Let me do the talking* look.

But the crew guy said, "I'm a *huge* fan of your dad's. Would you tell him that for me?"

Suddenly, there was oxygen to breathe again. Jules rolled her eyes. "I'll tell him."

"Thanks, Julia. I really appreciate it."

The crew guy left with a big smile on his face. Jules made sure the iPad was back to using her phone, and we walked toward town to pick up Otis at Dr. Joshi's.

"Does that happen a lot?" I asked.

"You have no idea," Jules said. "Today was actually good. Most of the time I don't have a name, not even a wrong name. 'Oh, look! Isn't that Ed Buttersby's daughter?' 'Hey, Ed Buttersby's daughter! Get me a part in his next movie?' 'Smile, Baby Buttersby!' They all know me from his Twitter or *People* magazine."

I understood what it felt like to have people think they know you based on something you can't control. I tried to imagine what it would feel like if people were constantly asking me for favors from my dad. Or being nice to me because of my dad. Or doing me favors because of my dad. Bad, probably. Also annoying and insulting. And maybe occasionally convenient.

Suddenly, I remembered why we were there in the first place. "Let's check and see if the spy-cam works," I said.

Jules typed on the glass screen and toggled up the volume. Fitz's voice boomed:

"Somebody get rid of this garbage egg sandwich and bring me two-forty MLs of my energy powder in a soy-almond base! And up the enzymes—my head's killing me from having to listen to all the morons!"

"It works," Jules said.

She turned down the volume a little, and I wrung out my sweatshirt one-handed.

"What's with the spoon?" Jules said.

"Don't ask."

CHAPTER TWELVE

True Fact: Sometimes the only thing worse than knowing
is not knowing.

I told Mom and Dad that Jules had offered to help me
with my water project so they wouldn't wonder why we
were always together, and we spent the next week searching the bottom of the bay in ten-square-foot chunks. Even
though I still didn't want Jules there, I had to admit the
search went a lot faster now that there were two of us and
we each had our own view bucket.

While we searched, Otis snoozed or gnawed or kept
watch for rogue seagulls. We couldn't see the *Windfall*
because we were at opposite ends of Gardiner's Island.
Instead, we kept Jules's iPad running with just the audio
from the spy-cam, since the sun made it impossible to
view the video. Plus, it's possible I got marine glue on
the camera lens, because when we tested it indoors all

we could see was blurry mush. We were now experts in what every member of the *Windfall* crew liked for lunch. We also knew that Sonia, the documentary director, thought crew-guy Damon was annoying, and that other-crew-guy Marc missed his boyfriend in Chicago. Also, everybody hated Fitz.

But most important of all, we knew that so far the *Windfall* had found exactly the same thing we'd found: nothing.

At the end of each day, I came home and checked the mailbox for a letter from Nora. At first I knew there was no way there'd be one, but I checked anyway. Now it'd been a week, though. Nora must have gotten my going-away card, but I still hadn't heard from her.

"This is dumb, Otis. Nora and I don't keep score." Otis shook raindrops off his fur on the front porch. "I'll write her again now, and her letters will get to me when they get to me." Otis and I went upstairs to my room. He took the bed and I took the desk.

Dear Nora...

Too formal.

Nora...

Too cold.

Hey!

I crumpled the paper and tossed it into the trash basket under my desk.

I'd never written Nora a real letter before. I'd never had to. If this had been any other summer of our lives, we'd have been bowling or going to the beach or maybe writing a dictionary for Old Country, the secret language we invented in second grade after our class trip to the Renaissance fair. I should've been talking to Nora every day, but instead, I had no idea what she was doing or who she was doing it with, and she knew the same about me.

Nora would understand about Jules. She'd say, *Think of Jules as a circus clown. She prances around the big tent, doing silly clown things, piling into cars, honking noses. While you, Blue, you watch and say, "Ha! Look at that slightly amusing and rather annoying clown! I will laugh at her, and then I will go about my business ruling the world."*

I decided I'd try writing again after dinner and went downstairs to help Mom. Since it was raining, we were eating in the kitchen instead of outside on the back deck like usual. Mom sat shucking corn directly into a garbage can wedged between her knees, her hair piled on top of her head and secured with two pencils.

I moved a giant vase of mixed flowers to the counter so Otis and I could set the table, our nightly chore. "Lamb's ear feels like Otis's ears," I said, rubbing a velvety leaf between two fingers.

"And its flowers smell like pineapple," Mom said.

I sniffed, but the flowerless leaves didn't have a smell. "Napkins, Otie."

Otis took the yellow napkin holder off the counter and carried it to me in his mouth by the handle. On the radio, the DJ was "spinning songs from the seventies" at WLNG, the local Sag Harbor station.

A rock song came on, and Mom did her best air guitar to the opening riff. I just watched, thinking about Nora and letters we hadn't written and ballast piles I hadn't found.

"Blue, you left me hanging!" Mom held out empty hands.

I admit it: I air-guitar with my mom. And we lip-sync instead of sing because I inherited my lack of musical ability from her and we both know it.

"Sorry. I'm just not feeling it tonight," I said, trying to force a smile.

She brushed a piece of hair out of her face with her forearm. "Still no letter from Nora?"

"Not yet." I folded another napkin.

Mom gave me a good long look. "How about we make that potato-rosemary bread you love tonight so we can toast it with cheese for breakfast tomorrow? We haven't done that in a while."

"Maybe." I wished I could talk to Mom about the hunt.

I hated keeping such a huge secret from my parents. But Pop Pop and treasure were very sore subjects for Dad. I wished, for the zillionth time, that I knew why.

Dad came in from the patio, where he'd been grilling under an umbrella, raindrops spattering his favorite Pearl Jam T-shirt and his hair, which is black and curly like mine. He put the plate with the burgers on the table. "Head hug," he said.

I leaned over so he could wrap an arm around my head and squeeze. Mom put the corn in a big pot of boiling water.

"How's the project going, Belly?" Dad crouched over Otis, giving him a massive belly rub while Otis's whole body corkscrewed around in a state of ecstasy. Dad claims he's Otis's favorite belly rubber, a title I challenge. He also says he's Otis's favorite wrestling partner and jogging buddy, but I remind him he's Otis's *only* wrestling partner and jogging buddy.

"The project's going okay." It turns out guilt tastes like spoiled grapes, mushy and sour.

"It's good to see you making new friends. Being alone all the time isn't healthy."

I pretty much dropped off the planet friend-wise last fall when Pop Pop got sick. At first, I'd visit him during the times we'd usually sail together. I'd read aloud from his favorite books about a sea captain and his doctor /

spy best friend from the 1800s. Pop Pop would interrupt every few lines to make sure I knew all the nautical terms, which made it kind of hard to follow the story, but I didn't complain. Later, when Pop Pop got sicker, I visited every day and read pages and pages until he fell asleep.

"Spending every day with Jules isn't healthy," I muttered.

"You wouldn't have to spend every day with Jules if you'd done your homework during the school year like you should have," Mom said in a singsongy voice. "It's your own fault you're in the doghouse."

Every time Mom tells me I'm in the doghouse for something, I want to point out that Otis's house is *our* house, so she's actually insulting her own home. But I never do, because no matter what Jules might think, even though I'm almost failing out of school, I'm not stupid.

Mom took the corn out of the pot and put it in a bowl lined with red-and-white-checked dish towels. "Dinner's ready."

Headbutt.

"High or low?" Dad said to Otis before I could get the words out. Otis gave Dad a high-five paw.

I glared at Dad.

"Sorry," he said.

"You're supposed to be letting me handle this," I said.

"I know." Dad held up both hands in surrender. "You're right. Old habits."

Otis dropped my kit in my lap, and I tested while watching my parents out of the corner of my eye. Mom was literally biting her lip.

A few seconds later the meter told me my blood sugar level was 180.

"Good high, Otis." I gave Otis his turkey jerky treat, and he lay down next to my chair to savor it. He looked relaxed, but I knew he was still on duty, sniffing whatever chemicals my body made that would let him know when my blood sugar went down to normal. "So that's forty-five grams of carbs for the corn and the bun." I typed the number forty-five into my pump.

"We're having strawberries for dessert," Mom said. "They were in season at the farm stand."

I entered another fifteen grams for the strawberries, and the pump calculated how big a bolus of insulin I'd need to bring me down from my high and cover the carbs. "Three and a half units," I told Mom and Dad.

The whole time I went through these steps, Mom and Dad watched me while pretending not to watch me. I understood why they wanted to double-check—no, *triple*-check—that I was doing everything right. Because what if I got it wrong? If my blood sugar went too high I could go into ketoacidosis, which is medicalese for feeling like your brain has the stomach flu. And if it went too low I could pass out. Or worse.

Diabetes has been around forever, but people started using insulin only about a hundred years ago. I think about that sometimes: If I'd been born in 1900, I'd have been dead before I was three. The only thing scarier to me than managing my diabetes myself is *not* knowing how to manage my diabetes myself.

"So tell us where you've sampled the water so far," Dad said, sneaking a piece of burger to Otis under the table. We have a strict rule against feeding Otis table scraps, which is why all three of us try to do it without the others seeing. Even Otis keeps up with the act. He never begs. He just hangs around the table, quietly available to helpfully snarf down any juicy chunks of meat that happen to fall his way.

"Oh, you know. Not much. Just some stuff near Shelter Island."

"Shelter Island? Aren't you supposed to be concentrating on the South Fork?" Mom said.

I choked on a sip of water. "Well, not really Shelter Island so much as Northwest Harbor. And, um, Springs." I'm a rotten liar. I stutter; I come up with dumb excuses; my nose may actually grow. Feeling guilty makes me even worse at it.

"Which is it? Shelter Island or Springs?" Mom asked.

"Um, both? I mean, I started at Shelter Island, because I forgot I didn't need to sample that. I mean, I didn't forget—I just thought it would be more accurate and thorough if I included the area near the big landmass in the middle of the fork. And then I did Northwest Harbor, and now I'm doing Springs."

"That's a lot for a week," Dad said, pointing at me with his fork.

"Yeah," I said. "I've been working hard. Really hard."

Rotten. Rot-ten. Rot.

Even though Otis wasn't alerting, I tested again to make sure I was back in a good range.

"Better?" Dad asked.

"One-oh-two," I said.

Dad's shoulders relaxed.

"How are things going with Jules?" Mom asked.

"Surprisingly okay," I said. The surprising part was that I wasn't lying. When Jules wasn't talking about life in LA or her favorite fashion designers, she actually had interesting stuff to say. Yesterday, for example, Jules had told me that back in the day, when sailors got shipwrecked and ran out of food and had to resort to cannibalism, they called it a "custom of the sea," a True Fact so good that I put it in my journal. It's possible that in her spare time Jules read things like history books and watched things like documentaries about physics.

"I'm glad," Mom said. "Because the fund-raiser is going to be big this year. Ed's really excited about it—he's got a million ideas—a silent auction, a fruit fair—"

"A fruit fair?" I said.

"A celebration of fruit," Mom explained. "Because it's a healthy carb."

"Maybe they should do a *fish fest* instead, since it's a healthy protein." Dad waggled his eyebrows at me.

"*Dad*," I groaned.

"It's going to be a real festive *o-cake-sion.*" He grinned.

"Hal, you're killing us," Mom said.

"Heh," Dad grunted with pride. Nothing makes him happier than a bad pun.

Fruit fairs. Huge crowds. Photo ops. "Can't they find some other kid to be their poster child?" I asked.

"Not all diabetic kids are as healthy as you, Blue. You're doing this for them too," Mom said.

How many times had I heard that line? I wasn't hungry anymore, but I had to finish my carbs anyway because I'd already taken insulin for them. I stuffed the rest of the bun in my mouth in one huge wad and dropped half the burger on the floor for Otis without even trying to hide it.

"So have you seen the *Windfall* out there?" Dad asked.

"Whuh?" I choked down the giant lump of bun that was stuck in my throat. "Oh. Yeah. But they haven't found anything yet."

ROT!

"What makes you say that?" Dad asked.

"I just figured if they found something, Fitz would have a big press conference about it," I said, for once in my life sounding halfway convincing.

"Well, I hope they keep looking for a long time. Pump some money into the local economy. They won't find anything," Dad said.

"How do you know? You can't be sure there's no treasure out there," I said, wishing yet again that he'd give me a real answer.

Dad pushed back from the table and picked up his plate, his good mood gone. "Trust me. I know."

He left the kitchen.

I growled and threaded my fingers through my hair. "What did I say wrong?" I asked Mom.

She sighed. "It's not you. Talking about treasure hunting reminds him of Pop Pop."

"I just don't get it," I said. "What's so bad that he won't talk about Pop Pop or the family stories? And why did he sell my VOC coin?" I was still mad about the coin. I probably always would be.

Mom pursed her lips, thinking. Maybe, *finally*, somebody was going to tell me something real. Something that wasn't "it's private" or "you wouldn't understand" or "when you're older."

Maybe not. "It's not for me to say, sweetie. It has to come from Dad," Mom said.

"But he won't talk about it!"

More thinking. At last Mom said, "I can tell you this: Dad misses Pop Pop. He misses him a lot. And the stuff with the treasure? It's complicated."

Which was more than she'd ever said before, but not by much.

CHAPTER THIRTEEN

True Fact: People think having a diabetic-alert dog means you can spend less time monitoring your diabetes, but actually it means you spend more time. I check my blood sugar as soon as I get up in the morning, before and after I eat, before I go to bed, and once in the middle of the night—plus, I do it whenever Otis alerts me.

The air conditioner in my room was broken, and the night was so hot and humid that every time I rolled over in bed I was afraid I was going to drown in my own sweat. I didn't even need my alarm to wake me for my usual middle-of-the-night blood sugar test—something else my parents used to do for me that now I do for myself—because I didn't sleep for more than twenty minutes at a time.

Poor Otis would have been way better off in my parents' room, where it was cool, but he knows my blood sugar tends to go a little crazy at night, so he stays close to me, even though he can smell my blood sugar from any room in the house, including when I'm upstairs in the shower and he's downstairs in the kitchen.

After melting all night—made way worse by the huge furry dog in my bed and my lowish blood sugar, which wouldn't go above seventy-five no matter what I ate—I was tempted to spend the whole day with my head in the freezer. Instead, Otis, Jules, and I were on the boat in choppy water, life vests on, Otis napping and Jules and me looking at nothing but swirling sand through our view buckets.

"This is pointless," I said. "Let's head back."

"Why should we head back? I don't want to head back."

"But we can't see anything." *And just a short twenty-minute boat ride from here there's a freezer at home that I can stick my head in. Plus, my blood sugar's still kind of low but I ran out of Skittles and I don't want to have to resort to the disgusting orange glucose tablets that Mom bought instead of the strawberry ones.*

"So? There's plenty of other stuff we can do." Jules seemed strangely hyper considering the air felt like steamed gym socks.

"Like what?" *Ice bath, iced tea, lie on my parents' bed with their air conditioner on . . .*

"Like . . . look at maps or clean the boat or . . . or . . ."

Jules *really* didn't want to go home. And I bet her whole house was air-conditioned, not just the bedrooms.

She plunked her bucket down.

"We need to embark on a campaign of misinformation."

"A what?"

"Send Fitz and the Fitzminions on a wild-goose chase. Tell them stuff that will make them think the treasure is someplace where we know it isn't."

I pictured the *Windfall* pulling up their anchor and motoring to Orient Point or Fishers Island or maybe East Shore, where the old nuclear power plant is.

Suddenly, the air felt a little less heavy. And the freezer could wait. Otis sensed my excitement; he lifted his head and sniffed.

"How do we do that?" I asked.

"Easy," Jules said. "We lie."

Turns out lying is like any other skill: It just takes practice. First I lied to Miguel at the Breakfast Buoy: "You know, my great-grandfather was part of a team that dredged the waters in Gardiner's Bay back in 1932, so, um, there's no possible way the *Windfall* will find any treasure there now." Then Jules lied to Laurie at the dock: "I found some old maps in the town library, and guess what? There used to be a strip of land that connected Gardiner's Point to Gardiner's Island, so there's no way there can be any treasure there now." Then we went to the gas dock and Jules lied to the guys who pump gas: "So, this lobster fisherman was at my house the other day selling three-pounders to my chef, and he said his traps keep getting caught in an old wreck about ten miles away from the *Windfall*."

Then we waited to see what the *Windfall* would do.

The next morning, Jules and Otis and I went to the Long Wharf, a pier at the harbor with a bunch of shops and restaurants and parking for cars on it. Small boats bobbed on one side of the wharf and gigantic yachts loomed on the other side. The air was even hotter and stickier than the day before, and it felt like it was going to pour any second.

Jules and I hunched over the iPad, sharing a pair of earbuds. Otis lay on the ground by our feet, panting.

"Do you think our lies worked?" I said.

"Shhhhh," Jules hissed.

The minutes crawled by. Nobody on the *Windfall* said anything about changing locations. Instead, the crew complained about the weather, and Fitz complained about the crew, and Sonia the documentary director complained about the light, until, finally:

"Hang on. What's that?"

"What's what?"

"*That*. That blob on the screen."

"You sure it's not a shell?"

"It's too big to be a shell."

"Here! Take the wheel—I've got a good feeling about this!"

After which there was a lot of moving around and static and yelling. Jules had my arm in a death grip, but I barely noticed because my body temperature had shot up to six hundred degrees.

Fitz's voice came out of the iPad:

"Listen up, people! Whatever we find down there—I don't care if it's the *Golden Lion* payroll or the lost city of Atlantis—you say nothing to nobody, hear me? From this second on, we are on information lockdown. You speak of it to no one, not even to each other. *I* control the information flow, got that?"

I yanked out my earbud and jumped up. Otis and I started pacing back and forth.

"We *need* to know what they found," Jules said.

"I know." *Pace, pace, pace.*

"They're not going to say what it is out loud," she said. "Fitz said they can't talk about it, 'not even to each other.' "

"I know."

Jules joined us. *Pace, pace, pace.*

"And we can't see it from the spy-cam because of the glue." She held up the iPad. Even in the sun, you could tell it showed nothing but blur.

"I know." *Pace.*

Jules stopped short. "We have to sneak up on them and look."

Otis and I stopped short. "Not while they're in open water. They'd see us coming a mile away."

"There's got to be *something*. Think!" Jules said.

There was something, but it was a crazy something. An illegal something.

A chill came over me, like an ice cube on the back of my neck.

"Every second that goes by is one second closer to Fitz putting whatever they found in a place where we can't see it," I said.

Jules smacked her forehead. *"Duh!"*

I looked down at Otis, who was standing at attention, ready for anything. Which was good, because we'd never done anything as dangerous as what we were about to do. But then again, Petra and Abraham were even younger than me when they survived a mutiny and somehow ended up with a stolen fortune.

Suddenly, the chill on my neck turned to heat.

"Boat!" I ordered, Otis at my heels.

"Where are we going?" Jules asked, jogging after us.

"The Ruins."

CHAPTER FOURTEEN

True Fact: Sometimes the thing you're scared of is
the wrong thing to be scared of.

An hour later, Jules and I stood at the wheel of the Mako,
scanning the coastline of Gardiner's Point, a.k.a. the
Ruins, a.k.a. a tiny speck of land due north of the tip of
the T-bone's pointy hat.

"Let me get this straight," she said, wind whipping
her hair around her face. "The government of the United
States of America says that no one is allowed to step foot
on this island."

"Right." My heart was back at the top of the death-
drop ride.

"Because they used it for target practice in World
War Two."

"Right again," I said. *Hands on the safety bar.*

"So now it's covered with unexploded bombs."

"Yup." *Whooosh...boom!*

Jules lowered her binoculars. "Have you ever been there?"

"No," I said. "But I've heard that high school kids sneak onto it sometimes."

She shifted the throttle into drive. "So it can't be that dangerous, right?"

"I hope not," I said, and took the wheel.

The only way to find out whether the *Windfall* had found an old shoe or something from a 350-year-old wreck was to sneak onto the far side of the Ruins, hike to the near side facing the *Windfall*, and spy through binoculars from the shore. So here we were, breaking the law again.

What would be next? Bank robbery?

"Here's what we should do," Jules said. "Let's look at the Ruins on satellite images so we know where to walk."

"I've tried," I said. "The government used to pixelate it. Even now, you can't zoom close enough to see anything." Blacked out. DO NOT ENTER. Not only are people banned from going to the Ruins; people aren't even allowed to *look* at it.

"That's so cool."

True Fact: It kinda was.

We motored to an old broken-down dock on the Ruins' far side that looked strong enough to tie the boat to, but not strong enough to stand on.

"We'll have to swim to shore," I said.

Jules and I both had bathing suits on under our clothes. We stuffed our shorts and T-shirts and some supplies into a waterproof gear bag, and then the three of us stared over the side of the boat at the water.

"There could be a bomb right here under us," Jules said, reading my mind. Except she said it in an excited front-car-of-the-roller-coaster kind of way.

"We'll slide in gently and we won't touch bottom," I said. "Okay?"

Otis woofed.

"I'll go first." Jules swung a leg over the rail.

"No, let me." I didn't trust Jules to be careful, and besides, this whole crazy mission was my idea.

"You sure?" Jules asked.

No! "Yeah." I climbed over the boat rail and hung from the side, questioning my sanity, then let go and started treading water. Otis watched me from the edge of the boat, ready to leap the instant I gave him the command. "Okay, give me the gear bag," I said to Jules.

She passed it to me, and I swam one-handed to shore, breathing much harder than I should have needed to. I waited until the last possible second to put my feet down.

I took a few seconds so my heart could stop racing. The sand was full of broken mussel shells and shards of old metal trash. Jules and I both had on flip-flops, but Otis was going to have a problem. We would have to carry my wet eighty-pound dog to the walking path.

We could turn back now. Before anything bad happened. Like a bomb going off or the Coast Guard arresting us.

But also before we saw what the *Windfall* had found.

"Your turn!" I called to Jules. "Be careful."

"Don't worry." She slid off the boat and swam to shore.

It turns out worry tastes sharp and bitter, like olive juice, which Nora once dared me to drink. I gulped and called, "Come, Otis!"

Otis jumped over the side and paddled toward us. When he got close Jules and I waded in and heaved him over the metal and shells to a rough, sandy path that led to the other side of the island. I had Otis's front half, and he licked my nose while Jules and I carried him. The lick was Otis's way of saying thank you, which I appreciated.

"Don't you think you should leave him on the boat?" Jules grunted.

"I would," I huffed, "but he'd never stay."

"Not even if you ordered him?" Jules said. "I thought Otis always did what you told him to do."

We set Otis down, and I said, "Otis's number one job is to take care of me. It's one thing if I'm in the living room and he's in the kitchen. But he can tell this is serious.

Even if I tied him to the boat, he'd chew through the rope and come after us. It's better if I just let him come." Plus, I felt safer having Otis around, but I wasn't going to admit that to Jules.

Jules's eyebrows scrunched like caterpillars.

"What?" I said.

"Nothing," she said, her eyes on Otis as she petted his head. "Just that it must feel really good to have somebody care that way about you. Even if he's a dog."

Otis cares about me more than he cares about anyone or anything in the world. My parents do too. Was there really nobody who felt that way about Jules? Not even her mom or Ed? For a second, I saw a different person, the girl with her mother in the photograph that Jules had shown me on the beach, only sad.

Thunder rumbled close by. The sky had turned gunmetal gray. A big storm would roll in soon. We hurried to put on our shorts and T-shirts.

"That way." I pointed straight ahead.

Gardiner's Point was so small that you could see the whole thing no matter where you stood. I got why they called it the Ruins. It was basically a big pile of rubble. No trees, lots of sand and broken boulders, and some big concrete blocks in random spots that looked like they'd rolled off what was left of the old fort, which wasn't much.

Another thunderclap.

Jules jumped from rock to rock while Otis and I carefully picked our way along the path.

"I don't think you should be doing that," I said.

Jules took a long leap to the next rock. I winced.

"You worry too much," she said. "I have excellent balance."

"What if you fall and land on a bomb?"

Jules paused, foot in the air, and shrugged. "You only live once." She jumped to the next rock.

"Jules."

"Blue."

"Fine, do what you want. But don't blame me when... you know..." I stepped around a chunk of cement, sweating all over even though the temperature had dropped about ten degrees.

"I promise I won't blame you if I get blown to pieces by a bomb." Jules jumped. "Actually, which do you think is worse: getting blown up or dying by falling out of a plane?"

I kicked a piece of metal away from Otis. "Definitely falling out of a plane. It's a slower death."

"But with the plane at least you have a few minutes of free fall before impact, so you get to have some fun before you die." Jules waved her arms up and down like an enormous yet graceful bird. It reminded me of flying around the Island Bowl parking lot with Nora the night before she left. What was Nora doing now? Definitely not tiptoeing through a bomb field on a spy mission—although she probably would have loved the idea as long as it was imaginary. Which this definitely wasn't.

"I don't think free fall is so fun if you know you're going to die at the end of it," I said.

"Maybe not." Jules jumped again. "But it's still better than a bomb and having no fun at all."

"Fine." I grabbed Otis's collar so I could brush some pointy rocks out of his way before he stepped on them. "Which do you think is worse: eating a giant plate of worms right now or going hungry for a week?"

Jules didn't even need a second to think it over. "Obviously eating worms now is worse. Hunger at any given moment isn't anywhere near as bad as eating worms. Plus, you'd lose a ton of weight if you went hungry for a week."

"You know that's insane, right?"

She shrugged. "Insane for Sag Harbor, maybe. Not for LA."

"Are you serious? I'm never moving to LA," I said.

"I *am* serious," Jules said. "And I don't blame you."

We'd reached the far side of the island. Jules stepped down from her last rock.

"There they are." I pointed at the *Windfall*, about a hundred yards out. "Do you see them?"

Jules squinted at the blob on the water that was the *Windfall*. "Barely."

I got out binoculars. Fitz and the crew were on the deck. Fitz was holding something over his head with his crew bunched around him. *Dancing.*

"Can you see what's happening?" Jules asked.

"Yeah," I said, fighting to keep my voice steady.

"Well, what did they find?" Jules grabbed the binoculars out of my hands.

We were too far away to see what the *Windfall* had found, but it didn't matter. We were close enough to see it was something that made them really happy, which meant it was something that probably came off a boat 350 years ago and not something like an old shoe. They were close to the treasure before and now they were even closer, and they were professional hunters with every piece of expensive gear known to humankind.

The rain started at last. Big fat drops.

Jules kept looking and looking through the binoculars until the drops slurred into sheets and she couldn't see anymore.

The wind blew through our soaked clothes, and I shivered from the cold. Otis pressed his wet shoulder against my leg.

"There really is a giant treasure somewhere in these

waters, isn't there?" Jules said, turning away from the *Windfall* and her celebrating crew.

"No," I said, rubbing my arms up and down. "I just made the whole thing up for the fun of it."

Jules was just as wet as me, but she hardly seemed to notice. "Seriously, I'm being serious. Like 'somebody else is wearing your dress on Oscar night' serious. These professional treasure hunters have just found an object that could be from a boat that carried the *Golden Lion* payroll. But the sorrowful hound is on the opposite end of Gardiner's Island from the *Windfall*. Tell me the honest truth. Do you *still* think we're looking in the right place?"

"Absolutely," I said automatically.

But the truth was, I didn't know anymore. My gut still said I was in the right place, but my eyes weren't so sure. Neither was my head. There were so many mysteries. Like how did a girl from Amsterdam end up with a boy from Java? And how did the payroll get from the *Golden Lion* in the Indian Ocean to whatever boat Petra and Abraham sailed across the Atlantic? And how did two twelve-year-olds get their hands on the treasure in the first place?

Jules pushed a wet clump of hair out of her eyes. "How can you be right if they just found something over there?"

My fingers sank into Otis's soggy ruff and combed the dense fur. "Because," I said, seeing it in my head. "Ships

112

don't always sink where they run into trouble. Sometimes they hit something and drift before they sink. The water near the *Windfall* at the northwest side of Gardiner's Island is full of rocks and shoals—"

"What are shoals?"

"Shallow water. Like from a sandbar. Probably the boat hit something bad, something they couldn't recover from. Maybe when they first hit, some stuff on the upper decks slid overboard. Then they drifted and maybe more stuff fell overboard until they finally sank near the sorrowful hound."

"Are you saying the payroll could've gone overboard before they sank?"

"No. It wouldn't have happened like that." I closed my eyes and pictured a square-sailed wooden ship. "The payroll was heavy. It would've been in the hold at the bottom of the boat. It wouldn't have just rolled off like a plate or a hammer or something on deck."

"You're saying this like you know, but you don't. You're just guessing," Jules said.

Her hair flopped around her head like a string mop in the wind. Otis looked like a shaggy otter with ears.

"It's more than a guess," I said, my gut getting stronger by the minute. "It's logic. It makes *sense* that it happened like that. Plus, I have something the *Windfall* doesn't."

"What's that?" Jules asked.

"Eyewitnesses. My great-great-great-great-great-great-great-great-great-great-great-great-grandparents were there. They lived through that wreck and they told me where to find it: *In view of paradise, watched over for eternity by a sorrowful hound.*"

Jules squinted through the rain at the *Windfall* for a few long seconds.

"In view of paradise," she repeated. She looked at the *Windfall* a little longer, then turned back to Otis and me. "Paradise sounds good to me." She smiled. "I'm with you and the hounds."

CHAPTER FIFTEEN

True Fact: Medical-alert dogs can smell blood sugar, cancer, seizures, heart attacks, and strokes. Humans need machines to do all those things. (TF supplied by Dr. Greene, the vet.)

Back at my house I moved a pair of gardening shears and some work gloves off the dining room table and unrolled sea charts in their place.

"Okay, here's Gardiner's Bay." I pointed to a sideways-U-shaped body of water with Sag Harbor on the left at the base of the U and Gardiner's Island (a.k.a. T-Bone Steak with Pointy Hat Island) on the right in the center of the mouth. "Here's the Ruins"—I x-ed the tiny speck of land straight up from the tip of the T-bone's pointy hat with a red pencil—"and here's the *Windfall*." I x-ed a spot just above the top of the T at the left end.

"What about the sorrowful hound?" Jules asked.

"He's here." I x-ed a spot on the left side of the bottom tip of the T-bone. If you drew a circle around the area near the hound, we'd covered maybe half.

"So you think the boat drifted from there...to there?" Jules said, tracing an arc from the *Windfall* to the sorrowful hound with her finger.

"Exactly." I sounded way more certain than I felt, though. Whatever my gut was telling me, it was still just a hunch.

"So where do you think we should look next?"

I studied the chart and tried to see Petra and Abraham on their sinking ship. Which way was the wind coming from? What was the current like? Was there a storm? Could they steer? Were they scared? When did they realize the boat wouldn't make it to shore?

Otis headbutted my leg.

Come to think of it, I did have a headache, and my hands were tingly.

Anything can affect a diabetic person's blood sugar. Food? *Check*. Exercise? *Check*. Weather? *Check*. Being sick, taking medicine, time of day, nothing that you can figure out no matter how hard you try? *Check*, *check*, *check*, and *check*.

"High or low?" I asked Otis.

Otis bowed.

"We'll be right back," I said to Jules.

Usually I keep better track of my blood sugar. It's like I have a computer program constantly running in my head that factors in everything I eat and drink and all the things I do. Not even Nora knows how much time I spend thinking about and dealing with diabetes. Only Mom and Dad know, because they're thinking about it all the time too. And Otis, of course.

Otis and I went to the bathroom, and I tested. "Good low, Magoats." I gave him his treat and texted Mom and Dad. "Get juice."

Otis went to the kitchen and came back to me at the dining table with a juice box.

"You can do your diabetes stuff in front of me, you know," Jules said, petting Otis's back.

I busied myself with opening the juice box. Ever since that humiliating first day of sixth grade, the only people I did my diabetes stuff in front of were my parents and Nora. Did I want to include Jules in that club?

"It's not like I haven't seen you do it on the boat every day when you thought I wasn't looking."

It's possible she had a point.

Keeping my voice as totally-casual-no-big-deal as possible, I said, "Otis just told me my blood sugar's too low. The juice will bring it up."

I held my breath. And then let it out when all Jules said was:

"Cool." She held out her hand palm-up. "Now do me."

People who don't have to do it every day think testing is fun. I tested Nora's theater friends once. They loved it, and I felt like a sideshow performer.

I unzipped my supply pouch and took out a flattish roundish machine about the size and shape of a good skipping stone. "This is a glucometer. It measures how much sugar is in your blood." Next I opened a plastic vial and pulled out a testing strip that looked like the kind of match you tear from a matchbook, and a tiny plastic stick about an inch long. I snapped off the top of the stick, revealing a sharp metal point on the end. "I'm going to prick your finger with this lancet so I can get a blood sample."

"Will it hurt?" Jules asked.

I jabbed the tip of her thumb with the point. "Nope."

I squeezed out a drop of blood onto the testing strip. Technically, this move is called "milking," but I wasn't going to tell Jules that. The word even grosses *me* out and I do it at least seven times a day and once in the middle of the night. So far, though, Jules didn't seem repulsed. She seemed kind of...interested. "You put this strip in the meter and drip a tiny bit of blood on the end. Wait five seconds and...one hundred and three."

"Is that bad?" Jules asked.

"Your blood sugar's perfect," I said.

And it always would be. Unlike mine. Which is something I try not to think about, but sometimes—like now—I can't help thinking about. Jules could eat a bowl of white sugar for breakfast and her blood sugar probably wouldn't go over 150. She'll never have to eat when she doesn't want to or not eat things she wants, and no matter what she eats—carbs, protein, fat, whatever kind and however much—her pancreas will give her exactly the right amount of insulin she needs.

"What's yours?" she asked.

"Sixty-four. Which is too low, but the juice'll fix it." I poked the straw into the hole and slurped.

"Don't you need to take insulin?"

"Insulin is for when your blood sugar's too high," I explained. "Carbohydrates are for when it's too low."

"*Wait.* You mean when your blood sugar gets too low, you have to eat carbs whether you want to or not?" Jules said "eat carbs" like someone else might have said "sacrifice baby animals."

"Pretty much, yeah," I said.

"That's the worst." She leaned toward me and sniffed. "I can't believe Otis can smell what's inside your veins." She sniffed again. "I don't smell anything."

"Gee, thanks." I pulled my arms in close to my body just in case.

"How did he get the box out of the fridge anyway?" Jules asked.

"There's a rope on the door handle that Otis pulls with his mouth. We keep juice boxes and some other stuff on the lower shelves so he can reach them." Raw meat goes in the vegetable drawer. Even Otis can't open that. "Otis, bring Jules a juice."

Otis loped off toward the kitchen.

"Otis, stop!"

He stopped.

"What's wrong?" Jules asked.

Otis was walking funny.

"I'm not sure," I said.

I got down on the floor next to Otis and ran my hands over his back left leg, the one he'd been favoring. He didn't yelp with pain, but that didn't mean anything. Otis doesn't complain unless something's really bad.

"Paw," I said.

Otis gave me his paw and I inspected it. I didn't see anything.

"Is he okay?" Jules asked.

"He was limping," I said.

Here's what I didn't say: Maybe Otis sprained something or tore a ligament or pulled a muscle. He could have an infection in his leg. Or even hip dysplasia, which a lot of German shepherds get. But whatever was wrong with

Otis probably happened at the Ruins, because he was fine before we went.

Which meant that whatever was wrong with Otis was my fault.

He needed to see the vet, but Mom and Dad wouldn't be home for hours. Otis never waits a single second to help me; no way was I going to wait hours to help Otis.

"I have to take Otis to the vet, but I need someone with a car to drive us," I said, trying to keep the flashing red siren of panic that was in my head out of my voice.

"And you don't want your parents to know," Jules said.

"That too." They'd have to know Otis had been to the vet if it turned out there was something wrong, but if we went now and nothing was wrong, maybe my parents would never find out.

"I'll get someone to come drive us." Jules typed on her phone, waited half a minute, and said, "My dad's massage therapist will be here in five."

"Let's go wait on the porch," I said. "Come, Otis."

He was definitely limping.

CHAPTER SIXTEEN

True Fact: I can _never_ be careless. _Never._

Something sharp had cut Otis between two of his paw pads. Something like a piece of metal or a shell or a chunk of cement at the Ruins. The cut wasn't deep, and Dr. Greene, the vet, said it would heal in a few days. But his paw was wrapped in blue tape halfway up his back leg. And no matter how many times I told him to stop, no matter how many chew toys and bones I gave him, Otis kept picking at it. He hated that wrap.

I didn't take care of Otis and he got hurt. And the worst part was that he didn't know it was my fault. While we were waiting for Dr. Greene, Otis alerted. Of course my stupid blood sugar decided this was a good time to blow past the juice I'd had at home and go high. Because there was no way Otis would stay in the waiting area with Jules while I dealt with it. No, he had to limp to the bathroom with me so I could test. And when I told him, "Good high, Otis," his tail wagged as hard as ever— even though his paw was hurting him, even before I gave him his treat—because taking care of me is Otis's favorite thing to do. I kneeled on Dr. Greene's bathroom floor and told Otis I was sorry over and over and over again, and he licked the tears off my face and had no idea why I was crying.

After Otis finished with Dr. Greene, the receptionist gave me a bill.

For $125.

I'd known the visit was going to cost something, but I didn't think it would cost *twelve weeks'* allowance. Before we left my house, I'd emptied my fake-book safe of thirty-five dollars, which was every penny I had.

Jules, on the other hand, had plenty of money. I'd seen her wallet. It was always full of twenties. And not one but two credit cards. Jules, whose father gave her forty dollars for the taco truck at the beach. Jules, who ordered $150 video cameras online that her father's accountant would never even notice. Jules, whose sneakers were custom-colored and monogrammed.

I'd rather eat my toes for breakfast than ask Jules for money. Or lick the sidewalk. Or solo dance at a school assembly.

But this was for Otis.

Jules was scrolling on her phone in the waiting area a few feet away.

"Jules?"

"Yeah?" she said without looking up.

I swallowed. "Can-I-borrow-ninety-dollars-to-pay-the-bill?"

"Sure." Jules said "sure" in a distracted kind of way, like loaning me ninety dollars was no big deal. She reached into her back pocket for a credit card, handed it to me, and went back to scrolling.

What was it like with her and her friends at home? I bet when they went out for pizza they didn't figure out what each person ate when they split the check. Or maybe they didn't go out for pizza. Maybe they went out for sushi.

After we left Dr. Greene's, Jules and her dad's massage therapist dropped Otis and me at home. Before I shut the car door, I said to Jules, "I *promise* to pay you back."

She waved her hand like she was shooing a fly. "Don't worry about it. As long as Otis is okay that's all that matters." She leaned out the open door and rubbed Otis's head. "Right, Otis McGoatis? All that matters is *you*."

Jules and I had that in common, at least.

When Mom came home from work, Otis was lying on the rug by the front door, and she noticed his blue paw right away.

"What happened?" She squatted next to him without taking off her sun hat or muddy shoes.

"He stepped on something sharp." Which was a partial truth.

"Where were you?"

"Um...the parking lot near the marina?" Which was a total lie.

"Poor baby," Mom said, stroking Otis's head. Otis stopped tugging at the tape and licked her hand. "Did you do this wrap yourself, Blue?"

I took a deep breath. *Here comes the hard part.* "Jules and I took Otis to Dr. Greene's. He said it would be fine in a couple of days."

Mom stopped petting Otis and looked up at me. "Did you get the bill?"

"Yes."

I knew the question Mom was going to ask next, and I really really didn't want to answer it.

"How much was it?"

I could feel my face flushing. "A hundred and twenty-five dollars."

"Oh, Blue. That's a lot of money for a cut paw. We could have taken care of Otis ourselves. Why didn't you call me?"

Because I was hoping there'd be nothing wrong and you'd never have to find out. But I was worried there was something really wrong and Otis needed a doctor. "I thought I was doing the right thing."

Mom pushed herself up slowly with her hands on her knees. "Next time call me, okay? We can't afford for Otis to go to the vet for every little thing. And speaking of what we can afford, how did you pay the bill?"

"How'd she pay what bill?"

Dad opened the screen door. I'd been so busy lying I hadn't even heard him come up the porch steps.

"Otis cut his paw, and Blue took him to Dr. Greene," Mom said, re-piling her hair on top of her head. "A hundred and twenty-five dollars."

Dad whistled. "Where'd you get that kind of money, Blue?"

I closed my eyes and willed myself to become as small as an ant so I could run away through the gap between the screen door and the floor. It didn't work.

"I had thirty-five dollars, and Jules paid the rest," I said. "I told her I'll pay her back."

Mom let go of her hair and it stuck out all around her. "Jules loaned you ninety dollars? That's *completely* inappropriate!"

I cringed. "It wasn't a big deal to her at all," I said, even though I knew Mom was right.

"Well, it's a big deal to us," she snapped. "I'll give you

the money to pay her back tomorrow. But you're not getting your thirty-five dollars back."

After dinner, Otis and I trudged upstairs to be miserable together in private. He parked himself on the bathroom floor and gnawed his wrap. If he didn't stop soon, I'd have to put the cone of shame around his head.

I sighed a long sigh and got into the shower, peeking around the curtain every couple of minutes at Otis, who was now lying belly-down on the bath mat with his chin resting on his front paws and his eyebrows crinkled, a look of utter pain and sadness that magnified my own.

I finished my shower and dried off. And then it was time for the thing I hated most about dealing with diabetes: moving my infusion set, the device that's plugged into my body and connects to my insulin pump through a long catheter tube. I'm supposed to move it to a different patch of skin every three days (even though I usually stretch it to four) so I don't build up scar tissue or get a skin infection. I can handle the cringy part when I peel off the adhesive tape and it tugs on my skin, and the Band-Aid smell of insulin that I taste in the back of my throat when I fill the reservoir. No, the part I can't stand is injecting the new catheter. You would think that a person who pricks her finger multiple times a day wouldn't care about one more needle. But there's something about pressing the inserter button and how fast the needle plunges—like shooting a nail gun or an electric stapler into my body—that freaks me out.

I was reconnecting the tube, half my attention on Otis, when my pump went flying out of my hands and crashed on the tile floor.

"Shih tzu!"

I retrieved the pump and looked it over. It seemed to be okay.

Otis, on the other hand, was now fighting with his wrap like it was a swarm of angry mosquitoes.

I kneeled in front of him.

"I'm sorry," I said for the thousandth time.

Otis kept gnawing.

"Otis, look at me."

He stopped. Big dark golden-brown eyes stared into mine.

Otis was seven years old. He wouldn't be able to be my medical-alert dog forever. Wouldn't be able to go to school with me forever. Or sleep in my bed with me forever.

I grabbed Otis by the jowls. Inspected his snout for white hairs. Then his chin. Otis didn't pull away. He understood that I wanted to comb through the fur on his face, and that was enough for him. He didn't need to understand why.

I checked every single strand and didn't find a white one.

But one day I would.

CHAPTER SEVENTEEN

True Fact: Too much sugar in your blood is like acid on paint. It eats away at you. You walk around looking totally healthy, but it adds up, bit by bit, episode by episode, year by year, until one day you've got a DIABETIC COMPLICATION, which is a nice way of saying that your heart doesn't work right or you have nerve damage or you need one of your feet amputated. Most diabetics, if they have the disease long enough, get complications.

"Four hundred and ninety. Still going up. Oh, man—"

"Shhh! Quiet, Hal, you'll wake her."

Wake who? Wake me?

"The reservoir's full and I keep entering the numbers in her pump, Em, but nothing's happening."

Dad.

"Did it come out?"

Mom.

"No, the infusion site looks good," Dad said.

"Here, let me," Mom said.

My eyes fluttered open.

The clock on my night table said 3:12. Mom sat on the edge of my bed and Dad kneeled on the floor next to her, both in pajamas. I could just make out their serious faces in the dim light coming from the hall outside my room. Otis stood behind Dad, giving my parents the space they needed to fix me.

"Hey, Belly," Dad said, picking up my hand and rubbing it between his. "Your sugar got high. We've been trying to get it down for a while."

"Four-ninety," I croaked, my throat so dry it felt like it was sticking to itself.

"I can't get the pump to work either, Hal. I think it's broken. That's why your sugar's so high, sweetie," Mom said. "You haven't been getting any insulin."

At least we had a reason. Half the time when my blood sugar goes crazy in the middle of the night we don't know why.

"Mom's going to give you a shot. Okay, Belly?" Dad said.

I nodded, too parched and nauseous to speak.

"Otis, where's Blue's kit? Oh, good boy," Mom said.

Otis already had my kit in his mouth. He knew the routine as well as any of us.

"Light on, Otis," Dad said.

Otis went to the wall next to the door and jumped up on his hind legs to flip the switch with his teeth, a trick he used to love to do over and over again when he first figured it out—especially in the middle of the night—until Dad trained him out of it.

Mom held up a hypodermic needle and a vial of insulin. "What do you think? Three units?"

"With her basal rate? Wait...let me think. Yeah, do three units. Give it to her in her arm. Belly, do you hear me? It's going to be fine. You're fine. Mom and I are here."

And so was Otis, who had climbed back onto my bed and glued himself to my side.

I barely felt the prick of the needle.

"I hate this," Dad whispered to Mom.

"I know," Mom whispered back.

"If Otis hadn't..."

"I can hear you, you know." I struggled to sit up a little. "Oh no," I moaned.

"Nauseous?" Mom fluffed a pillow and propped it under my head.

I nodded, which made my brain slosh. "And hot." Even though Dad had fixed the air conditioner.

Dad yanked the covers down. Then he fanned Otis and me with the sheet.

"Otis alerted us," he said.

Which meant I was so out of it that I didn't wake up when Otis tried to alert me, and he had to go get Mom and Dad. I tried not to picture him headbutting me and licking me and pawing me while I lay on the bed like a sack of wet cement.

"Let's test you again." Mom poked my finger with a lancet. A few seconds later: "Four hundred and ten." Ideal for me is under 140.

"Do you think we gave her enough insulin?" Dad asked.

"We could—" Mom started.

"Give it fifteen more minutes," I whispered.

We'd played this game so many times. Not enough insulin and my blood sugar wouldn't come down. Too much insulin and it would go down too far. But how much was enough and how much was too much were different every time.

"Okay, Belly, you're the boss," Dad said.

Mom got a wet washcloth and pressed it to my forehead while we waited. The cool heaviness felt good on my prickly skin.

"I have to pee," I said.

I tried to sit up, squinting against the glare of the overhead light.

"Here, let me help you. I'll take you to the bathroom." Dad scooped me up from the bed. I couldn't remember the last time he'd carried me anywhere.

"I think I might throw up."

"That's okay," Dad said. "You can throw up on me; I'm washable."

All four of us crowded into the bathroom. I was still dying of thirst. Dad put me down and I stuck my head under the faucet and gulped. Mom put my kit on the vanity so I could test again. Otis kept watch in the doorway.

"We'll give you some privacy," she said. "But come get us when you're out of the bathroom."

"I'm going to call Dr. Basch's service and have them page her," Dad said. "We need to know how much long-acting insulin to give you. And you're going to need more boluses of short-acting tonight. Mom or I will come in every fifteen minutes to test until you're back in a good range, okay?"

I nodded, too tired to get words out.

Mom and Dad left the bathroom, but Otis stayed. I sat down on the toilet.

490.

Four hundred and ninety.

See, the thing is, no matter what I do, no matter how

careful I am, even with the computer in my head, even with Otis, it can all go wrong. I know it. Mom and Dad know it. We don't need to say it.

My head felt too heavy to stay up on its own. I hung my arms around Otis's neck and buried my face in his fur, breathed in his dry-leaf doggy scent. "Thanks," I whispered.

CHAPTER EIGHTEEN

True Fact: An old toilet can be an important discovery.

The whole next day my skull felt like it was stuffed with wet socks. My body felt like it was wrapped in one of those lead aprons they make you wear when you get an X-ray. Forget the hunt—I could barely stay awake long enough to see Dr. Basch. I hardly had the strength to check the mailbox for a letter from Nora. Who still hadn't written to me.

Then again, I hadn't written to her either. I kept trying, but there was so much to say that I didn't know where to start. How would I tell her about Jules and Fitz and Otis's paw and last night? The letter would have to be a hundred pages long. Could I send another greeting card? Or maybe a postcard? I pictured the postcards on the rack at the Five & Dime: rainbow beach balls, rolling waves, the windmill at the entrance to the Long Wharf. *Greetings from Sag Harbor!* Ugh.

Dad took Otis on a beach run before he left for work, while Mom and I went to Dr. Basch's. She confirmed that my pump had broken, and gave me instructions—which Mom wrote down—about what kinds of shots I should give myself until the new pump arrived.

After Mom left for work, I texted Jules and told her about my high blood sugar and why I wouldn't be able to hunt today. Then Otis and I skipped the Indiana Jones marathon that was on TV and slept in my bed all morning. In between naps, my brain circled like a dog chasing its tail:

What damage did that 490 do to my body? What will happen when I'm older and Mom and Dad aren't there to wake me up? Did I break the pump when I moved the infusion set after my shower last night?

I remembered checking the pump after it fell on the floor. *What had I missed?*

Because I took Otis to the Ruins, he got hurt. Because Otis got hurt, he had to wear a bandage he hated. Because he was miserable and it was all my fault, I got distracted. Because I moved my infusion set while I was distracted, I broke my pump. *Because, because, because...all, my, fault.*

Jules called around noon while Otis and I were in bed

half dozing, half watching a documentary about penguins on my phone.

"What's the big deal? Your blood sugar's fine now, isn't it?"

"Yeah, but—"

"Do I have to remind you that the Fitzminions are out there right now, vacuuming your family's inheritance off the ocean floor?"

"I know, but my doctor said—"

"I can't believe I care about this more than you do."

"Jules—"

"Whatever. I'll see you tomorrow. Have a nice day *resting,*" Jules said.

Why are you being such a jerk?

Which I couldn't ask out loud because Jules had hung up.

The next morning I was feeling tired but better. Mom woke me before leaving for work and said I could go back out on the water for half a day as long as I followed a few rules.

"You need to test every hour," she said, sitting on the edge of my bed.

"I know," I said.

Otis dropped my kit on my pillow. I took the hint.

"Your new pump will be here tonight. But in the

137

meantime, you're doing shots instead of getting a slow drip. It feels different from what you're used to."

"I know, Mom. I've done it this way before." I finished testing and held up the meter. "Perfect. One-oh-five."

"Great." Mom stood up. "Text me your numbers while you're out."

"Absolutely," I said.

She paused. "You know, sweetie, this would be so much easier if you'd use a CGM. Then Dad and I would know your numbers automatically and you wouldn't have to text us."

I said nothing.

Mom sighed. "I need to know those numbers. Don't forget, Blue."

"I won't. I promise."

"C'mere."

I leaned over so Mom could head hug me.

Squeeze, kiss. "I love this head."

Mom had left for work, and Otis and I were watering the hanging planters on the front porch when Anna's hair colorist dropped off Jules at our usual meeting time. I hadn't been sure she was going to come. I definitely was sure I didn't want her to.

"Here." Jules held out a tinfoil log. "It's a whole wheat egg white and spinach wrap."

I crossed my arms in front of my chest. "I already ate."

"Fine." She shrugged. "I'll give it to Otis. How's his paw?"

"Better. The vet said the bandage can come off tomorrow."

Long awkward pause during which Jules peeled away the foil and carefully pulled out the egg whites for Otis, who hadn't been part of our phone fight yesterday and therefore wasn't holding a grudge.

Jules's iPad was still playing the usual *Windfall* soundtrack—boring nothings about wind and lunch and weather—when all of a sudden, Fitz's voice blared out:

"Listen up, people, I've got good news. My curator in Amsterdam says our little find here is a seventeenth-century jockum gage. Judging by the stamp on its bottom, it was made in Germany in 1655."

Crew Guy: "It's a what?"

Fitz: "A jockum gage."

Silence.

Fitz: "A member mug? Piss pot? A small vessel, in this case pewter, used by sailors for urination in lieu of a toilet."

Sonia (under her breath): "You know he just learned all that stuff yesterday from the curator."

Fitz: "Remember what I said—tell no one. But, friends, we can rejoice quietly amongst ourselves that Fitz Fitzgibbons is on track to finding one of the greatest missing treasures in history."

True Fact: Fitz and the gang had found a seventeenth-century port-o-potty.

The strange thing was, apart from the hilarity (a seventeenth-century port-o-potty!), and apart from the anxiety (I had so far found seventeenth-century nothing), and apart from still being exhausted and really mad at Jules, the fact that the *Windfall* actually found something gave me that tomorrow's-Christmas tingle in my stomach. It meant that my ancestors and my gut were right. It meant Pop Pop was right. There really was something down there.

We hurried into the house, snatched up our stuff, and headed out.

"Come on, come on, come on. Let's go," Jules said, pushing me down the dock.

Jules was a weird mix of hyped up and ticked off, but I was still too mad at her to care why.

"I'll drive," she said.

It was Jules's first time driving, but I figured she'd been watching me long enough. Besides, I was too tired to fight about it.

Jules turned on the engine and pulled out without crashing into the dock or running aground. I leaned back against the side rail.

"Watch the buoy," I said.

"What's a buoy for, anyway?" Jules said.

"They show you where deep water is, and they keep boats from hitting each other. Since we're going out, keep the red ones on your left and the green ones on your right. When we come back, you keep the red ones on your right and the green ones on your left. Remember: red right returning."

"Red right returning. Got it." Jules gunned the engine.

"Slow down! We have to stay under five miles an hour here."

"Are you always this annoying when you get high blood sugar?"

"Are you always this annoying every single day? Wait, don't answer that. I already know."

"Hey, you were the one sleeping on the biggest day of this whole thing!" Jules yelled.

"As it so happens," I snapped, "I almost died the other night—not that you could care less! And this treasure hunt is *my* whole thing, remember? Besides, what did you do all day? Shop for thousand-dollar lip gloss?"

Jules threw the engine into idle, and Otis slid across the deck. Her eyes were little slits of fire.

"You really want to know? First, I skipped breakfast because She Who Must Not Be Named was in the kitchen in her underwear. But then my dad asked me to go for a walk on the beach with him. And because I'm such a moron, I actually thought it was because he wanted to spend time with me. But then a hundred people stopped him every ten feet just like they always do, and of course he needed to bless each and every one of them with the full-on Ed Buttersby charm. I wasn't even sure he remembered I was there until he dragged us away from the crowd and put on his old fishing hat and sunglasses disguise, and I thought, *finally*, we're going to hang out and have fun. But no. Because that's when he started going on and on about how he'd found true love and he was 'happier than he'd ever been in his life.'" Jules put air quotes around that part. "And, no, I didn't ask him if that included the day he married my mom and the day I was born, because I actually thought he might say yes." She stopped for a breath. "*Then* I went back to the house to video-chat with my mom and her eyes were all wet and swollen because she'd been crying. At nine o'clock in the morning Pacific time. Like she's been doing pretty much every day since my dad dumped her for Anna."

I looked away from Jules at the water. It's possible her day had been worse than mine. It's possible she could look the way she looks and have a famous father and be really rich and not have a disease and her whole life could be worse than mine. *But still.* I ground my teeth and spun back.

"So you thought you'd just pay it forward and take your bad day out on me?"

142

"It wasn't a bad day!" she shouted. "It was the *worst* day I could possibly have had. And besides, you didn't *almost die*." More air quotes. "Four-ninety isn't lethal."

My hands started to shake. "Oh, so you looked up blood sugar online and now you're an expert? Yeah, four-ninety isn't lethal—unless it keeps going up because I sleep through it or Otis doesn't get to my parents in time or it's going up so fast that nothing anybody does matters before it's too late. So, yeah, I could've died last night. I could die pretty much *every* night!"

I glared at Jules with my hands on my hips. She glared back at me with her hands on her hips. And then her shoulders slumped and she said:

"I'm sorry you almost died and I took my bad day out on you."

I exhaled. And then I said:

"Thanks. I'm sorry you had the worst day you possibly could have had and we couldn't hunt because I almost died."

"I *did* buy a really amazing pair of shoes online," she said.

"Just one?" I said.

"Okay, three." She reached into her bag and pulled out a piece of paper. "But that's not all I did."

"What do you mean?" I asked.

She handed me the paper, her face like a TV game

143

show host about to announce the big winner. "Turns out staying home all day wasn't the worst thing in the world, because if I hadn't had all that time to kill, I never would have found *this*."

This was a web page printout with a list of names. Strange names like Jeronimo Lobo and Albert Joachim and Happy Jan. Next to the names were titles: *Gunner, Surgeon's Mate, Head Cook*. And where the people were born.

"It's a ship's log," Jules said. "I found it online on this Dutch website that lists every ship the Dutch East India Company ever owned and everyone who worked on them. They just translated it into English a few months ago."

"*Every* ship?" I asked.

"Look!" She grabbed the paper out of my hands, flipped it, then shoved it back. "Look there. Halfway down. *Look*."

Abraham Broen, Carpenter's Mate, Birthplace: Java, East Indies

My very own last name, right there in a Dutch ship's log from 1663. The same name in the old family bible that I'd combed through a thousand times: *Abraham Broen, Carpenter's Mate, Birthplace: Java, East Indies.* Teeny tiny Fourth of July sparklers ignited under my skin.

"Is this the ship I think it is?" I asked. Even though I already knew what she was going to say. I knew knew

knew it in my bones, because it could be only one ship in the whole history of ships.

"Uh-huh." Jules bopped up and down, practically dancing in the well of the Mako.

"Wahoo!" I yelled.

Otis woofed with joy. And then all three of us actually *were* dancing in the well of the Mako.

The *Golden Lion*. Jules found proof that my great-times-twelve-grandfather had traveled on it!

I grabbed the wheel. "We've gotta get back to the hound."

"Floor it!" Jules said.

CHAPTER NINETEEN

True Fact: <u>Pop Pop was right.</u>

We made it to Gardiner's Island in record time. Usually, scanning the bottom of the bay for hours put me into a kind of zen state where I'd zone out going from seaweed clump to seaweed clump. Today, though, every clump was possibly *the* clump. Every lump was maybe *the* lump. It was best-birthday-ever exciting.

Even with the distraction of having just made the most important discovery of my life (or, rather, Jules having made the most important discovery of my life), I tested every hour and sent the numbers to Mom. They were all in normal range. When we got hungry for a midafternoon snack, Jules brought out homemade nut clusters.

"I told my chef you had diabetes, so she made them with carob and fake sugar to keep the carbs low." She took a bite. "Oh wow, these are really disgusting."

"I like them." I tossed one to Otis.

Otis liked them too.

Jules and I were about to get back on the tube when a *Windfall* dinghy motored in our direction.

"They're not coming over here, are they?" Jules said.

"I hope not," I said.

But they were. And by "they" Jules meant the crew person driving the boat...and Fitz.

We watched them get closer and closer, and I gripped the wheel tighter and tighter, until the rubber side of Fitz's boat not-quite-so-gently bumped the Mako.

"Hi, girls." Fitz smiled like a shark: lots of teeth, dead eyes. He had on a polo shirt with an open neck that exposed a gold chain with a big medallion on it.

It was my first encounter with a famous media person without at least one of my parents present. Which may have been why my mind went blank and I lost the ability to speak. Jules, on the other hand, had met lots of famous, powerful people and knew exactly what to say in this situation:

"Hi." She peered at him over the top of her sunglasses, like a true movie star's daughter.

"What are you two up to?" Teeth, teeth, and more teeth.

"Nothing." Jules flicked her ponytail over her shoulder.

"It doesn't look like nothing," Fitz said. "What are you doing with those buckets?"

Once again, Jules was ready. "Just a school project. We need the buckets to take water samples."

"I see." Fitz shark-smiled again. "That's interesting, because my crew says those look like underwater-view buckets."

In an act of epic bravery, Jules tossed her hair and said, "So?"

Fitz did a double take, like this was the first time anyone had ever given him Jules Buttersby attitude, which it probably was. The shark-smile chilled into a stare, like Fitz might open his toothy mouth and chomp us at any moment.

"If you are looking for something in this water, you've got a problem. Unless, of course, you have an exploration permit?"

Jules looked at me. I shook my head. I'd never even heard of an exploration permit, but I didn't like the sound of it. And I really didn't like the sound of "you've got a problem."

"I didn't think so," Fitz said. "Well, I *do* have an exploration permit, and it lets me—and *only* me—search a ten-mile radius around Gardiner's Point. So *you* have to find somewhere else to do your little project. Today. *Now.* And don't let me see you here again." Fitz flicked his wrist at the crew person, his way of instructing him to head back to the *Windfall* since his business with us was done.

Before my eyes, Gardiner's Bay turned into a giant toilet with a giant handle that Fitz had just flushed. The water swirled around and down, disappearing into a sludgy mud hole, sucking away every dream of greatness I'd ever had. All that was left was three million florins of gold, silver, and copper, waiting for Fitz Fitzgibbons to plunge up.

My vision blurred. All I saw was mud. Mud, mud, mud, mud—

"Fine. Show us the permit," Jules said.

Fitz whipped around. "Excuse me?"

"How do we know you're not making the whole thing up?" Jules demanded. "Sorry. If you want us to go, you have to prove you have the right to make us leave. You do know that my friend's family has lived here for three hundred and fifty years, right? And you just carpetbagged in, like, when? Five minutes ago? Who do you think you are? Christopher Columbus? Well, that's just awesome. I mean totally awesome. And by 'awesome' I mean an awesome subject for a feature-length documentary about corporate greed and corruption. I'm Jules *Buttersby*, by the way."

Fitz actually flinched from the power of Jules's words. Or possibly because sunlight bounced from her golden hair into his eyes, temporarily blinding him. "Buttersby?" he said. "As in Ed Buttersby?"

Jules stuck out her chin. "He's my father."

Fitz pursed his lips, no doubt thinking evil thoughts. "Thank you, Jules Buttersby. You've just given me an excellent idea." The shark-smile was back. "But you still need to get out of here."

Another wrist-flick and Fitz sped off. Otis barked after him.

"Is that what your history papers sound like?" I asked, half-stunned.

Jules shrugged. "Pretty much, yeah."

"You were incredible. Thanks."

"Well, you were just sitting there like bald Rapunzel," Jules said. "Somebody had to find us another way down from the tower."

I touched my ponytail.

"It's a metaphor, Blue."

"I knew that."

CHAPTER TWENTY

True Fact: Even with the right actors and the best costumes and the perfect setting, the movie can still stink.

After we got back to the dock, I was tying up the Mako when Jules said a word that made me botch my bowline. I looked over at her. She was staring at something on her phone, half her hair hanging out of a bun.

"What are you doing tonight?" she asked. "Whatever it is, you have to cancel and come with me."

"Come with you where?" I said.

"My dad wants to take me out to dinner." Jules looked up from her phone, her face a mixture of amazed and uncertain. "He says he's sorry about what happened on the beach and he wants to make it up to me. He says there's an incredible burger place on the Bridge-Sag Turnpike."

"Um, you mean Harbor Burger?"

"He didn't say the name. Is it incredible?"

"I guess." They have hot dogs and hamburgers and you can eat outside at picnic tables if you want, which Otis prefers, dirt being his favorite habitat. Still, I'm not sure I'd call Harbor Burger incredible, especially by Buttersby standards. "They have tater tots with bacon." Jules looked unconvinced, so I added, "And they make their own ice cream." Which Otis likes a lot. Especially the blackberry.

"Homemade ice cream? I guess that constitutes incredible. Ask your mom if you can come. She has to let you."

"But if this is your dad's way of saying he's sorry, wouldn't it be better if it was just the two of you alone?" I said.

"No way. I need moral support." Jules looked like Otis during Fourth of July fireworks. Like she wanted to dive for cover. "Please, Blue? I'd . . . really appreciate it."

Jules's voice was quiet, and she was looking at me, not her phone. It was the first time she'd ever actually asked me for something instead of telling me or ordering me.

"Okay." *At least Otis will be there.*

I texted Mom, who wrote back, Fly! Be free! And then But don't forget to test.

Jules pulled a pink sundress out of the bottom of her bag. "Yes! I knew I had this in here." She held the dress up against her and smoothed out the wrinkles. "It's good enough. Oh, and in other happy news, Anna's not coming. It'll just be us."

We went inside so I could give Otis his precisely measured dinner of kibble, plus a bonus leftover pork chop from last night (*sorry, Dad*), and we waited for Ed, who said he'd pick us up at six thirty. Mom was working late, and Dad was at poker night with some friends, so we were alone.

Upstairs in my room Jules asked, "What are you going to wear?"

I looked down at my shorts and T-shirt. "This?"

"No, really. What are you—forget it. We'll just accessorize." She pulled a little makeup bag out of her bigger bag and took out two bottles of nail polish. "Love 'Em and Leave 'Em or Sky's the Limit?"

"The blue one." At least Sky's the Limit was a nice shade of blue. Like, well, the sky. I held out my hands.

"What's the best thing they have on the menu?" she asked, painting a thumb.

"Most people really like the milkshakes," I said.

"Perfect. I'll get a chocolate one. Or do they have fun flavors like salted caramel or s'mores? Or, no, wait. I'll go classic American, like the restaurant. Black-and-white malted. Do they have malt?" Jules dipped the nail polish brush in the little bottle and pumped it up and down like an engine piston.

"Um, I'm not sure," I said.

I'd seen Fierce Jules and Cool Jules and Snarky Jules and even Kind-of-Normal Jules, but Nervous Jules was new.

"Doesn't matter. Black-and-white is perfect. With or without malt." She screwed the cap back on the bottle. "You're done. Unless..." Jules beamed laser eyes at Otis, who was lying down watching us with his chin on his front paws. She shook the glass bottle up and down so the metal mixing ball inside sounded like a kitchen timer about to go off. "What do you think? Should we do Otis?"

"NO," I said.

Otis whined and scrunched backward away from Jules.

"You're right. It's six fifteen. I need to get ready."

Jules went into my bathroom to change into her sundress, while I blew on my nails to dry them.

"It's actually within the realm of possibility that we're going to have a good time," she said through the door. "When he's not being awful, my dad can be great. You'd really like him."

"I've met him, remember?" Even though I hadn't seen Ed since Mom and I went to their house for the CJDF meeting. Somebody else always dropped Jules off at my house, and we never went over to hers.

"No, you haven't. Not really. You met him with your

mom when he was being EDWARD BUTTERSBY THE FAMOUS MOVIE STAR. He's different when it's just us."

"How's he different?"

Jules came out of the bathroom. She had on the sundress and some lip gloss and a fresh coat of Sky's the Limit. "He looks at things in different ways from other people. Like, one time we went to a house that had belonged to a famous painter in the eighteen hundreds—you know, one of those houses that they turn into museums? We went up to the studio with all the pigment powders and brushes and easels exactly as the artist left them. But my dad didn't take pictures of the room or the art supplies. He took a picture of the doll that the artist's daughter had left on the window seat."

I pictured an attic with a slanty ceiling, tourists crowded around an unfinished painting, and Jules and Ed kneeling by a window, sunlight leaking through its dusty panes onto a yarn-haired rag doll left behind for a hundred years.

"My dad sees the things everybody else misses," Jules said softly.

So does Jules.

We went downstairs to wait. Jules only checked her phone twice because at exactly six thirty, a car horn honked in the driveway.

"He's here," I said.

Jules smoothed her dress one last time. "I'm ready."

CHAPTER TWENTY-ONE

True Fact: Everybody matters. Even sidekicks.

I put Otis's service vest on him so nobody would give us any trouble about dogs and food, and we all went outside.

Ed got out of his black SUV. *"Aw, shoot,* Julie. I was halfway out the door on my way to get you and Blue, and I get a call from my agent. Timing is everything, right?"

Nervous Jules stood at the bottom of the porch steps, fiddling with the clasp on her bracelet. She looked up at her dad through strands of hair that had fallen in front of her face, but Ed didn't wait for her to answer.

"He starts talking, and he keeps talking, and the whole time, all I'm thinking is *No way am I gonna be late for my girl. How fast can I get rid of this guy so I can get to my girl?"*

Ed opened his arms and Jules melted like a pint of ice cream in a pizza oven. "You're not late, Daddy. You're right on time." She dropped her bag and stepped into the hug.

"Phew!" Ed tilted her chin up with a finger. "Because the last thing I want to do is wreck our first big night out on the town."

Wait—their *first* big night? Jules had been here for more than two weeks already, and she and her dad hadn't gone out once?

"It's all good, Daddy."

Ed turned to me. "How are you, Blue? I'm almost as excited about getting to know you tonight as I am about spending time with my girl here."

Ed had this way of talking to you like you were the most fascinating person in the world. It wasn't what he said; it was how he looked at you and only you when he said it.

"I'm good, Mr. Buttersby."

"Otis?" Ed held out a treat he'd brought with him, so Otis was good too.

We got in the car, Jules up front next to Ed, Otis and me in back.

"So what happened with your call?" Jules asked.

"You know how it goes. More numbers, more rewrites, more meetings."

"The usual," Jules said.

She said this like she really did know how it goes with major movie studios, like she and Ed talked about this stuff all the time. Which they probably did. My parents talk about their work too, but that just means I know the names of lots of flowers and the difference between drywall and plaster.

When we got to the restaurant, it was crammed. As in, people were spilling out the door and there wasn't a single spot left in the parking lot. I'd forgotten it was Thursday, which is the night Harbor Burger has their weekly jazz jam, where people take turns sitting in with the band. During the year, when it's just locals, it's not so crowded, but in the summer, when half of New York City moves to town, you can barely squeeze inside.

Jules snapped to attention. "Did you have your PR guy tell them we were coming?"

"No. I swear it, Jules. This crowd has nothing to do with me." Ed sounded like he meant it, but then again, he was a professional actor.

We parked down the road and walked back. Inside was a big front room with a bunch of tables, Sky's the Limit walls, and lots of windows. All the tables were full, and people lined the walls, waiting for other people who were waiting for other people to get up. Luckily, we had Otis with us. People tend to make way for a service dog that looks like a wolf.

The band was set up at the near end of the room. All the musicians were oldish men, except for the guitar player, who was a girl in tenth grade at Sag Harbor High School. At the far end of the room a huge food line snaked to the counter. We got in line to order, which was good because Otis had just alerted and I was starting to feel woozy in a low-blood-sugar way. Ed and Jules talked about something called film noir, while I zoned out staring at the big whale-shaped sign on the wall that listed all the burger toppings.

"You thinking cheddar or Swiss, Blue?" Ed asked, breaking away from his conversation with Jules.

I dragged my eyes from the whale sign to Ed. Otis headbutted me and bowed. I ignored him. I didn't want to go through the whole medical alert thing in front of Ed.

"I'm having more of a pickles or onions dilemma," I said, trying not to slur.

Before Ed could give an opinion, the woman behind us said, "Excuse me, you're Ed Buttersby, aren't you?"

Ed clicked on a charming half smile. "Yes, but don't tell anyone. I'm here with my daughter and her friend tonight, and we're having some family time."

"I knew it was you!" the woman said. "I told my husband, but he didn't believe me. Do you mind if we take a quick selfie with you?"

"Well, I—" Ed started.

"And then I swear we'll leave you alone for the rest of the night." The woman yanked over her embarrassed-looking husband by the wrist.

Ed let out a sigh that the woman ignored, and leaned in so she could take a picture with her phone.

"You play drums, don't you?" The husband raised his voice a little to be heard over the music. "You should sit in."

"No sticks." Ed held up empty hands. He looked down at Jules and mouthed *Sorry* even though he didn't look all that sorry.

"You should totally do it," said another woman in line near us. "Sorry, I couldn't help overhearing."

Next thing we knew, a crowd of burger eaters was begging Ed to sit in with the band. It'd taken all of two minutes for us to go from being just another group waiting for dinner to being the center of attention for the whole restaurant. It was like Cinderella turning into a princess and bathing all the little forest friends in her glow. (Just to be clear, in this scenario, Ed was Cinderella, Jules was the mouse footman, and I was the assistant to the mouse footman.)

"Dad . . . ," Jules said, her voice a warning.

"Jules, if I don't do it, they'll never stop. You know how this goes," Ed said with a smile. I was learning that actors have a whole range of different smiles that regular people don't have. This one was Ed's *I'm irresistibly charming so just let me do what I want* smile.

Jules grabbed his arm. "This was supposed to be our night."

"It'll just be one song. So they'll leave us alone." Ed's eyes were on the band, not Jules.

"You *promised*," she pleaded.

He pried Jules's fingers off his arm and backed away. "Five minutes max. Then I'm all yours."

Jules didn't answer. I'm not sure Ed noticed.

Jules and I smooshed against the wall to wait, and I put Otis between us so no one would step on him. Luckily, service dogs are trained to know how to make themselves as small as possible. We could hear Ed, but we couldn't see him. Not that I cared. I had bigger problems. I could feel my blood sugar dropping fast. My head hurt and I was getting shaky. Otis kept whining and headbutting. If I didn't eat soon he would start to bark. Also, if I didn't eat soon, I might pass out.

Before I wrecked things for Jules or embarrassed myself, I'd test my blood sugar and see how bad the situation was. Unfortunately, there was no way to make it to the bathroom through the crowd.

Jules was in a corner, swaying on her toes, trying to see the band over people's heads.

"Can I switch places with you?" I asked. If I stood in

her spot with my back to the room, I could test and no one would see.

"Why?"

"I need to test my blood sugar."

Jules's head snapped in my direction. "Are you okay?"

"I'm fine. I just need to test."

We switched places and I unbuckled my diabetes kit from Otis's carrier. My hands were trembling. Otis licked them.

"Do you need help?" Jules said, watching me.

"I'm okay."

I opened the vial of testing strips but couldn't get one out.

"Let me." Jules took the vial before I could answer and pulled out a strip. "In this little slot at the end, right?"

I nodded and she stuck the strip in the glucometer. I pricked my index finger with a lancet (twice—it was time to throw this dull lancet in the trash and start using a fresh one) and squeezed out a drop of blood.

Five seconds later: fifty-nine.

"Good low, Otis." I gave him a treat. "Sorry I made you wait."

"How bad is it?" Jules asked.

"It's not great," I said, "but I've got candy in my kit. I'll just eat some now and it'll tide me over until dinner."

I had to be careful not to eat too much, though, because dinner would push my blood sugar up more.

"My dad didn't know," Jules said. "Or else he never would have left."

"I know." But there were other reasons Ed shouldn't have left.

I crouched next to Otis and he licked my cheek. Actually, it was nicer on the floor, like being surrounded by a little forest of legs. I texted Mom and Dad, and then I poured half a fun-sized pouch of Skittles into my mouth and slumped against the wall to wait for the sugar to kick in. Jules slid down next to us while Otis stood guard.

Looking up, all I saw were arms with cell phones snapping pictures, taking videos.

The band finished the song and everybody cheered. Jules jumped up. I was halfway to my feet when she kicked the wall and plunked back down.

"What's wro—"

The band started up again. Ed was playing a second song.

CHAPTER TWENTY-TWO

True Fact: A human chain is stronger than a riptide.
(TF supplied by Jules Buttersby.)

The mood in the room went from fun to freaking out. Ed played a solo that sounded like somebody taking a kitchen's worth of pots and pans and dropping them on the floor, and people clapped and woohoo-ed.

"This'll be all over the Internet in an hour," Jules muttered. "I wonder if he knew about the jazz jam the whole time. I bet that's the real reason we came here."

"No, that can't be true," I said, trying to sound convincing. "He seemed so excited to hang out with you."

Seemed. But there was no way for Jules to know for sure.

"He's not even good," Jules said.

True Fact: The drummer before Ed sounded way better.

A mom near us said to her daughter, "Can you believe this? Honey, you have to understand—Ed Buttersby is one of the most famous actors in the world."

And then the dad said, "Even though his last three movies flopped."

Jules, scrunched on the floor next to me in the corner of the room where no one could see us even if they wanted to, even if they had been looking, peeled Sky's the Limit off her fingernails while strangers talked about her father like she didn't exist. I didn't know what to do. I was glad it was too loud to talk much because I had no idea what to say.

I tested again without bothering to hide it, since nobody was paying any attention to us. My blood sugar was up to the seventies.

Actually, it wasn't true that no one was paying attention to us. Otis hadn't taken his eyes off me and Jules. Now that my blood sugar was normal, he relaxed, but he never stopped guarding us. Jules buried her hand in Otis's ruff, something I know from experience is guaranteed to make a person feel better.

Two more solos and thousands of photo ops later, Ed finished the second song. I hoisted myself up—a little shaky from my blood sugar swing—so we could shove our way back to the burger line, but Ed waved us over to a smaller dining area off the main room, where the manager was waiting to take our order personally.

Everybody's eyes followed us as we snaked through the restaurant. I imagined people thinking, *Who's that kid with Ed Buttersby?* For once, the answer didn't have to be Diabetes Girl. I could be whoever I wanted: Sailor Girl or Treasure Hunter or Rising Eighth Grader (if I ever finished that science project) or Future First Person to Land on Mars. I got to decide, not them. Jules, on the other hand, didn't get to decide tonight. She could only be Ed Buttersby's daughter.

Even though there were loads of people still waiting in line—and plenty who had been waiting longer than us—the restaurant had cleared this whole room and a manager was waiting on us, just because Ed was famous. Which made me feel important and embarrassed all at the same time.

Otis wedged himself underneath the table where he wouldn't be in anyone's way and so I could slip my feet out of my flip-flops and massage him with my toes. Maybe now that we were finally sitting down just the four of us, Jules could have her special dinner.

"So what did you think of your old dad, Julie? Not bad for a guy who makes movies for a living, right?" Ed said. His face was red and sweaty, but he looked really happy. And bigger. Like cut flowers after my mom puts fresh water in the vase and leaves them on the back deck to soak up the sun.

"Did you make the manager boot someone from this table so he could give it to us?" Jules demanded.

"Oh no," the manager said. "Somebody was already getting up."

"You know I'd never do that," Ed said.

"Whatever," Jules said. "Let's order. Blue's blood sugar is low from waiting for you. She needs to eat."

"You okay, Blue?" Ed asked.

"I'm fine," I said, giving Jules a look that said *NOT okay to play the diabetes card.*

I asked for a cheeseburger medium—with pickles *and* onions—and tater tots. Jules asked for a salad with no dressing.

"How 'bout a milkshake with that, Julie?" Ed asked. "They make their own ice cream here."

Jules, who had been so excited about her classic American dinner only an hour ago, said, "Just water."

"You sure? I hear they're great," Ed said.

"Water's fine."

Ed squeezed Jules's hand. "Blue can't have a milkshake, so you're not having one either. You're a good friend."

Ed really didn't get it. Or maybe he didn't want to. He had ruined their special night. The classic American dinner would have just made Jules even sadder. Besides, Jules knew that I wouldn't have cared if she'd ordered a milkshake, and anyway, if I really wanted one, I could take a big bolus of insulin and have it.

Through the doorway and a big pass-through window thing, I could see other diners. A lot of them stared at us instead of at the band. Some of them pretended not to stare at us, but you could tell they were staring anyway because the blank wall over our heads couldn't possibly have been that interesting. *Do apes in the zoo feel this creeped out?*

"Um, excuse me?"

A hipster guy in his twenties hovered in the doorway with that look you get when you really need to pee and you're about to ask if you can cut the line.

"I'm sorry to interrupt your dinner, but I just need to say—I mean I just want to tell you how much your work means to me. *There and Back* is what made me want to be an actor. So, uh, thank you."

"Thank *you*," Ed said, smiling at him and only him. He half stood to shake hands. "And good luck."

"Mr. Buttersby?" Another guy. "Can I just ask—I've always wondered—what did you think happened to your character at the end of *Plutonium*? My girlfriend said he was dead, but I think—"

A woman: "*Space Voyager* is my favorite movie of all time. You have no idea..."

So many famous people come to the Hamptons during

the summer that regular people usually pretend to ignore them. But after one person stepped through the doorway, it was like floodgates had opened and another person came after them. And another and another and another. And then they weren't staying near the doorway; they were coming right to the table.

"Oh wow, I can't believe it's actually you!" a girl shrieked.

Jules flinched. More people came. Surrounded us.

"Dad," she begged, "do something!"

Somebody touched my hair. I turned. A little kid with pink ice cream on her chin stared at me. Otis pushed out from under the table.

Jules squeezed her eyes shut. People crushed in, shrinking the room smaller and smaller. Otis swung his head from side to side, trying to clear space. I felt like a pair of lungs having an asthma attack.

Ed held up a hand. "All right, everybody, let's just—"

Cameras flashed. Otis barked.

Ed stood up, still friendly, still soaking up the sun. "Let's dial it back now, everyone!"

"Ed!" somebody yelled. "Ed Buttersby!"

Jules smacked the table. "Forget it! Let's just go."

Ed looked over his shoulder. Saw Jules's puffy face. Saw, finally, the room, the people, no dinner on the table, no big night out. He leaned close to Jules. "I'm really sorry, babe. This is a disaster, but I'll fix it, I promise. You two go wait outside at the car. I'll get our food to go and we'll have a picnic."

But Jules was frozen, blinded by camera flashes, deafened by all the *me*s and *my*s and *need*s. Each person was like an octopus arm, studded with suction cups, glomming on to us. It made me want to Incredible Hulk through the wall, and I was just the mouse footman's assistant, the sidekick of the sidekick. If I'd been in Jules's shoes, I'd have been feeling so many things: mad at Ed, sad about the big night out being a big pile of dog poo, mortified in front of all these people taking pictures of the movie star's daughter crying so they could post them online.

I jumped up. "Otis!"

But Otis was already by my side. Ready. I grabbed his collar and took Jules's hand so we were one unit and no one could separate us. I squeezed and Jules squeezed back.

"Out," I commanded.

Otis was like Moses parting the Red Sea. A German shepherd on a mission is no joke. The electricity sizzling from his nose to his tail curled the hairs on my neck. Parents shot out their arms to shield their kids. We marched straight for the door, one solid chain, and nobody stood in our way.

Right before we got outside, Jules tugged on my hand. "Look."

I followed her gaze back over mobs of people, over the jazz band, and through the pass-through window. The chaos was over. Ed had gotten all the fans to line up so he could sign autographs and pose for selfies one at a time. He was smiling again, looking like there was no place in the world he'd rather be.

Outside on a table, someone had left a burger with only one bite taken out of it and a full cup of fries. We snagged them and walked the mile home with Otis between us.

Ed finally called right when we got to my house. Jules said, "At Blue's," and then listened without saying anything more, head down, hair hiding her face. After a minute, she covered the speaker with her hand and whispered, "He says he's done with all the fans and he'll pick me up. Or he can pick us both up. For a beach picnic."

Where we can get mobbed by fans again.

"Or we can go to my house."

And play board games with Anna.

"What do you want to do, Blue?" Jules asked.

I thought about that. What *did* I want to do?

I opened the screen door. "Tell him you're staying here with us tonight."

We found Mom in the kitchen. Flour dusted the counters, the table, and the floor around her feet like a thin coat of snow. Even the peanut butter sandwich next to her—Mom's go-to dinner when she doesn't feel like cooking—was floury. Otis, who cleans floors better than any mop, got right to work.

"I'm making that potato-rosemary bread we keep talking about," she said. "You can have it for breakfast tomorrow."

"Excellent," I said. "Can Jules sleep over?"

"Hmmm." Mom pretended to think about it. "For a price." She plopped a lump of dough in front of Jules and then another one in front of me. "Knead."

Jules followed my lead. We washed and dried our hands, and then we each sprinkled a patch of flour on the table. Then, using the heels of our hands, we pushed the dough forward, folded it, turned it a quarter turn, then pushed again, adding a little flour when it got too sticky.

"That's right, Jules," Mom said. "Really lean into it."

The dough smelled of warmed yeast and fresh-cut rosemary from Mom's herb garden. Delicious.

"How was dinner?" Mom asked. She kneaded her dough twice as fast as we kneaded ours; Mom is a champion dough kneader.

I waited for Jules to answer—I didn't know what she'd want to tell my mother about her disaster of a night—but she stayed quiet with her eyes on her dough. So I jumped in and said, "It was okay. Really crowded, though, because of the jazz jam. Do you mind if we go up to my room?"

Mom must have noticed Jules's sad mood because she said, "Of course not. You two go ahead. I'll do the cleaning up."

Upstairs, Jules studied my bookshelf with its pictures of the Gutter Girls and me and Nora, cool rocks I'd found at the beach, and other knickknacks. "Do you do stuff like that a lot? Make bread with your mom, I mean?"

I do, especially when it's not summer. Mom and I do puzzles together, and I help her plant the herb garden every year. We also have an ongoing game of gin rummy with scores somewhere in the thousands.

"Sometimes," I said. "Do you do stuff with your mom?"

Jules picked up my New York City snow globe and rocked it gently from side to side. "We go shopping. And she used to read to me a lot when I was little." She put the globe back on the shelf and watched the snow fall. "You're so lucky, Blue."

I'd never thought of myself as lucky. But now I wondered which was worse: having diabetes or having parents like Jules's.

"I'm sorry about tonight," I said. "All those people at the restaurant—it was awful."

Jules half smiled. "Thanks."

The crowds weren't the worst part, though, and we both knew it.

Otis nudged Jules's hand and she sank into the beanbag chair, after which he stretched the front half of his body across her lap. I sat next to them on the floor.

"Is it always like that with your dad?" I asked.

Jules nodded, just once, like her head was too heavy to do more. "Pretty much, yeah."

"That's hard," I said. "Really really hard."

We were both quiet after that. Not an awkward quiet, a sad quiet. Jules stared down at Otis and stroked his head, and I tried to think of what I could possibly say that would make her feel better. Finally, since I had no magic words, I reached for a beat-up box on the bottom shelf.

"Would you like to do this oversized fifty-piece dinosaur puzzle for ages four and up with me?"

Jules looked at me holding the box like a display model with a goofy smile on my face. She gave a little laugh. "Who wouldn't?"

She squirmed out from under Otis, and we dumped the pieces on the rug. Jules took the blue T. rex and I took the pink stegosaurus. When we finished, we swapped and started again.

CHAPTER TWENTY-THREE

True Fact: Everything that can go wrong does go wrong.
(TF supplied by some guy named Murphy.)

Two days later, it was pouring rain. Zero visibility. The water so murky and choppy that trying to find the treasure would be like looking for a penny in a washing machine on suds cycle. The *Windfall*, on the other hand, didn't need eyes, human or mechanical. Not when they had towable underwater machines capable of detecting the presence of iron by disturbances in the magnetic field.

Which was why they were out treasure hunting, and I was in the garage grooming Otis. Because just like it's Otis's job to take care of me, it's my job to take care of him.

Otis loves being groomed. He goes to his happy place—stands very straight with his eyes half-closed, and every now and then his whole coat shivers.

A car pulled into the driveway with Jules's dad's yoga instructor at the wheel. Jules got out, and the car drove away.

"This blows," Jules said.

I put down the comb and picked up the nail clipper. Otis gave me a front paw. "Agreed." I snipped. "But I have a plan. We need to make sure Fitz was telling the truth about the permits. Maybe he made the whole thing up just to get rid of us. And if he does have one of these permit things, maybe there's an exception for students or something like that. Other paw."

Otis obliged.

"Good," Jules said. "And even if there's no exception, we keep looking anyway. What's he going to do? Tow us out of the water?"

Otis rolled onto his back so I could do his rear paws and Jules could rub his belly at the same time. I didn't like to think about what the *Windfall* would do if we kept looking. Fitz had a tough reputation: When he bought his airline, he fired the president—who also happened to be his wife. For his kids' tenth birthdays, he made each of them spend a week alone in a Maine forest with nothing but a canteen and a hunting knife. One time, on a bet, he went waterskiing behind a blimp with a broken arm. I learned all this on the Internet.

"Teeth."

Otis pretended not to hear me. He hates getting his teeth brushed. If his breath didn't smell like fish I wouldn't bother, but it does so I do.

"Teeth, Otis," I said, using my *I mean it* voice.

He stuck his nose in Jules's armpit. She laughed.

"Give me back my dog's head or I'll tell him to lick your face," I said.

"Ew." Jules pushed Otis away.

Otis knew he was defeated. He drooped his head and bared his fangs. I pulled up his lip and brushed.

After I finished, I stood up. "Okay, let's go talk to Laurie."

"Aren't you going to wash your hands?" Jules said.

Why would I? "Of course," I said.

Since there was no lightning, we motored to town in the boat. We had a choice: wear foul-weather gear and be hot but dry, or wear bathing suits and be cool but wet. We picked cool but wet. The water was rough, so we all wore life vests, including Otis.

"Can I be totally honest with you for a minute?" Jules said, over the sound of the engine.

"When do you ever hold anything back?" We entered the channel to the harbor, and I dropped our speed to five miles an hour.

"Fair point. The thing is, these tankinis you wear? They're hideous. Do you want me to go with you to the surf shop to find something cuter?"

That feeling you get when your foot falls asleep? It happened to my entire body.

Why is it that when there's something you're mortified about—say, a giant pimple on the end of your nose, or finding out you've been walking around with toilet paper stuck to your shoe for half a day, or maybe wearing an ugly bathing suit to cover up a weird machine that's stuck in your body—hearing somebody else talk about the thing out loud is even more mortifying than the thing itself?

"Thanks," I said through numb lips. "But I'm good." *Except no, I'm not good, and can we please talk about humidifiers or toe fungus or pretty much anything else?*

"You mean you actually *like* wearing a mom-suit?"

I could tell Jules wasn't going to let it drop. To her, I was a fashion emergency. "It's not a question of like. I need a two-piece so I can get to my infusion set, and the tank top covers that and my pump."

"Who cares if people see your infusion whatever? If it were me, I'd rock a bikini and let my diabetes flag fly."

Easy for you to say. You don't have a catheter tube hanging out of your belly.

I pictured myself strolling along the beach in a bikini, shoulders back, head high, flying my diabetes flag. Shining sun, rolling waves, some little kid screeching, *What's that?* The mom offering an apologetic smile. *Hush, sweetie, it's not nice to stare.*

"Point taken," I said.

"It's just a suggestion," Jules said. "As your friend."

"I *said* point taken."

Jules held up her hands. "*Okay.* I was just trying to help."

We found Laurie in the harbormaster's office on the wharf. She looked up from her desk and smiled when we walked in. Laurie has tan skin with white lines around her eyes from squinting in the sun. Like Pop Pop's but not so tigerish.

"Hey, girls. Hi there, Otis." Laurie got up and gave Otis a big rub. His tail wagged like a loose garden hose with the water running full blast. The fact that she didn't mind getting sprayed by my wet dog made me like Laurie even more. "How's everything going with the diabetes benefit?" she asked. "It's coming up soon, right?"

Ugh.

"July Fourth," Jules said.

Three days away. *Ugh, ugh, ugh.*

Awkward pause while I tried to figure out how to ask Laurie what I wanted to ask her without telling her why I wanted to know. Finally, lightning struck my brain. "I'm doing this science project for school—"

"Because she failed the class," Jules interrupted.

I mentally glared at her. "I have to collect water samples in Gardiner's Bay." I explained what happened with Fitz and how I needed to be in the bay for my project. "Is it true? Does he really have one of these permit things?"

"I'm afraid he does," Laurie said.

Jules and I exchanged a look of misery.

"So *nobody's* allowed to go near the area?" Jules asked. "Not even students?"

"Sorry, girls," Laurie said, shaking her head. "Not without the *Windfall*'s permission."

Jules looked as hopeless as I felt. We slunk to the door, and I had my hand on the knob when Laurie said:

"You know, Blue, it's funny that the *Windfall* is searching in Gardiner's Bay, because that's where your grandfather searched for years."

"He did?" Something that maybe possibly could have been a spark of hope started to flicker in me.

"Yup. I used to see him out there all the time when I was in high school. You should ask your dad about it."

Jules raised her eyebrows at me, which I took to mean *Did you know that your grandfather spent years searching for treasure right where we're looking?* I shook my head. There were so many other places to look that I'd never asked him about Gardiner's Bay, and he'd never mentioned it.

I flung open the door. "Thanks, Laurie!" I called over my shoulder.

Jules, Otis, and I ran outside, oblivious to the rain waterfalling off the eaves of the harbormaster's office.

Fitz or no Fitz, no way were we stopping now.

CHAPTER TWENTY-FOUR

True Fact: In 2008, some miners accidentally found a five-hundred-year-old shipwreck with a chest full of gold...in the Namibian desert. (TF supplied by Scouring the Seas.)

"Why does he have to be dead?" Jules wailed.

Seriously? "Gosh, Jules. I'm really sorry my grand-father got cancer."

"Don't feel bad." She patted my back. "It's not your fault. It's just, this would be so much easier if we could ask him what he knew about Gardiner's Bay."

The thing was, I knew exactly how Jules felt. Or rather, she knew exactly how I felt. There had been so many times I wished I could talk to Pop Pop. So many questions I wanted to ask.

What do you think, Pop Pop—does that rock look like a dog's head to you?

You know, BB, it just might.

I tried to remember the last time I'd heard Pop Pop's voice in my head or imagined him steering the boat next to me. It had been...a while.

I closed my eyes. I could still smell his smell and see his tiger stripes. But when I tried to remember his voice, I only heard the soft rasp from last winter, when he was sick, like when you can't remember some of the lyrics to a song and you have to make them up.

What would I have left of Pop Pop if I lost more words to his song?

I bent over to retrieve Otis's already full water bowl so Jules wouldn't see the expression on my face, then carried it to the kitchen sink to empty and refill it.

"Let's go ask your dad about it," Jules said, following me.

"My dad's on a job in Water Mill. We can't ride our bikes ten miles in the rain to interrupt him in the middle of his work to ask him about his father hunting for treasure back in the twentieth century." Plus, with the way Dad feels about treasure, we'd be crazy to try to talk to him in front of everybody at work.

"You're right. He might get suspicious. We'll stay here and wait for him to come home." Jules took Otis's bowl from my hands and put it back on the floor. "If it turns out your dad doesn't know anything, though, what do you want to do about Fitz?"

I knew exactly what I wanted to do about Fitz. "Like you said, what's he going to do? Tow us out of the water?"

Jules grinned. "Good."

It took precisely six episodes of bad TV, one frozen chicken burrito, two rounds of checkers, and a totally lame hide-and-seek game with Otis (you can't play hide-and-seek with a scent-alert dog; they have no ability to hide and they find you in about thirty seconds) for Dad to get home.

We heard his truck in the driveway and ran downstairs to meet him.

"Hi, girls." Dad tossed his keys on the table by the front door. His hair was gray with plaster dust. This time of year everybody in the Hamptons wants their guest houses built yesterday. Dad got down on his knees to rub Otis's head and so Otis could give his face a welcome lick. "Mom's on her way home with dinner. Jules, you want to stay?"

"No thanks, Mr. Broen. My dad's girlfriend's trainer is picking me up soon." Jules beamed laser eyes at me.

"Hey, Dad. You'll never believe it. Jules and I ran into Laurie today. You know, Laurie from the marina? It was totally random and coincidental, and she happened to mention to us that Pop Pop—you know, your father, Jerry?—that when he used to hunt for treasure, he'd do it in Gardiner's Bay. Just like Fitz Fitzgibbons!"

Jules looked at me like I'd grown three heads, which,

184

because I'd developed the ability to see things from her point of view, I took to mean *Worst liar ever!*

Which was pretty much true.

Dad blinked at me. Maybe I *had* grown three heads. "I thought you couldn't work on your water project because of the weather. What were you doing at the marina?" he asked.

Before I could make things worse, Jules said, "We motored into town so I could get new sunglasses. I just broke my third pair of Ray-Bans. My dad is so mad at me. Eye health is really important to him, and sun damage is a leading cause of blindness."

This time Dad blinked at Jules. "Let's talk in the kitchen." He grabbed the mail from the hall table.

Jules and I leaned against the counter while Dad flipped through the mail. He gave up after the third bill and got a beer out of the fridge. "So Laurie talked to you about Pop Pop, huh? What did she say?"

"Just what I told you. Is it true?"

I expected Dad would refuse to talk about it, but he took a long swig and nodded. "Yeah. He studied all the currents and old charts and weather maps, and he came up with this whole big theory that Gardiner's Bay was where he was going to find the *family treasure*." Dad said "family treasure" in the woo-woo way that most people would say "UFO" or "Bigfoot."

Pop Pop's reasons didn't sound mythical to me, though. They sounded logical. *Provable.* The hair on my arms prickled.

Dad went on, "He used to drag me out on the boat with him all the time. We'd lean over the side of his dinghy and stare into the water for days, just like you used to do with him."

I crossed all my fingers, willing Dad to give the answer I wanted to hear, before I asked, "Did you ever find anything?"

"Tons of stuff." Dad went to sit at the kitchen table, and Jules and I followed him. "A chunk of somebody's rudder, an old rubber tire, some nice driftwood. One time Pop Pop found a mug that he was convinced came from one of those German spy boats that landed off Amagansett during World War Two."

"But no actual treasure?" Jules asked.

Dad took another swig of beer. "Oh, no. We found treasure."

The prickles on my arms turned to chills. "Well?" I asked, and then, when Dad didn't say anything: "*What was it?*"

"Ambergris." Dad plunked the can on the table.

"What's *amber grease?*" Jules and I almost shouted at the same time.

Amber was valuable, wasn't it? And gold-colored? Maybe

186

the treasure was more than gold bars and coins. Maybe it was *gems*, too, maybe—

"Whale poop." Dad grinned.

Maybe not.

"The stuff hardens into rock, and it's worth a fortune," he said. "They use it to make perfume. Pop Pop found a big hunk and sold it for over a thousand dollars."

Jules rolled her eyes. I groaned.

"Dad," I said through gritted teeth. "That's not treasure."

Dad lobbed his empty beer can at the recycling bin. He missed. "A thousand dollars was a lot of money in 1975, Belly. Heck, it's a lot of money now."

"You know what I mean," I said.

"Blue." Dad had stopped kidding around. "Pop Pop was a dreamer. His father told him those old family stories just like he told you, and he believed them. When he didn't find anything in Gardiner's Bay, he came up with another theory and then another one after that. Trust me, there was never any ship of gold. The sad truth is Pop Pop wasted his life looking for something that wasn't there." Dad got up and put the beer can in the bin. "So forget all your dreams of fame and glory. Whatever Fitzgibbons finds, it's got nothing to do with our family."

That's what you think.

As far as Dad was concerned, the case was closed. He

went back to the mail. "Bill, bill, junk, *bra catalog*—" He waved the catalog in the air.

"Dad!"

"Oh, here's one for you, Belly. Looks like a letter from Nora."

He handed me a square yellow envelope with pictures on it. As in, instead of the words "Camp Footlights," Nora had drawn a stage with its curtains open in the return address box. And my first name was a blue square she'd colored in crayon. She'd written my street address in regular numbers and words so the letter would actually get to me.

Jules looked over my shoulder at the envelope. "Your friend writes with crayons? How old is she?"

I pressed the front of the letter to my chest. "Nora's very creative."

Jules scowled. "She sounds fun." She took her phone out of her back pocket and started texting. "I have to go home now."

Is it possible Jules was jealous of Nora?

"I think you'd really like each other," I said, holding out the envelope so Jules could appreciate the unique zaniness of my best friend. "Maybe we could all hang out when she gets home from camp."

"Maybe," Jules said, scowling a little less.

I wanted to rip open the envelope right that very second,

but I didn't want to read the letter in front of Jules or Dad. For the whole half an hour it took for Anna's personal trainer to pick up Jules, I could practically hear it screaming, *Read me! READ me! READ. ME. Read! Read! Read! Now! Now! Now!*

At last Otis and I were upstairs in my room on my bed, just the two of us.

> Blue!
>
> Camp is great. Greater than great! Even though I'm exhausted from being in tech all week for <u>Into the Woods</u> (I'm the baker's wife!) and in chorus for <u>Beauty and the Beast</u> at the same time. Last week I was rehearsing <u>Beauty</u> and crewing for <u>Les Mis</u> on the fly floor, which was possibly—no, definitely—the most terrifying experience of my entire life. But fun. Funner than fun. People here are incredibly talented. The two leads in <u>Kate</u> are from LaGuardia and Ellington! The TD for <u>Rosie</u> thinks he rules the world, but the MD is like a musical fairy godmother, so life is good. Except I miss you like crazy!

How's Otis? What's happening with the hunt?? And Jules the evil dog-hater??? WRITE SOON!
Love and xoxoxoxoxoxo,
Nora

P.S. True Fact: The original B&B story is based on a real boy who was covered in hair and got kidnapped and given to King Henry 11 of France as a present!

P.P.S. I'm SO sorry it took me this long to write. Please don't hate me! As punishment I will blanket my face with the fluffy cloud kittens from your anniversary card, even though I'm allergic.

I let the letter float to the floor. "True Fact, Otis," I whispered. "Nora wrote me a letter all about her life at camp, and I don't understand half of what she said."

CHAPTER TWENTY-FIVE

True Fact: The problem with being a girl my age is when it comes to dressing up, you have two choices: kindergartner or beauty queen.

I'd prayed for appendicitis, scanned the skies for a freak tornado, and, when those didn't pan out, considered hiding under the house with the rabid raccoons. Instead, my worst nightmare came true, and here I was: in Dad's truck with Otis and my parents arriving at the CJDF gala.

I had on an aqua sleeveless dress with white piping that was shaped like a tent. At least it didn't have ruffles or ducks. But it did have a tiny hole that I cut so I could thread the tube to my pump through it and hide my pump in one of the pockets.

"I look eight years old," I muttered.

"You don't look a day younger than eleven," Mom said.

Dad looked even more miserable and uncomfortable

than me in his jacket and tie. Probably because it was about eighty-five degrees outside at six o'clock.

Otis, who loves a party, was totally psyched. He sat next to me in the back seat, straight and tall, with his fur neatly brushed—very Noble King Otis—but the tip of his tail was wagging. He carried my diabetes kit in a pouch on his service vest.

Mom—cool and comfortable in a long flowy silky dress—was also psyched. Last year's party raised $600,000. We'd already blown past that this year, and the party hadn't even started yet. She had a list of more potential donor names inked on her palm, which she'd written in Sharpie so they wouldn't sweat off. Knowing Mom, we wouldn't go home until she'd wrangled a check out of every one of those people.

A quarter mile from Jules's house, local police directed traffic to the valet line. A young woman in a black dress with super-high heels, a body mic, and an iPad leaned into the driver's window and checked us in.

"Okay, gang. Let's go cure diabetes," Dad said.

He gave his keys to one of the valet parkers, and then we piled onto a shuttle. By "shuttle" I mean a chauffeur-driven golf cart with a cooler of champagne.

The shuttle took us to the house, where a gigantic white party tent filled the middle of the front yard. Over to one side, a reggae band played chill tunes for a few hundred guests. Waiters with fruit tower hats wobbled around with silver trays of mini burgers the size of postage stamps. Security guards patrolled the grounds on Segways.

Nora would have had plenty to say about this scene. But would I have understood any of it? Back home I kept rereading her letter. I went online and found out LaGuardia and Ellington are arts high schools; an MD is a musical director and a TD is a technical director; and I'm pretty sure the B&B story is actually just *Beauty and the Beast*.

I never used to have to look up any of Nora's words. But now I might need a dictionary if I ever wanted to talk to her again.

As soon as we got off the shuttle, cameras started flashing: *Ladies and Gentlemen: Diabetes Girl!* A CJDF person sent over a makeup artist, who descended on Mom with a giant powder brush while her assistant went after Otis with a comb. After she finished with Mom, the makeup lady attacked me. She didn't go for Dad, though.

"It's because I'm gorgeous just the way I am," Dad said.

"It's because you're a man, so no one cares how you look," Mom said, rolling her eyes. "A thirteen-year-old girl needs makeup, but a middle-aged man takes a shower and he's distinguished."

"No one's ever called me distinguished before." Dad kissed Mom on the cheek. "Thank you."

"Broens!"

Ed and Anna, along with a video crew, floated across the grass. The photographers abandoned us to snap them. Ed had on a linen suit with no tie and flip-flops. Anna was wearing a long shimmery skirt and a man's white ribbed tank top, with a gardenia in her carefully messed-up hair as her only accessory.

You know how cartoon characters will smile really big and a little bolt of light will bounce off their teeth with a *ping* sound? Turns out that happens to some people in real life, too.

After photo ops, introductions, air-kisses, and paw shakes, Ed said, "So, Blue, how's the guest of honor?"

Miserable. "Great," I said.

"What do you think of the fruit theme?" Anna asked.

"Very low on the glycemic index," I said.

Mom gently stepped on my toes.

"No, really," I said. "It's incredible. Everything's incredible. Thank you so much, Mr. Buttersby. This is definitely our biggest and best event ever."

"Call me Ed, and you know how glad I am to help. Hey, listen, let's get out of this heat before we all melt. The CJDF folks are waiting for us."

I figured that meant we were going inside the house, but no. Ed led us to the party tent. Which was air-conditioned.

About ten years into a discussion of timelines, pro-
ceeds, and head counts, Jules finally showed up. She had
on a slinky white dress with a hole over part of her rib
cage. She looked like a stranger from a magazine with
her dark eyeliner and her hair pulled back, and also like
she'd grown five inches, which was probably because of
her gold platform sandals.

"Julie Jules, you look amazing!" Anna leaned over to
kiss Jules on both cheeks. "Mmmm. You smell delicious.
What perfume are you wearing? Jo Malone?"

"Whale poop." Jules grabbed my arm. "C'mon, Blue,
let's go mingle."

We made our escape.

CHAPTER TWENTY-SIX

True Fact: Public mortification isn't the worst thing that can happen at a party.

As soon as we got out of the tent, Otis headbutted me and high-fived. No surprise. Being nervous always makes my blood sugar high. I tested and took insulin behind a seven-foot neon banana while Jules snagged some kiwi on a skewer from a waiter with pineapples stacked on his head. We tried to disappear anonymously into the hordes, but it was impossible. Not with my face plastered on the invitations like one of those baby seals you can save for fifty cents a day. I could feel people's silent questions—*She looks so healthy. How can she have diabetes?*—and dumb suggestions—*Have you tried eating paleo?*

But not everybody was silent. From behind us, a man's voice said, "I've been looking for you, girls."

Jules and I turned around slowly, like two humans

in a zombie movie who just heard a noise coming from *inside the house*. I tightened my grip on Otis's leash.

Fitz.

"One of my crew saw you back on the water today."

Actually, we'd been on the water the last two days, but Jules and I weren't about to tell that to Fitz.

"What part of 'stay away' did you not understand?" Fitz leaned in so only we could hear him. "Don't make me escalate this. *You'll regret it.*"

I lost the power to breathe, let alone talk.

Fitz leaned back and shark-smiled. "Oh, and thanks for that great idea you gave me, Jules. It's happening. All because of you."

He grabbed a microscopic crab cake from a waiter dressed like a raspberry, tossed it in his mouth, and walked away without saying good-bye.

"Jules—" I started.

Jules swatted the air, like Fitz was an annoying gnat she could brush away. "Forget him. He's just trying to scare us."

"Well, he succeeded! And what did he mean about the 'great idea' you gave him?"

"Who knows? It's probably just some lie to scare us because he likes to torture children. Nothing's changed. We keep looking unless somebody makes us stop, remember?"

I let out a slow breath. "You're right. He's just a bully."
A big, powerful, billionaire bully.

Jules took Otis's leash from me. "C'mon, let's get out of here."

The three of us hid under a big weeping willow tree in a corner of the property away from the party. Inside the droopy branches, it felt like a secret fort. Jules and I sat next to the trunk, and Otis stayed near the perimeter so he could keep watch and sneak nibbles of leaves at the same time.

"How's your mom?" I asked.

Jules shrugged. "I haven't talked to her in a few days. But I'm actually thinking maybe that's a good thing? Maybe it means she's busy."

"That's great," I said. "If she's busy she must be feeling better."

"Maybe." Jules pulled out hunks of grass like the ground was a dead chicken that needed plucking. "I hate this party."

"I hate my dress," I said, picking at a section of piping that was unraveling.

"I hate *my* dress," she said.

"Really? I think you look incredible."

"It feels like everybody's staring at me." Jules wrapped her arms around her waist like she was trying to cover herself up.

"Yeah, because you look incredible," I said.

She rolled her eyes and attacked the grass again.

"Jules, what do you want? I mean, really?" I said.

"What do you mean, what do I want?"

"What do you wish for most when you wish on birthday candles and eyelashes?"

Already Jules had plucked an impressive pile. "According to Anna, I should wish that when I'm done growing, my thigh-to-calf ratio is somewhere between one point four and one point five to one," she said.

"Seriously? Is that a thing?" What did those numbers even mean?

"It's a really important thing. Any bigger and your thighs are too fat."

"Says who?" I looked down at my legs. Were they too fat? What was too fat, anyway?

"Says Anna the super-starlet and every magazine you've ever seen." Jules rolled her eyes again. "Which obviously means it has to be true."

I thought about girls and women I knew and tried to remember what their thighs looked like and whether the people with smaller thighs were happier than the people with bigger thighs.

"That's the most ridiculous thing I've ever heard," I said.

"Yes, it is," Jules agreed. "But just because it's ridiculous doesn't mean that people don't believe it."

"But *you* don't have to believe it," I said. "Jules, there's got to be something else you really want other than a good leg ratio."

She stopped plucking. "Fine. I just want *one thing* in my life to be about me and not about my dad."

"You mean the way there are five hundred people all here for the Ed Buttersby Saves Diabetes Girl show who don't even know our names?" I said.

We both laughed.

"Yeah," Jules said. "Something like that."

The alarm on my phone went off.

"We have to go," I said. "It's time for the speeches."

I got up and brushed the back of my dress. I could feel my thighs through the material. Was that fat or just skin? *Ugh.* I hated that Jules put that question in my head, and I decided to 100 percent refuse to care.

"Do you mind if I stay here?" Jules said. "I know you've got your speech, but my dad told me he's got some big announcement, and I don't want to hear it."

I signaled Otis to come so I could put his leash back on. "It's probably just something to do with the fundraiser," I said. "Like a donation." I really needed Jules there for moral support. Plus, I wanted someone to look at who wasn't my parents or a stranger or a celebrity. Or Fitz.

"I don't think so," Jules said. "There was something about the way he said it. I'm worried..."

"About what?" I said.

Jules didn't answer right away. She stayed on the ground, digging the heel of her sandal into the soft earth. Finally she said, "I'm worried maybe he's going to announce his engagement or something."

My hand froze on Otis's collar. "Haven't they only been dating for a few months?"

"Yeah, but that would be totally like him. Stealing the spotlight at a party for dying children—no offense—"

I shrugged.

"—to tell the world he's in love."

That *would* be totally like Ed. And awful for Jules. "I get it," I said. "And I'm *really* sorry to ask. But...I don't think I can get through this speech if you're not there."

Which was true. And Jules looked as surprised as I was to hear me say it. Somewhere in the craziness of the last three weeks, we had become friends.

Jules stopped digging and plucking. "Really?" she said.

I nodded.

She stood up and took Otis's leash from my hand. "Okay, team, let's get this over with."

We got to the tent just as Ed was saying the words "brave," "overcome," and "shadow of death."

201

"That's your cue," Jules said, shoving me toward the stage.

I staggered a few steps, and the piece of paper with my speech on it went flying out of my hand and landed next to table nine. And then a man who was sitting at table nine stepped on it. I'd just gotten down on my hands and knees to pry it from under his shoe when I heard, "Sag Harbor's very own hero, Blue Broen!"

If only my head hadn't been under a dining table. If only I hadn't tried to stand up too soon. If only that table had been loaded with balloons instead of dishes and glasses for ten people.

For the record, not everything fell over. Just maybe about half of everything. And not the table itself. Just the stuff on it. Also, there was no food yet, just drinks. Lots of drinks.

Turns out half a table-load of crystal and china all crashing at the same time makes a really really loud noise.

Really loud.

Otis sprang into action, woofing a chesty danger bark: *Get back! Something bad is happening and I need to protect Blue!* He broke away from Jules and stood over me while I inched out from under the table, licking and sniffing me, checking for injuries. People were calling my name, but Otis wasn't letting anyone near me. He gave me his back

202

to lean on to help me get up. My head throbbed where I bonked it, but I was basically okay.

Table nine was another story. Red wine splattered the party guests like *Nightmare on Lily Pond Lane.* Waiters with strawberry headdresses swarmed the scene with brooms and hand towels.

Jules was still standing at the edge of the tent. Bent over and laughing her head off.

Dad was out of his seat, and Mom was holding him back. *You all right?* she mouthed. I nodded.

Ed said, "Okay, everybody. No harm done. Just a few dishes. Look at that, it's cleaned up already. Dry cleaning's on me! Blue, why don't you come on up now?"

Why don't I teleport to China? Or swim to the moon?

I slithered to the front of the room, trying to pretend I didn't look like an oversized preschooler with a drinking problem.

I uncrumpled my speech and leaned toward the microphone. Most of what I had written was smeared.

I cleared my throat. "Um, thank you, Mr. Buttersby."

The tent was filled with people from town plus hundreds of unfamiliar faces, all waiting to hear what the clumsy diabetic girl had to say.

Plus Fitz.

Dad gave me a big thumbs-up. Jules toasted me with her ginger ale.

203

It didn't matter that I couldn't read my speech; I pretty much had it memorized since I basically gave the same one every year. It was all about what it's like to have this lousy disease that no one can see that's only going to get worse unless everybody in the room opened their wallets right this second and paid for a cure.

I was so sick of being the sick girl.

I cleared my throat again. "I want to tell you..."

Otis pressed his body against my leg. I sank my fingers into his ruff.

"Um, let me tell you..."

Mom. Dad. Jules. A cool lady with a birdcage for a hat.

Otis ducked his head under my palm. I scratched between his ears and thought about all the things I was expected to say that I didn't want to say.

I'm done talking about the sick girl.

I took a deep breath, and...

"Let me tell you about my service dog, Otis."

Mom and Dad gave me a *Huh?* look. They knew this wasn't how my speech was supposed to start.

"The funny thing is," I said, "we didn't mean to get a medical-alert dog when we got him. Actually, we didn't even mean to get a dog. We were just trying to get my teeth cleaned."

Only a few people laughed at my joke. I glanced over

at Jules, who circled her hands in a *Keep going* motion. So I did.

"I was at the dentist's office for a checkup one day when I was six. There I was, in the chair with the spit-suction thing dangling out of my mouth, when all of a sudden, I heard a cry."

I'll never forget that cry. It was soft and soulful and sad. Full of yearning and loneliness. Starved for love and understanding. Or at least that's what it sounds like now in my memory.

"See, Eloise, the hygienist, is also a dog trainer, and she'd heard about a German shepherd shelter puppy nobody wanted. He was a runt, he was hyper, and he was scared of kitchens. The first owners gave up on him. I mean, who would want a pet like that?"

I scanned the audience. People seemed to be paying attention, or at least no one was checking their phones, which I took as a good sign.

"Anyway, Eloise had told the shelter she'd try to work with this hopeless, possibly mentally ill dog, and she had him with her at work that day. After the cry, I was out of the chair in a second. I didn't even bother taking the paper-towel-on-a-chain thing off my neck." That got a few more laughs. "I followed the cry to a crate in the corner of the exam room, kneeled down..."

I paused for dramatic effect.

"And there was *Otis*."

Another pause. How could I possibly describe the epic humongousness of Otis entering my life? I looked down at him, my hand still on top of his head, and Otis twisted his neck around so he could lick my palm.

"Otis was so little back then!" I said, remembering every adorable detail. "Just a pair of big maple-syrup eyes in a fuzzy black face. He had crooked puppy ears and a skinny puppy tail that thumped *thwack, thwack, thwack, thwack.*"

Exactly in time with the beat of my heart.

"So, guess what? It turns out that it's really hard for parents to say no to a free puppy for an only child, especially when nobody in the family is allergic."

That got a bigger laugh. Maybe this public-speaking thing wasn't so bad after all.

"It also turns out, as you can see for yourselves, that Otis is the opposite of a runt. He was hyper because he's ridiculously smart and bursting with brainpower. And he doesn't hate kitchens. He just has a crazy-sensitive nose, and when he was little he got overwhelmed by too many smells."

Mom and Dad were holding hands. Dad winked at me.

"At first, Otis was just like any other puppy—assuming any other puppy was the world's best puppy. He loved food and naps and sniffing things and finding things and eating left shoes and rolling in mud and running like a maniac on the beach."

And me. He loved me most of all. Which was good because I loved him most of all too.

"After a while, my parents started noticing that whenever I had a blood sugar episode, Otis would plaster himself to my side and lick me until my levels were back to normal. They didn't think too much about it, though, because he did the same thing when I fell down or got sad. But then he started doing it before I noticed I was feeling bad. And then there was the day that Otis pushed open the screen door, found my dad in the garage, and whined and nipped at him until my dad followed him back into the house and up the stairs to my room, where I was half-unconscious with a blood sugar level of forty-five and dropping."

Quiet murmurs from the audience, who were no doubt picturing six-year-old me lying on my bedroom floor, clammy and pale.

I kept going. "Eloise worked with us for two full years to get Otis's scent training solid, so that he would do it right every single time and even wake up from a dead sleep to alert us. My parents did most of the work, but I'm the one who still plays scent games with him to make sure his training stays fresh."

I felt Otis tilt his nose up, and I smiled down at him. He wagged his tail like a windshield wiper on high. "That's right, Otis—I'm talking about you."

The audience awwww-ed. I looked out again. Anna was wiping away tears.

"You saw tonight the way Otis helps me and protects me. What you can't see is that he understands diabetes better than anyone in this room, including me. Otis saves my life every day. I don't know what I'd do without him."

I tried to picture it—life without Otis—but I couldn't. There's no version of Future Blue walking down the street, reading in bed, or doodling in English class without Otis.

The audience waited for me to finish my speech, but what more could I say?

"Um, thanks?"

I didn't expect the tidal wave of applause. Usually when I finish my speech there's some polite clapping, which I can barely hear because most people go back to eating and chatting by the time I'm halfway through speaking. But tonight, the sound filled the tent. I froze, not sure where to go or what I should do.

Luckily, Ed was ready with an exit line. He came back to the microphone. "Thanks, Blue. Now, folks, I hope you'll all be as good a friend to Blue and kids like her as Otis is. But with your wallet, not your nose."

People smiled and nodded, and more than a few of them reached for the donation envelopes on their tables.

Ed held up his hand. "I know everyone's ready for dinner, but I have one more announcement to make."

The murmuring died down.

"Some of you may know I have a new partner. A new partner in work and in life. Anna, would you please come up here?"

Anna made her way to the front of the room and stood on Ed's other side. I looked over at Jules from my spotlight of awkwardness onstage. Her face was a total blank.

"Anna and I have decided to embark on a new journey together. An exciting journey that will bring the past into the present."

Otis's panting was now the only sound in the tent.

"Anna Bowdin, the beautiful, talented Anna Bowdin and I..."

Anna, gazing adoringly at Ed. Ed, gazing adoringly at Anna. Jules, frozen.

"...are teaming up with Fitz Fitzgibbons and director Sonia Jacobs for their documentary about Fitz's search for the *Golden Lion* payroll. Anna will narrate, and I'm coming on as producer. Best of all, folks, Fitz is giving the first hundred thousand dollars he finds to the Cure Juvenile Diabetes Foundation! Fitz—come on up!"

And that's when the fireworks started. And the band launched into "The Star-Spangled Banner."

"Isn't this great?" Ed shouted.

Otis dove for cover between my legs, and I nearly fell on top of him. Half-blind in the stage lights, teetering over my dog, I squinted over the crowd, searching for Jules. All I saw was the back of her head as she ran from the tent.

CHAPTER TWENTY-SEVEN

True Fact: Up until the Middle Ages, people diagnosed diabetes by drinking pee to see if it tasted sweet. (TF supplied by Dr. Basch.)

"So your dad and Anna are on the *Windfall* right now?" I said.

Otis, Jules, and I were back on the water less than twelve hours after the CJDF fruit fail. So far we'd covered about three-quarters of the area near the sorrowful hound. We were running out of time *and* space.

"Yes. Thanks to my last name and my brilliant idea to threaten Fitz with a documentary, Fitz asked my father and his likely future daughter-wife to be part of the one that Fitz and Sonia Jacobs were already making. They're all there together, as we speak, doing light studies and camera tests," Jules said. "We'll probably hear them on the spy-cam any second."

As if on cue, Anna's voice came through the speaker:

"Can we do something about this wind?"

Sonia: "Like what?"

Anna: "I don't know. Block it? With a...thing?"

Jules yanked on the tow rope to the tube like she was an evil dentist going after a healthy molar. "I should have known he'd find a way to make the treasure hunt all about him," she said. "I won't let him. Not this time. We *have* to find the treasure first."

Jules was all business since Ed's big announcement. No more debates about wedges versus platforms or lectures about why the millions of bacteria that live in our guts will be the medicine of the future. Just bucket, bucket, bucket.

Which was fine with me. Every second that went by, somebody was getting closer to the treasure. And Jules was right: That somebody needed to be us.

The water today was calm and clear, and the bright sunshine meant we could see straight to the floor of the bay about twenty-five feet down. Perfect hunting conditions. We paddled from section to section, finding the usual rocks and seaweed.

Until I spotted the hunk.

"Jules." I tried to keep my voice normal even though there were smoke detectors going off in my head.

"What?" she said, her voice muffled by her bucket.

212

"Look here and tell me what you see." I moved over on the tube so she could take my spot.

Jules scooched over and put her bucket where mine had been. After a few seconds she said, "The seaweed?"

"No." I stuck my arm in the water and pointed. "The hunk to the right of the seaweed. About two o'clock from the seaweed."

Jules scooched a few more inches off the tube into the water. "I see the seaweed, and some sand, and—" She gasped.

The hunk stuck up half-buried in the sand, black, lumpy, about the length and shape of a quart-sized milk carton but skinnier. I'd been looking at lumps and bumps and hunks for weeks, and this one didn't look like anything I'd seen.

Jules took her head out of her bucket to face me. "Can we get down there?"

"It might be too deep," I said.

"Let's try anyway," she said. "Now. Like, right now."

"My thinking exactly," I said.

But distance wasn't the only problem. Because the water was deep, there'd be a lot of pressure as we swam closer to the bottom, holding our breath. The thing is, pressure is really bad for diabetic people's eyes, which tend to do things like hemorrhage. Not blood-spurting-out-of-your-face hemorrhage, but little-burst-capillaries hemorrhage, the kind that over time, if you have enough of them, can make you blind. So when Jules asked, "Want me to try first?" I gritted my teeth and said yes even though I was dying to shout, *No way!*

Jules took off her shorts and T-shirt and tossed them into the well in the middle of the tube. She had on a plain blue one-piece underneath. Very swim team. Not very Jules. She slid off the tube and treaded water.

"Let's not get overexcited. It's probably nothing," she called.

"Probably," I agreed. "But worth checking out."

"Definitely," she said, and dove down.

Otis stuck his head under the boat rail and stared at the spot where she'd been. Or possibly at the jellyfish, which there were kind of a lot of.

I watched Jules through the view bucket. She was a good swimmer. She went straight for the hunk, but before she even got close, she turned around and came back.

"I ran out of air," she said, breathing hard.

"How was the pressure?" I asked.

"I thought my ears were going to explode, but whatever. I'm going again."

Jules tried again. And again. She treaded water next to the tube after the third time, catching her breath.

"It's too far down to swim," I said, my brain scrambling for a backup plan.

"Yeah. Sorry. I—oh, *shih tzu!*" Jules yelled. "Oh! Ow! Jellyfish! Get me out of here!"

Otis barked. I slithered half off the tube and reached. "Grab my arms!"

Jules grabbed and I pulled.

"Oof!" she groaned.

I gave one last heave and Jules rolled all the way onto the tube, clutching her leg, which had a big red sting mark on it.

"Oh, wow, it hurts. It hurts!"

I yanked the rope to bring the tube to the Mako. Jules crawled on and curled into a ball. Otis hovered over her.

"Do something!" she begged.

I climbed on after her and got a small plastic spice bottle out of the gear bag.

Jules eyed me suspiciously from her fetal position on the deck of the boat. "What's that?"

"Meat tenderizer," I said, holding up the bottle. "It takes away jellyfish pain."

"Are you sure that's okay for my skin?" Jules frowned. "I don't want to get a rash."

"Well, the other thing that works on jellyfish stings is pee," I said. "Do you want me to pee on you?"

"Ew, no."

I kneeled next to her and sprinkled some of the white powder on her leg. Otis tried to lick it off but I distracted him with a bone. After that Jules seemed like she was feeling a little better. At least she wasn't whimpering anymore.

"Would you really pee on me if you had no meat tenderizer?" she asked seriously.

"I guess," I said. "If you needed me to."

Jules teared up.

"What's wrong?" I said. "Does it hurt?"

She sniffed. "I don't have a single friend back home who would do that for me."

The jellyfish sting seemed to have affected Jules's brain even more than her leg.

"Well, obviously you need to get some new friends," I said.

We laughed, and I helped her sit up.

"Could you tell what the hunk was?" I asked.

"No," Jules said, fanning the sting with her hand. "But it definitely doesn't look like something we've seen before. The size, the shape, those lumps all over it that make it look like it's been corroding for a really long time. Maybe we can find a way to bring it up instead of going down to get it. Do you have some kind of scooper thing?"

I shook my head. "I don't want to move it without knowing what it is. What if it breaks apart?"

"So what are we going to do?" Jules said.

Simple. There was only one thing to do.

"Do you know how to scuba?"

Jules gave me her *Duh* look. "Please. I've been going to Maui every year since I was five."

She was definitely feeling better.

CHAPTER TWENTY-EIGHT

True Fact: Taking a dive can be a leap of faith.

The problem was, we couldn't tell anyone we wanted to scuba. Nobody—not my parents, not even Ed—would let two middle school kids go off and dive on their own, not to mention go down without a buddy. Which was why Jules told Ed she was sleeping at my house and why we were loading gear into the Mako at midnight.

At least we had Otis with us. Not that he could scuba or drive the boat, but he had an air of authority. Otis didn't understand the words "sneaking out of the house in the middle of the night while Mom and Dad are sleeping," but he knew something was up. I could tell by his ears, which were especially tall and pointy.

"This is my first night dive," Jules said, clicking the waterproof flashlight on and off over and over again. "It's going to be really cool." *Click, click, click, click.*

"Shhhh," I hissed. "Do you want people to hear us?"

We used oars to paddle away from my house and then motored out to the hunk site without talking so we wouldn't add to the engine noise. Plus, I wasn't sure I could talk without my head erupting.

The thing is, people with diabetes have to be really careful about scuba diving. It's not just the pressure, which isn't too bad if you know how to breathe right and you don't go too deep. It's that spending time underwater can give you low blood sugar. Sometimes super-low blood sugar, which can make you go into a coma.

Sometimes people don't wake up from comas.

Dr. Basch says it's okay for me to dive, but there are a lot of extra rules I have to follow. Like I have to test my blood sugar an hour, a half hour, and ten minutes before a dive, and then every hour after a dive for twelve hours. I can't dive deeper than fifty feet. And I can't dive if I've had a recent "major blood sugar episode" without checking with Dr. Basch first.

The hunk was only twenty-five feet down, but getting up to 490 is definitely a "major blood sugar episode."

Which was why Jules was going to be the one to dive down and get the hunk that could possibly be part of the *Golden Lion* payroll instead of me. Which was why my head might erupt. Because I was super-angry-fuming mad.

After we found the hunk, Jules and I had marked the site with a shot buoy we made with one of the weights from Dad's dive belt, some rope, and a plastic water bottle wrapped with reflective duct tape. Now I swept the general area with the flashlight until I found the bottle.

I killed the engine. "Check your gear," I ordered Jules.

I heaved the anchor overboard and let out some slack while Jules put her mask on top of her head. The oxygen tank was heavy, and she rolled it toward her instead of picking it up like she should have.

"Hey! Be careful," I said. "You need to keep that upright."

"It slipped," Jules said.

She started putting on the buoyancy compensator vest.

"Don't you want to attach the vest to the tank first?" I asked.

"Oh. Yeah. I forgot."

Jules took off the vest and fiddled with the tubes and straps in a fumbling, clueless, I've-never-done-this-before kind of way. She caught me looking at her. "Usually my instructor does this part."

"Jules," I said, trying, and failing, to keep cool. "How many times have you scuba dived?"

"Technically—"

"Not technically. Actually. In an ocean, not a swimming pool."

"Actually? Once."

I pressed both hands against the sides of my head.

Once?

I've dived dozens of times, before *and* after I got certified.

My brain ping-ponged between bad choices.

Jules diving once was not enough.

Four hundred and ninety was a major blood sugar episode.

But once was not enough.

But 490 wasn't because of my body; it was because of my broken pump. Which had been replaced by a new pump that was now plugged into my hip, releasing insulin in a slow, steady trickle to balance my blood sugar, which was currently a healthy pre-exercise 150. Which I happened to know because I'd tested it thirty minutes ago, and thirty minutes before that.

Just in case.

Otis tilted his nose down and stared up at me like a mean librarian. It's the face he reserves for occasions like when I debate whether to jaywalk across Main Street, or the time our cove froze over and I shuffled onto the ice so I could say forevermore, and with total honesty, that I, Blue Broen, had walked on water. I hate it when he gives me that face.

"Sit, Otis. Stay."

Otis obeyed, but he kept giving me the look.

"Hand over the gear," I said to Jules.

She looked up from the zipper on her vest that she was trying and failing to unzip. "What? We decided I was the one who was going down!"

"That was before I found out you don't know how to dive."

"I do so know how to dive!" She clutched the vest to her chest.

"Jules." I held out my hand.

"You said your eyes might bleed."

"Not at this depth." I hoped.

"Blue, it's dangerous." She flicked her fingers to make little exploding motions next to her eyes.

"Jules, it's not. Trust me." I hoped again.

"Fine." She shoved the vest at me. "But don't expect me to clean eye glop off the mask when you're done."

Which was Jules's way of saying she was worried about me. And which would have made me smile if I hadn't been about to embark on the most exciting and tied-with-the-Ruins-for-the-most-dangerous adventure of my life.

I strapped on my gear and checked the airflow. Depending on how nervous I was and how much I breathed, the air would last between thirty minutes and an hour. But I shouldn't be down anywhere near that long.

I was pretty nervous.

And also ridiculously excited.

I sat down on the edge of the boat and tested my blood sugar one last time. Good to go.

The reflective tape on the water-bottle shot buoy glinted in the moonlight. I swung my legs over the side.

"If I'm not back in fifteen minutes, call for help."

Jules put her hand on my shoulder. "Are you serious?"

I shrugged her off. "Death-by-drowning serious."

I wedged the regulator mouthpiece between my teeth...

...and jumped.

CHAPTER TWENTY-NINE

True Fact: Rich people and celebrities aren't the only ones who love Hamptons beaches. <u>Great white sharks</u> do too.

I could hear my breathing through the regulator, loud and heavy. *Nice and even, stay calm; not too big, save air.* I swam to the water-bottle shot buoy. As long as the weight hadn't gotten dragged by a passing boat or eaten by a monster crab, I'd be able to follow the rope right to the hunk. I felt like Goldilocks: If I gripped the rope too hard, I might move the weight; if I gripped it too lightly, I could lose it. I had to hold the rope just right.

I exhaled and pushed the button on the vest to release air so I'd descend. Not too fast, not too slow. *Goldilocks.*

Except it turns out that diving at night is nothing like diving during the day. Below water, the world grew blacker than black. I couldn't see my body, couldn't see the gauges. The only reason I knew which way was up was because I could feel myself going down. The bay may be vast, but I felt it shrinking around me.

I fumbled with the clip on my waterproof flashlight. All I knew was darkness, one thin rope, and the sound of my own breathing bubbling through the regulator. Breathing that was getting faster and deeper. I had to slow down or I'd run out of air before I even got to the bottom.

Calm down, Blue!

Deep breaths were the worst thing I could do right now. I needed something to stop the panic, something soothing, like chamomile tea or one of those lilac-scented pillows you put over your eyes. Or a lullaby.

Baa, baa, black sheep, have you any wool?

I sang the tune in my head, picturing fluffy sheep and green meadows and ladies in hoop skirts, until my breathing slowed. Unhooked the flashlight, clicked it on, and...I'd lost the rope.

Lost. The. Rope.

Still sinking, I swept my arms around, stretched my fingers as far as they could reach. In the silty water, I could see maybe four feet in front of me.

Nothing.

Think, Blue, think.

I could go back up to the surface, find the bottle, and start over, but that would take too much air, and besides,

I didn't want Jules freaking out even more than she already was. If I just kept going the way I was going, I'd reach the sea bottom, in just another—

Now.

My fins touched the sand, and I quickly inflated the vest and exhaled into the regulator to stop my descent. More Goldilocks: Too much air and I'd ascend; too little and I'd sink. I fiddled until I found hover. Water, water, water, and below me, muddy sand and rocks.

But no hunk. And no dive-belt weight.

Shih tzu.

I checked my gauges. Depth about twenty-six feet. Air pressure about three-quarters. Blood sugar? No idea. It could be high from nervousness or low because of exercise. Could Otis smell me through twenty-six feet of water? Was he alerting to Jules right now? I pictured him headbutting her leg over and over, bowing or high-fiving, trying to get her to keep me from dying.

There was nothing I could do about my blood sugar except find the hunk and get back to the boat. And I had to do it fast because Jules was going to call for help in eleven minutes. I flattened out and glided slowly in a random direction, sweeping the flashlight below me. Shells, more shells. A big fish wafted by my ear.

The hunk was at two o'clock from some seaweed. What else? You stared at it forever, taking brain pictures. Long and rectangular like a skinny black milk carton, lumpy, sticking up almost straight in the sand. What else was nearby? A rock. No, two rocks. Or maybe one big rock. Sand. Oh, and a dive-belt weight.

It had to be close. I'd come straight down. Unless I'd gotten pushed by the current...

I checked the compass. I'd make a circle around my landing spot by covering pie-shaped sections, slice by slice.

Slice one: rocks, sand, sand, more sand.

Slice two: air pressure at fifty percent.

Slice three: sand, sand, rubber boot.

Half a pie: air pressure forty percent.

Slice five: plenty of seaweed, no sign of my hunk, until—

Slice six.

Half-buried. Snuggled next to a dive-belt weight at two o'clock from some seaweed.

My hunk.

I descended just enough to touch it with a finger. It felt sturdy. I brushed away the sand. Black, hard, rough, rectangular. Heart pounding, I dug it out. Solid metal, heavy in my hands, pockmarked from salt water. I clutched the thing against my chest, my eyes welling up inside the mask. Pictures would confirm it, but I knew what I had.

Ballast.

I found it, Pop Pop!

Air pressure thirty percent. *So long, black sheep!* I zoomed up as fast as my fins could get me there.

As soon as I broke the surface, I spit out the regulator mouthpiece and waved my arms. "Jules! Jules!"

"Did you get it?"

"Yes! I got it!"

I raced to the boat, which was only maybe ten yards away. Jules helped pull me on. Otis barked his ecstatic greeting bark and licked my face but didn't alert, which was a huge relief.

"What is it?" Jules demanded. "Show me!"

I pulled the lead brick from my pocket and held it out, a giant grin stretched across my face.

Jules took it and turned it over. "It looks like a piece of garbage."

"It is!"

"Then why are you so happy?"

"It's not just any garbage," I said, getting happier by the second. "It's *ballast.*"

I took it back from Jules, ran my fingers over the rough, pocked surface. After 350 years rotting away in salt water, a lead bar would look exactly like this thing I had in my hands. I know because I've seen pictures on the Internet. *Find the ballast, find the ship.*

We sped back to my house, whooping, laughing, barking, and high-fiving. My blood sugar was normal, and I had a hunk of seventeenth-century ballast in my gear bag. It was possibly the greatest moment of my life.

Until we went around the house to stow the gear in the garage and found Mom, Dad, Ed, and a squad car from the Southampton Police Department in the driveway.

CHAPTER THIRTY

True Fact: It's possible to want something so much that nothing else matters.

"WHERE HAVE YOU BEEN?"

"WHAT HAPPENED?"

"ARE YOU OKAY?"

"WHY ARE YOU WET?"

The last one was Mom, after she went to hug me and then jumped back like she'd stuck a plug in a bad socket. As her eyes took in the wet suit and scuba gear, her face morphed from panic to horror to fury.

"How about you girls tell us what's going on here?" the police officer said, in an official *Keep calm everyone* voice.

I looked over at Jules, but she was staring at the ground.

We'd done a lot of stupid things:

1. We snuck out of the house in the middle of the night.
2. We went on the boat in the middle of the night.
3. We went scuba diving in the middle of the night.
    i. It was my first time diving at night.
    ii. I had no diving buddy.

The question was how to explain these stupid things in a way that wouldn't get us sent to jail or grounded forever. But before I could come up with anything, Jules announced:

"It was my fault."

"Jules?" Ed said with a shocked look that I was 99 percent sure was real.

Jules pulled the elastic from her ponytail and shook out her hair like everything was perfectly normal except maybe she was slightly bored, and definitely *not* like she was getting questioned by the police in the middle of the night. "I was playing with my watch today on the boat, and I accidentally dropped it in the water. I told Blue we *had* to go get it. She didn't want to, but I made her."

"Wait." Dad held up a hand like he was stopping traffic. "You went diving alone at night for a *watch*?"

"It's a Cartier Tank," Jules said, as if that explained

everything. "And we knew exactly where it was. We even marked the place with a shot buoy. I was going to go down myself, but Blue didn't think I had enough diving experience and she insisted. She did it to protect me."

Being careless with an expensive watch, coming up with a crazy scheme to get it back—the story was so totally Jules that even I kind of believed her.

"Did either of you think about how dangerous this was?" Mom said, sounding less like herself and more like a demon had taken possession of her body and was about to burst free.

"Blue wanted to ask you for help, but I wouldn't let her." Jules turned to Ed, her face as heartbreaking as a cocker spaniel at a kill shelter. "I was afraid of getting in trouble, Daddy. I didn't want you to think I was irresponsible and be disappointed in me."

"Oh, babe—" Ed said, reaching to hug Jules at the same time that Mom threw her arms up and said, "IRRESPON—"

"Look," Dad cut in. "The most important thing is that the girls are safe. Officer, we're sorry for dragging you out here in the middle of the night. Ed, what do you say we talk about this in the morning?"

I only had a few seconds alone with Jules while Ed and my parents thanked the police officer. "You shouldn't have done that," I whispered. "It was my idea to scuba in the first place."

Jules shrugged. "Yeah, well, no one would ever believe you would do something so crazy. I'm used to everyone thinking I'm shallow and immature."

Jules could act like she didn't care all she wanted, but I knew the truth.

"Jules, you're not—"

"Blue!" Dad barked. "In the house. Now."

We couldn't delay any longer. It was time for Jules to go home and for Otis and me to meet our fate. I turned and took a couple of steps toward the house. And then I wheeled around and grabbed Jules's hand. "You're *not* crazy; you're *not* immature. I know what you were trying to do and I wish you hadn't. We're in this together, got it?"

Jules just nodded.

Otis and I followed Mom and Dad inside to the kitchen. Dad and I sat at the table; Mom stood next to the counter with her arms crossed. I shivered even though the night was warm and Otis was lying on my feet.

"My blood sugar's normal," I said before they could ask. "I tested on the boat."

Dad scrubbed his face with his hand. "Blue, what were you thinking?"

All the lies I'd been telling them were piled up between

us like the biggest pyramid in Egypt: the fact that I hadn't even started my science project, that I'd been secretly treasure hunting, that the dive was all my idea. Now was the time to tell the truth.

But even now all I could think about was the ballast in my gear bag and *How soon can I get back on the water?* If I told my parents the truth, the answer would be never.

"I wasn't thinking," I finally said. "I just...wasn't."

"Aw, forget it, Blue." Dad pushed back from the table. "Just go to bed."

Otis and I went up to my room, and I sat on the edge of my bed in the dark, still in my wet suit. The clock said 2:55 AM.

I pulled the ballast out of my gear bag. Held it in both hands. Felt its weight, its roughness like honeycomb. Three hundred and fifty years ago, some sailor unloaded this block of lead—smooth and new—from a sack or a cart and carefully set it down in the bottom of a ship next to dozens of other lead blocks just like it. The boat was made of wood. Below deck the ceilings were so low you couldn't stand up all the way. Up top were big square sails sewn from canvas and waterproofed with pine tar. Maybe the sailor died on that trip—maybe he got sick or got killed in battle or fell overboard when the ship hit the rocks. Maybe he died with no children, and that was the end of him. Maybe he lived and had ten kids, and I go to school with some of their descendants. Or maybe that sailor was my very own great-times-twelve-grandfather Abraham Broen.

This ballast meant there was more down there. Like the wreck of the ship and all her cargo. It meant my family stories were true.

Why did the Great-Times-Twelves have the *Golden Lion* payroll, and what did they do to get it? Did they steal it—and if they stole it, was it rightfully mine? What was *I* willing to do? I was willing to break the law twice—once by entering (and installing a camera on) the *Windfall* and once by going to the Ruins. I was willing to bring Otis to the Ruins, where he got hurt; to lie to my parents over and over again; to do something dangerous and let Jules take the fall for it.

I was willing to risk our lives.

Otis whined softly and dropped a pair of pajamas on the bed.

"Am I a bad person?" I asked him.

CHAPTER THIRTY-ONE

True Fact: Sometimes bad skips worse and goes straight to total catastrophe.

Mom and Dad were still home when I got up the next morning. We went into the kitchen, where Dad and I sat at the table, Otis lay on my feet, and Mom stood by the counter with her arms crossed, just like last night. Except for the sun being up, it was like the five hours since the driveway showdown hadn't even happened.

Dad said, "Mom and I have talked and we both agree: Jules didn't make you do anything last night. You made your own decisions every step of the way, and every decision you made was lousy. No watch, no matter how expensive, is worth more than your life or your friend's life. And you know what, Blue? You knew that. You knew better."

Dad paused so I could say something. I nodded once to show him I agreed. "I know. I'm really sorry."

"I'm glad you're sorry, but sorry isn't enough," he went on. "There have to be consequences for your actions."

"I understand." I sat up straight. "No TV, no Internet—"

"Not those kinds of consequences." Dad glanced at Mom. She hadn't said a single word this whole time. "Big consequences. Consequences that reflect the seriousness of what you've done."

"Okay..." A sick feeling swirled in my stomach.

"You're grounded for the next week," Dad said.

I exhaled. A major setback, but Jules and I could handle it. Well, we couldn't—not with Fitz out there getting closer to the treasure by the minute—but we would. Somehow.

"While you're home, you can clean out the basement," Dad said.

I almost groaned, but I stopped myself in time. Dad was using my punishment as a way to get him out of doing his job. But what choice did I have? "Okay."

I thought that was going to be it, but Dad kept going. "And, since you've shown us you're not responsible enough to use it safely, no more boat for the rest of the summer."

"What?!" I jumped up out of my chair. "No, I—"

Dad cut me off. "No more boat and no more Jules. She's a bad influence."

"Jules is *not* a bad influence, and I *have* to use the boat!" My brain scrambled for some good reason that would change their minds. All I could come up with was "What about my science project?"

"Mom or I will take you out on our days off."

"You can't mean that!" I looked at Mom, who was still leaning against the counter with her arms crossed and her mouth pressed into a thin, tight line. Why wasn't she saying anything? "I won't be able to finish before school starts!"

"We mean it, Blue. You should have thought about that beforehand. No boat, no Jules. I'll be checking the engine hours every day, so don't even think about sneaking out while we're at work."

"Dad, can't we—"

He got up from the table. "No, we can't. I have to get to work now. I'm already late. *Do not, under any circumstances, see Jules or leave this house today.*"

Dad left but Mom stayed, watching me silently while the biggest dream I'd ever had and my whole future dropped dead.

"Why didn't you help me?" I pleaded.

More silence. Seeing Mom so cold and closed-off terrified me.

"I know I did a really stupid thing," I said, "but why won't you talk to me?"

Her face argued with itself for a minute. Finally, she shook her head. "*Talk* to you? I can hardly *look* at you. Do you understand that last night you could have killed the person I love most in the world? *What am I supposed to do with that?*"

My eyes welled up and over. All this time I'd been so worried about Mom and Dad not letting me search for the treasure that I didn't think about why they wouldn't *want* me to search—because they were afraid I'd get hurt, or even die.

"I'm sorry. I'm really really sorry," I said, my voice shaky.

Mom waited for me to explain myself, but I couldn't. Not when there was even a speck of a chance that I could figure out a way to get back on the water. I wanted to tell my mother the truth, but I wanted to look for the treasure more. Because as long as I had the hunt, I still had Pop Pop. *And because I can't go back to being Diabetes Girl. And Jules can't go back to being Ed Buttersby's daughter.*

I clamped my lips shut.

Mom stomped out of the house and slammed the door behind her.

I was slouched at the kitchen table, replaying Mom's words—*You could have killed the person I love most in the world*—when Jules showed up. It was like she had ESP and she knew the second Mom walked out the door.

"Obviously, my dad's calling my mom today to tell her what a bad person I am," Jules said as she helped herself to a can of seltzer from the fridge. "But meanwhile, he's decided the problem is that I'm spoiled and I don't know what real responsibility is, so every single day from now on I have to do *chores*."

I almost laughed. "Your punishment is chores?"

"You have no idea. I have to make my bed—that's not so bad. I can just pull the duvet over everything. But I also have to unload the dishwasher, which is so annoying."

"You're kidding, right?"

Jules opened the can and slurped. "I'm child-slavery serious. I don't know where anything goes in the kitchen. It takes *forever*."

Silence.

She plopped down in the chair across from me. "Just kidding. I know it's a totally lame punishment."

"I'm not supposed to see you ever again," I said.

"I can still see you, but you're a bad influence," Jules said.

"You're a bad influence too." I took a deep breath and dropped the bomb. "I can't use the boat for the rest of the summer."

Jules opened her mouth, but no words came out.

"Before you ask," I said, praying the lump in my throat wouldn't turn into full-on tears, "the answer is no. There's no way my parents are changing their minds. Gardiner's Bay is too far to row. I can't borrow someone else's boat—they'd find out. And there's nobody we can ask for a ride."

Jules's shoulders curled. A piece of hair had come out of her ponytail and was stuck to her neck.

Just so we could torture ourselves, Jules got the iPad out of her backpack and we logged on to the *Windfall*. There was nobody on the bridge.

"They must be out on deck." *Or diving because they found something*, which I didn't say out loud but we were both thinking.

We kept listening, hunched over the iPad, waiting for bad news. We were concentrating so hard that we didn't hear the horn honking in the driveway until it stretched into one long blare.

Jules and Otis and I ran to the front porch. Dad had swerved his truck in front of the house instead of parking in his usual spot by the garage. He was standing next to the truck, leaning into the open driver's side window with his hand on the horn.

"Dad?" I said.

He whipped around, his face red. Then he saw Jules standing next to me and his face turned purple.

Dad started to speak, stopped himself, started again, stopped. Finally, he took a deep shaky breath through his nose and said, "I'm getting creamed at work. I'm late, I've gotta 'rock a whole house in two days, and my best Sheetrock guy's out getting an emergency root canal. Next thing I know, some guy in a suit shows up at my job site and gives me *this*." He grabbed an envelope from his back pocket and slapped it against his other palm. "So I leave my hundred packs of Sheetrock, and I come home, and here you are with Jules." He jabbed the air in our direction. "The person I *specifically* told you you were not allowed to see less than one hour ago!"

I had never once in my life seen my dad this mad. I didn't know what to say. I didn't know what to do. Next to me, Jules was shaking.

Dad held out the envelope. "Read," he commanded.

Otis followed me down the steps. My feet felt as heavy as two hunks of seventeenth-century ballast.

I took the envelope from Dad without meeting his eyes. The letter inside was from a lawyer, and it was addressed to my parents. I read the words "cease and desist." I saw the names Fitzgibbons and *Windfall*. I don't speak legalese, but I knew that this letter told my parents that Jules and I had been in Gardiner's Bay every day looking for something that we weren't supposed to be

242

looking for, that we had no right to be there, and that if we didn't stop, somebody was going to jail.

I looked up from the paper. Jules came down from the porch and stood by my side.

"Start talking," Dad said.

I put my hand on Otis's head for courage and began.

CHAPTER THIRTY-TWO

True Fact: Sometimes the whole truth is easier to tell than one more lie.

I told Dad everything, starting with my theory about the hound, explaining about the Dutch website, how Jules and I covered the territory, our inner tube–view bucket technique. Everything.

Okay, maybe not everything. I didn't tell him about installing the spy-cam that was still going strong on the *Windfall*, or about our trip to the Ruins. I'm not that insane.

The whole time I talked, Jules was silent and still, and Dad did a weird thing with his hands where he kept clenching and unclenching them so they looked like Venus flytraps opening and shutting. When I finished he said, "So you're telling me this whole time you've been chasing some pipe dream instead of doing your science project?"

A blast of heat shot from my gut to my chest and straight out the top of my head.

"It's not a pipe dream!" I yelled. "Haven't you listened to a single thing I said?"

Dad smacked the hood of his truck. Otis whined—he doesn't like it when anyone in my family fights—but Dad was so angry he ignored him. "It *is* a pipe dream, Blue! I spent my whole childhood stuck on a boat while my dad chased that dream instead of doing things like playing Little League while he watched in the stands. Why do you think I sold that VOC coin after he died? I didn't want you growing up like I did. And now I find out you didn't just waste your time—you could have died. And for what? For *nothing*."

Jules flinched when Dad said "nothing," but the word just made me even madder. "I didn't waste anything and it's *not* for nothing. And I can prove it!"

I blew past Dad and raced up the porch stairs.

"Where do you think you're going?" Dad shouted.

"To prove you're wrong! Jules, let's go. Otis, come!"

The three of us ran inside and straight up to my room. I snatched the gear bag off my bed. Otis and Jules watched me with identical worried eyebrows.

"Blue, wait, what are you doing?" Jules asked.

I wrenched open the zipper and checked the contents of the bag, then slung it over my shoulder. "Showing him he's wrong."

Jules and Otis followed me back downstairs, where Dad was rereading the letter and fuming in the front hall, the junk from the basement that he *still* hadn't gotten rid of piled up between him and the kitchen.

I yanked out the ballast.

"What's that?" Dad snapped.

"What does it look like?" I snapped back.

"A piece of junk you almost died for."

"Really, Dad? Really?" I stuck the ballast in front of his face. "You spent your whole childhood on a boat, and Pop Pop never told you what you were looking for? He never showed you any pictures? They had pictures back then, right? In books? You know those things made of paper with all the pages?"

I was channeling my inner Jules. I had never talked to my dad that way. Never ever. But I'd also never been so mad.

Dad snatched the lead out of my hand.

"You think this is ballast?" he said, a hair quieter.

"I *know* it is."

We locked eyes until Dad huffed and broke away. He ran his fingers over the ballast, held it up to the light.

"It *could* be," he said.

"It *is*," I insisted.

"Even if it is, there's no proof it has any connection to our family's ship."

"Come on, Dad. How can you say that? Abraham Broen is right there in the living room, in our family bible. He was a carpenter, just like you, just like Abraham Broen the carpenter's mate who sailed on the *Golden Lion* with the payroll."

Dad set the ballast on the hall table and turned his back to us, pinching the bridge of his nose. "Aw, crap," he whispered. "Crap, crap, crap, crap."

"Dad?"

"The thing is, Belly," he said in a choked-up voice, "even if you're right, you can't do this. Not on your own. Not like this. This isn't just taking a couple of water samples. It's too dangerous."

I pressed my hand to my chest. "I swear I won't dive anymore."

Dad turned back around. "It's not just the diving, Belly. The whole thing is too dangerous for you. You're not like other kids. You have to be more careful."

I wished Dad had punched me in the stomach. I wished the roof had collapsed on my head. I wished I had fallen down the stairs and broken my leg in three places with the bone sticking out. Because any of those things would have hurt less than what Dad had just said.

"You're right." Jules took a brave step toward him. "Blue's *not* like other kids. She tests her blood sugar at least four times a day when we're on the water, and she thinks about every bite of food she eats. But she also taught me to drive the boat and how to navigate and how to think about currents and wind and red right returning." Jules talked faster and faster, like she was trying to cram in as many words as she could before Dad stopped her. "She can tie a hundred different knots and rig an awning for Otis out of beach towels and fishing line. I don't know a single other kid who can do any of those things."

"You're great on the boat," Dad said to me after Jules finished. "I never said you weren't."

"I'm great with the diabetes stuff too," I said. "Plus, I've got Otis."

Jules cleared her throat.

"And Jules," I said. "She's the one who found the *Golden Lion* ship's log, and her chef makes me sugar-free nut clusters."

"That taste like hay," Jules said.

Dad stared down at me for a long time. Otis stood between us like he was trying not to take sides.

Finally, Dad shook his head. "There's a cease and desist letter, and I'm not going up against Fitz Fitzgibbons and his lawyers."

"Mr. Broen—"

"I'm sorry, Jules, but this isn't one of your dad's movies where the hero risks everything and saves the world and nobody we care about gets hurt. This is real life, where the playing field isn't even and bad things happen. In real life you have to learn to live within your limits."

"Dad—"

"Enough, Blue. Discussion closed."

CHAPTER THIRTY-THREE

True Fact: Most of the time, the middle of the night is when bad things happen, like nightmares or stomach flus where you throw up so much that you have to sleep on the bathroom floor with a towel for a pillow. But every now and then, the middle of the night is when you find a teeny tiny glimmer of hope.

I couldn't sleep. How could I sleep? Jules and I got so close, and now Mom and Dad were taking it all away. My heart used to feel like a doughnut with a big hole where Pop Pop should've been. Now it was Swiss cheese with a hole for Pop Pop, a hole for the hunt, a hole for Jules.

And a hole for Nora.

She'd sent me another letter.

Blue,
     Is everything okay? Not to play the pinkie-swear card or anything, but I've written you twice, and you did take an oath . . .

I turned on the night-table light and pulled a notebook and pen out of the drawer.

Dear Nora, Glad to hear camp is so great...

Dear Nora, I'm sorry I haven't written you back...

Dear Nora...

I threw the pad and pen on the floor and turned off the light. I missed the Nora who already knew everything about me. For the first time ever, I was afraid she might not totally understand me, that she might have to look up some of my words just like I had to look up some of hers.

I lay in bed using Otis's body as a pillow, tying and untying a monkey's fist knot in the dark with a length of rope.

"It's not fair," I said.

Otis licked my head.

"I hate it. Hate. Hate. It." I rolled over and faced him. "I hate diabetes."

Otis put his chin on his paws and crinkled his eyebrows.

"I know you get it. I don't hate you." I kissed his nose and rolled back over. "Just everybody else."

Otis and I went downstairs for a drink because kitchen water tastes better than bathroom water. Only the light over the table was on. Dad was sitting there with his laptop and some books. And the ballast.

He looked up when we walked in. "What's up, Belly?"

"Nothing," I said.

Otis opened the fridge, and I got out the water pitcher. We'd get our drink and go. I wasn't about to stick around and chat. Not after Dad had used my disease as an excuse to ruin the most—the *only*—important thing I've ever done or cared about.

"I've been researching ballast," Dad said, like we hadn't had the biggest fight of our lives that very morning.

I didn't answer.

"You might be onto something."

Not gonna answer.

"This book I found in the basement has a picture of lead ballast from a seventeenth-century wreck that looks a lot like yours."

Still not answering, but willing to look at the picture. For research purposes.

The ballast in the book looked pretty much identical to the ballast on the kitchen table. *Of course it does. Because they're made of the same thing and they came from the same century. Because the ballast on the table is real.*

"Tell me again why you think the ship of gold is in Gardiner's Bay," Dad said.

I wasn't going to answer, but Dad asked in this quiet, sad voice. The room was dark except for the one light hanging over the table. I was standing up, and Dad was sitting down, and his face looked like it hurt. Like he might cry. My dad doesn't cry.

So I told him again about the rock that looked like a hound and how Gardiner meant Garden of Eden, which meant paradise, which was why I thought the Great-Times-Twelves' ship was a few miles from our house with the *Golden Lion* payroll still on it.

"It's our legacy," I finished. "Pop Pop was right about the treasure being in Gardiner's Bay, only he didn't have proof. He was just going on a hunch and a family story. But now we *know* that Great-Times-Twelve-Grandpa Abraham was on the *Golden Lion* with the payroll, and this"—I picked up the ballast—"is proof the ship is still there." I sat down next to Dad. "Please let me keep looking."

He sighed a big long sigh. "You can't be sure the wreck is there, Belly. Pop Pop looked all over Gardiner's Bay. He

253

searched for years. After work, every weekend. Even in the winter."

Which meant that when Dad was growing up, if he wanted to spend time with his dad, he had to do it on a boat with his face in a bucket. I tried to imagine how that must have felt. None of the feelings were good.

"I get why you hate this," I said.

"I don't hate it," Dad said. "I just don't want you to get hurt. Or be disappointed like I was disappointed."

"But I'm not the same as you," I said, searching for the words that would make him understand. "I *loved* going out on the boat with Pop Pop. I *still* love it."

Maybe, though, the reason that I could love being with Pop Pop on the boat was because I had a dad who built me miniature igloos out of cheese cubes when I was little and who always came to my school plays and bowling tournaments.

Dad's face softened. He didn't look like he might cry anymore. "I know you love it, Belly, and it makes me happy that you got all the best parts of Pop Pop. He had a lot of good parts."

My stomach twisted like a clove hitch knot. "I wish he'd given you all his best parts too."

"I got plenty." Dad rubbed Otis's head. "Don't worry about me."

The clove hitch loosened a little. Maybe Dad would listen now if I tried to explain to him why the hunt was so important to me.

"Dad? There's, um, something else," I said.

"What's that?"

I folded my hands on top of the table to keep my fingers from tapping. "When Pop Pop died I promised I'd find the treasure for him. If I stop now, it means I broke my promise. I *have* to keep looking."

"Blue—" Dad warned.

"Plus," I said, in my most logical, reasonable, how-could-anyone-possibly-object voice, "if I don't finish the search, I'm definitely going to be disappointed, and you said you didn't want me to be disappointed."

Dad didn't say anything. Which meant he was thinking. Which meant there was hope.

I kept going. "Fitz, on the other hand, might be very *un*-disappointed when he's the one who finds the treasure that your father spent his whole life looking for."

"*Fitz.*" Dad said "Fitz" like most people say "sewer rat."

"*Fitz,*" I agreed.

Dad shook his head. "Even if I said yes, there's the cease and desist letter."

"Are you sure there's nothing we can do about that? Maybe we can fight it or get a permit or something."

"I doubt it, Belly," Dad said. "Fitz is lawyered up."

"So let's get our *own* lawyer. Please, Dad. Can't you at least ask someone?"

He thought it over. "I guess I can ask Marisol." Dad's friend Marisol is a lawyer in town who also happens to have been his high school girlfriend, which should be awkward but somehow isn't.

"Thank you."

"And while I do that, you clean the basement."

Dad stuck out a fist. I bumped it.

"Deal," I said.

CHAPTER THIRTY-FOUR

True Fact: Everybody needs extra help sometimes.

The next morning I woke up just as the sky was turning from pink to blue. Otis had claimed my pillow. I stroked the bridge of his nose with my thumb while he slept.

"You were really tired last night, weren't you?" I whispered.

My blood sugar had been low when I tested in the middle of the night, but Otis, who was still totally exhausted after our scuba misadventure, had missed it. He didn't wake up to alert me, he slept through my alarm, and he even stayed asleep while I ate a pack of Skittles.

Otis can't always take care of me.

But if I was going to manage my diabetes, if I was going to catch as many highs and lows as possible, I needed Otis to back me up.

And Otis needed a CGM to back him up.

But I'd known that for a while, hadn't I? I just hadn't wanted it to be true. I wanted—I *still* want—Otis and me to be everything for each other forever. Even though it's impossible.

Otis opened his eyes and nuzzled my hand, calm and peaceful. So I knew, even before I tested, that my blood sugar was normal. I didn't need to worry, because right now, and hopefully for a long time to come, Otis was taking care of me.

After I got dressed, Otis and I walked Dad to his truck. Dad slid behind the wheel but left the door open.

"Now listen." He held up his phone. "You're still grounded. I'll be checking your phone finder app all day. If I see you're not home, the deal is off."

"Got it," I said.

"And the deal is that you'll clean the basement today, and I'll talk to Marisol."

"Got it," I said.

"And no Jules. I'm calling Ed with an update."

"Will Ed even care?"

Dad gave me a Mom-look.

"Sorry," I said. "Can I at least *talk* to Jules?"

Dad thought it over. "Yes, but only on the phone. Not in person."

A small victory, but still a victory. I hid a smile.

"Otis!" Dad called.

Otis stood up on his hind legs with his paws on Dad's thigh in the front seat. It was only because Otis was huge that he could reach.

"Take care of Blue."

Otis woofed.

Otis and I were good. Obedient. The minute Dad left, we headed straight down to the basement.

I pulled the string on the overhead light.

Shih tzu.

See, the thing is, lots of people have messy basements. And usually, the longer you've lived someplace, the messier your basement is. Well, my family has lived in this house for two hundred years. That's two hundred years of ancient clothes, books nobody will ever read again, broken baby furniture, weird posters my parents hung on their walls in college, my great-grandfather's pinch pots, a framed embroidered Lord's Prayer, cracked litter boxes, fire pokers, a headless dressmaker's dummy, an old-timey bicycle with a missing seat, record albums, dented hamster cages, mystery boxes, mystery crates, and a butter churn. And that was just what I could see in front of me.

No wonder Dad is two psychological wrong turns away from being a hoarder. It's in his genes.

I took a picture with my phone and sent it to Jules. A minute later she texted back: Impressive

> **Jules:** Did you know that people's ears and noses grow their whole lives?
>
> **Me:** Really???
>
> **Jules:** Yup. Just saw it on the Science Channel

I looked down at Otis, who was sniffing a wicker basket filled with homemade rag dolls with black cross-stitches for eyes.

"No eating the zombies."

Otis gave me his *Who, me?* look and lay down. We both knew this was going to be a long day.

"We need a plan," I said. The basement has three main rooms, plus the creepy cobwebby crawl space from the original house in the 1600s, where no one ever goes. "We'll start with the room we're in now."

I could see that Dad had already cleared one corner. His mistake, I decided, was bringing all the stuff to get rid of upstairs into the main part of the house, where it could live forever in the hall like some kind of modern-art sculpture.

"We'll open the cellar doors and bring everything outside—because, let's face it, everything here is garbage nobody would want, right? That way, Dad will only have until the next time it rains to haul it all to the dump. Sound good?"

Otis woofed, and I gave him a head hug. I picked up the basket of rag dolls.

"Let's get these out of here before they suck out our souls."

It's amazing how many armloads you can carry out of a basement and when you come back it still looks like you haven't started. Piece by piece, I lugged stuff up and out to the grass by the side of the house. Then I'd go back to Otis and the room would still look like a jungle. Was new stuff growing where the old stuff had been?

It was sweaty, dusty work, but the hardest part was not getting sucked into a time warp whenever I came across a family heirloom. Because mixed in with the junk were some pretty intriguing finds.

Like the zombie dolls. I pictured some long-ago great-grandmother of mine in a flowered cotton dress and a white apron, maybe a bonnet, maybe some bloomers—all excited because she'd been begging her mother for a doll forever and when she turned six her mom made her one for every birthday she'd ever had. But maybe that was all wrong. Maybe that great-something-grandmother made those dolls herself when she was my age. Maybe she wanted to sell them to buy, oh, I don't know, penny candy or chewing tobacco. Or maybe Mom got them at a flea market and meant to use them for scarecrows, and I was getting sappy for nothing.

It's weird growing up as part of a family who've lived in the same place for centuries. The libraries are full of local history books that mention our ancestors, and the towns are full of streets with our last name. Broen Lane is just down the road from my house. Sometimes I'll pull over my bike and wonder about my great-great-great-great-uncle Herman Broen, who used to live there, and whether people would knock on his door in the middle of the night for emergency doses of the medicines he concocted at his pharmacy on Main Street. Had any of his five kids looked like me?

And had any of them died before they were three years old from a mysterious sugar sickness?

When I came back from dumping a bag of rusty pie plates and cookie cutters, Otis wasn't in his spot anymore.

"Otis?"

A small woof from the next room. Otis had decided to explore.

"No eating anything!"

I wiped my face with the bottom of my T-shirt and surveyed my progress. The pile outside was growing. Dad had warned me he might not be able to reach Marisol right away, so I tried not to check my phone too often. I also tried not to think about Fitz or the ballast pile or things like *What if Marisol is on a bucket-list trip to Tasmania for six months and can't help us?*

"Otis?"

Woof.

"Just checking."

Old stereo equipment. Mom's wedding dress packed in tissue paper in a foil-wrapped box (which I didn't throw away). A red wagon. I burrowed all the way to the corner of the room. Some kind of medieval torture instrument or possibly a pair of stirrups. An antique cabinet that was too pretty to trash and too heavy to lift anyway.

Hoooooooooowl!

I dropped a box of broken power tools. "Otis?"

Squeals and thrashes came from somewhere deep in the basement.

"Otis! What's wrong? I'm coming!"

I barreled through the clutter, shoving junk out of my way, following the sound of Otis running—or chasing something?—from one room to another and knocking stuff over like he didn't care what he crashed into.

"Otis, stay!"

But Otis didn't stay. Not until he got to the last room in the basement. The crashing stopped, but I could still hear whimpers, which I followed to the farthest far end of the room.

"Otis?"

Whimper.

The room was dark, with not even a cellar window to let in a trickle of light. I waved my arms around, looking for the string I knew was nearby, afraid of what I would find when I switched on the light.

What if it's a squirrel?

Or a raccoon?

Or a rabid *raccoon?*

Didn't matter. Whatever was in there, Otis needed me. I used the flashlight on my phone to find the string. Pulled—

Nothing. No wild animals. Not even Otis. Just heavy panting.

"Oh no, you're not..."

But he was.

Hiding inside the creepy cobwebby crawl space, the only part left of the house that used to be here 350 years ago. Possibly with the carcass of a diseased rodent.

I took a deep breath, ducked down, and shined the flashlight into the space.

"Oh, *Otis.*"

Otis's fur was covered with mousetraps. The glue kind that my mom leaves all over the basement baited with peanut butter. Which Otis loves. I held back the hysterical laughter that was threatening to burst out, because friends don't laugh at friends in their hour of need. Judging by the placement of the traps—stuck to his chest, his back paw, the tip of his tail, and dangling from his snout—Otis must have tried licking some peanut butter and then freaked out when the trap stuck to his face, running and jumping in circles, stepping on more traps, freaking out more, until he fled to the smallest, darkest corner he could find. Even if I hadn't been fluent in Otisese, I would have known he was thinking that this was the most miserable, humiliating day of his entire life.

"Come on. We'll go upstairs and I'll fix you up."

Otis shrank back. He *cowered*.

"Come, Otis," I tried again.

He lowered his head and turned his back to me, revealing a trap stuck to his rump that I hadn't noticed before.

I sighed. And then I got down and crawled into the crawl space with my dog. It was empty except for us and three and a half centuries of dust. The crawl space was about as wide as a small walk-in closet, with ceilings high enough for sitting but too low for standing. Unlike the rest of the basement, which had cement floors and brick walls, the whole crawl space was paneled with smooth wood and strips of black metal, even the floor and ceiling.

I wedged myself next to Otis and laid my head on a trap-free section of his back. Ignoring the lumpy chunk of metal poking my butt, I petted the top of his head and told him he would be okay. Nobody but us had to know about this terrible, embarrassing thing that had happened to him. I would get all the traps off and it wouldn't even hurt. *Promise.* There would be treats. Many treats. And a super-long belly rub and a new antler to chew.

Gradually, I coaxed Otis out, persuaded him to come

upstairs, and made good on all my promises, including peanut butter sandwiches—creamy for me, double extra crunchy for him.

We went back to the basement, and Otis stayed by my side while I lugged. The pile outside grew and grew, but I hardly noticed and didn't care. Desperate for news, I kept checking the time, checking my texts, checking for missed calls from Dad, for low battery, bad Wi-Fi, a freak tornado. Nothing, nothing, nothing, nothing, nothing. Until, finally, at precisely 5:40 PM, which was an hour earlier than my parents' usual get-home time, I heard two trucks pull into the driveway.

CHAPTER THIRTY-FIVE

True Fact: <u>Play by the rules. Obey the law. Do what you're told. Ask permission first.</u> Let's just say there are exceptions to everything.

Otis and I raced upstairs to the front hall. "What did Marisol say?"

Dad looked at Mom. Mom looked at Dad.

"Let's talk in the living room," Dad said.

The ballast was on the hall table, where I'd left it that morning. Dad picked it up, and we went into the living room, where no one ever goes except maybe once a year when my parents have a party. We sat around the coffee table, Mom and me on the couch, Dad in a chair next to me, and Otis in front of the fireplace. For a second, I was four years old again, next to Pop Pop in this exact spot when he first showed me the family bible all those years ago.

Dad weighed the ballast in his hand and sucked in a deep, long breath.

My whole future was in that breath.

He exhaled. "I told Mom already and we decided to give you the news together. It's a no go, Belly."

"What!"

"We're sorry, Blue," Mom said.

"Are you *sure*?" My brain was spinning in my skull like one of those toy tops you pull with a string.

"A hundred percent," Dad said.

No. No. Not okay. NO. "What *exactly* did Marisol say? Did you ask her about special permission for students? Or people whose families have lived here for hundreds of years? Or—"

"I asked her all those things," Dad said. "And more. The bottom line is that Fitz has a legal right to search those waters and we don't. And there's nothing anyone can do about it."

"But that's not fair!" I stood up. I needed space to move, air to breathe. "Pop Pop worked so hard! And our family brought that payroll here in the first place! Why should Fitz—"

"*Life* isn't fair," Dad interrupted. "Never has been, never will be. It's a game with rules that people like us are supposed to follow. And then there are people like Fitz, who get to break those rules. And take extra turns.

And maybe they get to play by a few extra rules that the rest of us don't even know about." Dad thwacked the ballast down on the table. "You need to accept that or else you're going to be walking around ticked off at the world for the rest of your life."

My eyes burned and the living room turned to melted wax. "You think *I* don't know life isn't fair? Me? *The only kid in Sag Harbor Middle School who sticks herself with needles every day?*"

Everyone went quiet. Suddenly, the air was full of all the stuff we never say out loud. It felt almost too heavy to breathe. So we didn't. Not even Otis.

Finally, Mom got up and gently pulled me back to the couch. "Enough about what's fair. We need to get to the bottom of all this, once and for all. What are you still holding back?"

I ground the heels of my hands into my eye sockets to keep the tears from leaking out. And then I told them all the really bad parts that I'd been hiding from them. Because what did it matter anymore? When I said we'd gone to the Ruins, Mom's eyes got really big and Dad's got really small. But when I told them about entering the *Windfall* and installing the spy-cam, my parents imploded. As in, instead of yelling and screaming, they got very very quiet.

"Do you realize what you did on the *Windfall* was a felony?" Mom said.

"Um, what's a felony?"

"A serious crime," Dad said.

"Then yes."

"And a bomb on the Ruins could have exploded?" Dad's face was so red I worried his head might explode.

"But it didn't!"

"That's not the point," Mom said, her voice rising. "Blue, the things you've done—insane, dangerous, illegal things, including lying to us and keeping the whole thing secret and putting Otis in danger—why? What's going on with you? That's what I can't figure out. Why would you do all this?"

"I told you!" I shouted. Otis whined. I lowered my voice. "I did it for Pop Pop."

"Pop Pop wouldn't have wanted you to take all these risks. You know that," Dad said. "There has to be something else you're not telling us."

"I just—"

The words caught in my throat, packed into a big, hard baseball.

"I—"

"What is it?" Mom took my hand. I took it back.

"Diabetes is expensive," I said at last. They weren't the words I was trying to say, but they were true. My insulin costs almost $1,200 a month. Insurance covers a lot, but it doesn't cover everything. Not even close.

"You mean you want to find the treasure because you think we need the money?" Dad said.

"Well, don't we?" I said. "I hear you on the phone fighting with the insurance company all the time. Why do you think I wait four days instead of three to change my infusion site?"

Mom gasped, horrified. "You wait four days?"

I flung up my arms. "Yes! Because insurance only covers enough for every three days, and if I stretch it I have spare sets, just in case."

"That's not safe, Blue. You'll build up scar tissue," Mom said. "You have to promise you'll change it after three because if you can't manage your diabetes responsibly—"

"My skin is fine, and I know how much extra infusion sets cost," I grumbled.

"That's not something for you to worry about, Belly. That's our job—Mom's and mine," Dad said.

"But it's so much *money*," I said. "Thousands and thousands of dollars. And it never stops and it never will for the rest of my life."

The word-baseball throbbed in my throat. It hurt to breathe.

Mom reached over and brushed a stray piece of hair off my cheek. "It's true diabetes costs money. But we're lucky—our insurance *does* cover a lot of it—"

"Especially when we fight with them," Dad interrupted.

Mom smiled at him. "And Dad and I have jobs that cover the rest."

"But—"

"It's okay, Belly," Dad said. "We're okay. We have food on the table and a roof over our heads and clothes to wear, and don't we go skiing with Aunt Jen every Christmas at her house in Vermont?"

"That's not the point," I said.

"Then what *is* the point?" Mom asked.

"The point is that everything always boils down to diabetes," I whispered. "And I just want..."

I stared up at the ceiling to keep the tears from pouring over. Swallowed.

"Blue?" Mom said.

"I just want..."

"Want what, Belly?" Dad said.

Swallowed again. Hard.

"This!" I held up the ballast. *"This!"* The baseball shot out of my throat. "I want to find one of the most famous missing treasures in the world. I'm so *sick* of the biggest thing in my life being my stupid blood sugar. There has to be something more to me than that!"

Otis licked my knee and put his head on my lap.

"There's *plenty* more to you than—" Dad started.

"And besides," I cut Dad off before he could start

listing all my unique, wonderful qualities. And before he could remind me that treasure hunting is too dangerous because I have a disease. "I got here, didn't I? I mean, I didn't find the treasure, but I got close. And lots of bad stuff could have happened, but it didn't."

Mom and Dad looked at each other for what felt like an hour but was probably more like a minute, during which they were having a whole silent conversation with their eyes. Then Mom finally said:

"What's done is done. And we can't fight Fitz. But from now on, no more secrets. No more lies."

Whatever flicker of hope that was still alive in me turned to smoke. The hunt was over. There was nothing more to lie about, no more secrets to keep. "None. I promise."

"And, Blue?" Dad said. "You may not believe this, but I really am sorry about how everything turned out. It doesn't seem fair to me, either."

We had a depressing, awkward chicken dinner, where pretty much nobody said a word, and then Otis and I went up to my room, and I wrote new True Facts in my journal (TF: Failure tastes like curdled milk, lumpy and foul) while Otis gave himself a bath. I knew I should text Jules to tell her the bad news, but before I could make myself do it, the house phone rang. A minute later, Mom stuck her head around my door. "It's for you," she said. "Jules."

I picked up in my parents' room. Otis and I lay down on their bed, and I put a pillow over my head.

"What's with the landline?" I said.

"My dad took away my cell, and I had to look up your number," Jules said.

"Are you serious?"

"Amish serious."

Jules without a cell phone was like Planet Earth without oxygen.

"Let me guess," I said. "He talked to my dad?"

"Ten points for Gryffindor," Jules said. "Don't worry about it. I get the phone back tomorrow."

I pushed the pillow off my face. It was too hot under there. Otis, who has no shame whatsoever, sprawled on his back with all four paws splayed out, taking up most of the bed.

"Is this How to Punish Your Teen, Hollywood Edition?"

"This is my dad trying to instill responsibility in me, even though he's actually ecstatic that the documentary just went Oscar supernova now that the producer's daughter is trying to scoop the billionaire."

In other words, Ed was looking out for Jules a little and looking out for himself a lot.

"Did you get a cease and desist letter too?"

"Are you kidding? Why would Fitz want to tick off the world-famous actor who's producing a movie about him?"

But Fitz has no problem at all ticking off the local guy who builds houses.

"Listen, Jules, I have to tell you something."

"That doesn't sound good."

"It's not."

I told her what Marisol had said.

Jules listened. And then she paused. And then she said, "So?"

"What do you mean, 'so'?"

"I mean, so what?"

I sat up and put the phone on speaker so I could crush the pillow tight to my chest. Otis, picking up on my change in mood, wriggled himself into a more modest position. "What do you mean, 'so what'? So we can't hunt anymore. The whole thing is over!"

"Don't be ridiculous," Jules said. "Did Henry Hudson have permission from the Dutch authorities to sail west when he founded New Amsterdam? *No.* Was Clara Barton following the rules when she treated wounded soldiers on the battlefields of the Civil War? *No*, she most certainly was not." Jules's voice trumpeted through the speaker. I could almost hear the sound of a marching band playing behind her, like she was in one of those movies where the coach yells about spirit and guts and the underdog team goes on to win the championship. "Did my friend Kaylee's older sister Izabelle have permission when she hacked the school's emergency contact system and sent messages to every high school family canceling school for the day so all the kids could go to Coachella? That's right, she didn't. Because people who do great things don't ask for permission. They just do the great thing, no matter what." Jules paused, her voice still ringing in the air.

Do the great thing, no matter what. Fair or not fair. Rules or no rules.

Just like nobody ever asked me if I wanted diabetes, nobody ever offered to wrap up the *Golden Lion* payroll with a big red ribbon and dump it in my lap. There was nothing I could do about diabetes, but there was something I could do about the treasure. I could go back to the place where I knew it was buried…*and take it.*

"Blue, are you really going to let a creep like Fitz tell you what you can't do?" Jules asked.

"That's exactly what she's going to do."

Dad. Who was standing in the doorway. And had heard Jules's whole speech.

"Right, Blue?" Dad asked. Even though we both knew it wasn't really a question.

This was it—I could feel it: my do-the-great-thing moment. I slid off the bed and stood as straight and tall as I could, facing Dad with my hand on Otis's ruff for courage.

"No, Dad. Not right. Our family searched for years and years and years—and now Fitz gets to keep the treasure just because of some permit? We already know exactly where to look—find the ballast, find the ship, remember? Besides, Fitz might not even see us there. And even if he does see us, by the time he tries to do anything or call anybody, we'll have found it. We just need *one* last day to go get it." I let go of Otis's ruff. In my head the marching band was playing for me now. "Think of it like civil disobedience! Let's stand up for what's right."

Dad's mouth hung half-open, which I took as a good sign.

"*Please*. One day is all we ask."

Dad squeezed the bridge of his nose, and his head bobbed from side to side like two debate teams were competing for the nationals in there. Finally, the match ended and he announced the winner:

"*One* day," Dad agreed, then added, "As long as it's okay with Mom."

And it was like that moment in *The Wizard of Oz* when Dorothy lands in Oz and the movie goes from black and white to color, except without the evil flying monkeys and the witch with the green face.

I wrapped my arms around Dad and hugged him as hard as I could. He hugged me back just as hard. "Thank you," I whispered.

Dad let me go. "When you get off the phone with Jules, come downstairs so we can go over your plan as a family."

"Absolutely," I said.

"A benevolent dictatorship family, not a democracy family," Dad said. "Where your mother and I are the dictators, and you are the oppressed citizen."

"Agreed," I said.

Dad left.

"You know," Jules said from the speaker, "if you did more of that at school you might actually get some decent grades."

I'd promised no more secrets. Which meant there was still one thing I had to do before getting everything ready for tomorrow.

I found Mom folding laundry on the dining room table. "Can I talk to you for a minute?"

"Absolutely. As long as you fold at the same time."

Mom handed me a T-shirt, still warm from the dryer. I laid it flat on the table, smoothed out the wrinkles.

"I've been thinking..." Tucked in one sleeve, then the other. "I've been thinking that I want to get a CGM."

Mom paused for just a fraction of a second and then shook out a dish towel. "You sure?"

"Yeah." Which was true.

"What changed your mind?"

I half shrugged. "You were right." Which was also true. "Otis can't be on sniffing duty all the time anymore. He needs backup...and I do too."

Mom looked up from the towel she was so carefully folding into thirds. There were tears in her eyes. "C'mere." She opened her arms and I stepped inside.

CHAPTER THIRTY-SIX

True Fact: Everybody should get to tell their own story.

By seven forty-five the next morning I'd loaded the Mako with provisions and an airlift pump. I'd even scrubbed three weeks' worth of dirt and gunk off the boat. And I had Nora's letters tucked in my shorts pockets so she would be with me today, no matter what happened. I promised myself—and Nora—that as soon as the hunt was over, I'd write and tell her everything. No matter how many trees I had to kill to do it.

We were 100 percent totally ready to go. Dad had to be at a job site to make sure the foundation of a house got poured right, but he promised to take a break for a couple of hours at lunch and meet us on the water later.

At eight thirty Jules still wasn't at my house. She wasn't there at eight forty-five either. Meanwhile, our one day to search was leaking away like air from a bike tire with a nail in it. I texted. I called. Nothing.

And then, finally, at 9:03, while Otis and I were eating microwavable mac and cheese on the front porch, Ed's black SUV swung into the driveway. Ed, Anna, and Jules got out. Ed had a fancy video camera in his hand, Anna was patting sunscreen on her cheekbones with her fingertips, and Jules's eyes were doing that laser thing where they got fierce and squinty, and it seemed totally possible that they could incinerate things.

"Hey there, Blue," Ed called, his *I'm irresistibly charming so just let me do what I want* smile lighting up his face. "Anna and I thought it would be fun if we came along with you and Jules. Get some exciting action shots on the big day."

Jules shook her head like Otis does after a swim and mouthed *NOOOO*.

I searched for a good reason why I could tell Jules's father he wasn't allowed to accompany his daughter and her friend on a possibly dangerous mission that involved boats and evil billionaires. Come to think of it, why wasn't Ed with Fitz right now? The movie was supposed to be about Fitz, not us.

"Um...I don't think my parents would want me to be in a movie, Mr. Buttersby." I felt proud of myself. Maybe I

281

was getting good at the whole finding-convincing-excuses-on-the-spot thing. It helped when they were true.

"Don't worry," Anna said. "Ed checked with your dad already."

Maybe not. But either way I was positive Ed had lied. No way would Dad have agreed without checking with me first.

"Besides," Ed said, "don't you want to be famous?" Without waiting for an answer, he motioned for all of us to follow him and headed around the house toward the backyard. "This way, right?" he said to me.

Anna clapped her hands. "Come on, Otis!"

Otis ignored her and waited for me to give the go-ahead before we caught up with Jules by the side of the house, next to the piles from the basement.

"What's going on?" I whispered. "He's lying about my dad, right?"

"Of course he's lying." Jules was so mad I could see the muscles bulging in her jaw. "He talked to your dad this morning—"

"My dad said he was calling him yesterday," I interrupted.

"Well, he didn't until today," Jules said. "Whatever. *The point is,* your dad told my dad about the *ballast.*"

Which explained how Ed knew today was the big day

and why he'd want to be there if—*when,* I reminded myself—
we found the treasure. The death-drop ride was back in my
chest again.

"There's more." Jules pulled me close to her by my
T-shirt. She lowered her voice. "After he got off the phone
with your dad, my dad called Fitz and told *him* about the
ballast."

Whoosh...boom.

"Why would he do *that?*" I said, my voice cracking.
But what I meant was *When did Ed turn into an evil
overlord?*

"He's trying to make the movie more exciting," Jules
said. "It's all he really cares about."

Her eyes weren't laser-ish anymore. They were just sad.

Otis licked Jules's hand, and she squatted down and
scratched him behind both ears at the same time. Otis,
who is not only an expert blood sugar sniffer but also an
expert sadness sniffer, gave Jules a long, wet sympathy
lick on her face. Which Jules didn't even complain about.
She hung her head for a few seconds, and when she stood
up, the laser eyes were back.

"Stop!" she yelled at Ed and Anna.

They turned around, confused.

"What's wrong?" Ed said.

"Everything!" Jules said, marching toward them with

Otis and me bringing up the rear. "Stop means no. As in, *no*, you can't come with us. This is our thing and you can't take it over and make it your thing like you always do."

"Girls." Ed smiled at us and only us. "I promise you, I'm not taking anything from anybody. You two are heroes! You're stars! You're the underdogs fighting the corporate titan."

"You're doing that thing again," Jules said, pointing a finger at Ed's chest.

"What?" Ed said.

"Telling the story your way. Blue and I aren't heroes or underdogs—we're just us. Blue and Jules. Not Ed and Blue and Jules."

"Babe, this movie's got everything. It's going to be huge. There's plenty of room for everybody. For Blue, you, me, Anna—" Ed and Anna shared a lovebird-ish look. Gross.

Jules shook her head. *No no no no no.* "There's no such thing as *everybody* with you, Dad. There's only *you*." She clenched her fists into tight balls of anger. "How could you even have agreed to produce this thing in the first place?"

"Hey, I had no idea you were involved when I signed on. Maybe if you hadn't kept it a secret—"

"That's not even the point!" Jules interrupted. "As soon as you found out, you should have dropped it. Fitz Fitzgibbons is a *bad person*, and you picked *him* over *me*."

Ed's smile dimmed, and suddenly he was the dad in line at Harbor Burger before the crowd got hold of him and switched his Hollywood star back on. He opened his arms to Jules. "Jules...Julie, honey, you *know* why this documentary is so important to me."

Jules took a step back. "And you know why this treasure hunt is so important to *me*. For once I want to be somebody other than Ed Buttersby's daughter."

"What are you talking about? You're much more than my daughter. You're..." Ed did a swirly thing with his hands in the air. "You're you. Anyway, I *promise* it's going to be okay this time."

"*No,*" she said. "It won't."

Ed let out a huge sigh. And then the Hollywood star switched on again, but this time he was the villain in a horror movie. "Let's go. Move. Now."

Ed pushed Jules, Otis, and me ahead of him and Anna so they could keep an eye on us, and he herded us to the dock.

"I tried," I whispered to Jules.

"I know," she whispered back. "I tried too. We failed, but we totally tried."

At the dock, Jules climbed onto the Mako and started untying stuff. Otis jumped after her.

I tried one more time. "The ballast is fake," I said to Ed.

285

"Your dad didn't seem to think so," Ed said.

Jules turned on the engine; I got on the boat. Anna started climbing on after me.

"Okay, look this way, girls."

I turned toward Ed, who had the fancy video camera on his shoulder—and almost lost my balance when Jules revved into reverse and pulled out. Anna, who had one foot on the dock and one foot on the boat, fell into the water.

Which was really bad for her. Because of all the jellyfish.

Anna screamed a word that sounds like "shih tzu" but isn't "shih tzu." Ed screamed something even worse. Otis woofed a victory bark.

"Take the wheel," Jules said. She picked up a wooden scrub brush that I'd left on the seat and hurled it at Ed, knocking the camera off his shoulder and into the water.

"JUUULES!" Ed yelled.

"Nice shot," I said.

"No, it wasn't," she said. "I was aiming for his head."

CHAPTER THIRTY-SEVEN

True Fact: The only predator that can kill a great white shark is a human. (TF supplied by the online article "Famous Shark Attacks in the Hamptons.")

Forget the five-mile-an-hour-inside-the-cove speed limit. I gunned the engine.

Jules tidied up the dock ropes with the efficiency of a navy commander.

"Do you need a snack or insulin or anything?" she said, tossing a freshly coiled line into the storage locker.

"Nope, I'm good." I'd tested and eaten right before Jules got to my house. "You good?"

"I'm good. Let's do this."

We zoomed past the marina, and I prayed to Lara Croft and Indiana Jones that Laurie wouldn't see us speeding and arrest us.

The adventure gods heard my prayers. We made it to the water-bottle buoy with nobody coming after us.

Which would have been great if someone else hadn't gotten there first.

Fitz.

And the Fitzminions. And the *Windfall*, which looked gigantic even from fifty feet away, especially since we were at sea level and the *Windfall*'s deck was twenty feet higher. They'd rigged a diving platform off the side of the boat, and the crew were on it, with Fitz barking orders from above. One guy was lowering a big grid-shaped net down to another guy who was treading water in full scuba gear. The submarine drone bobbed next to a huge white inflatable dinghy.

Fitz must have decided to come look for the ballast pile himself after Ed told him what we'd found. The water-bottle buoy floated next to us—Fitz and the minions probably thought it was just garbage, if they'd noticed it at all.

"They're not even looking at us," Jules said. "Let's get started. How do you work this thing? It looks like R2-D2 had a baby with a giraffe."

She wasn't wrong. "This thing" was the airlift pump that Dad and I had rigged out of an air compressor, some PVC tubing, and one of Mom's garden hoses (Dad is a big believer that with a couple of rolls of duct tape, you can make pretty much anything). The idea was that Jules and

I would lower the tube down to the sea bottom, and the compressor would create a vacuum so it slurped up all the sand and mud, and hopefully uncovered one of the most famous missing treasures in the world. Assuming the treasure was even there. And the hose didn't leak. And the compressor was strong enough. And we didn't mess up. And Fitz didn't chase us away. And Ed didn't find us.

"Have you ever used a vacuum?" I asked Jules.

She rolled her eyes. "What do you think?"

Of course not. "You just push the end of the tube around the sandy bottom. We'll take turns. I'll go first so you can see how it works."

I slid the PVC tube off the side of the boat and lowered it hand over hand deeper into the water. When I felt the tube hit bottom, I stopped. The tube was just long enough for me to hold the end and still have enough leverage to drag it.

"Okay," I said. "Turn on the airlift."

"Mutant robot giraffe baby activated," Jules said.

The tube vibrated in my hands. Pretty soon there was a whirring, whooshing, glug-glugging noise as it sucked up sand and rocks. I stayed in one spot for a few seconds and then moved the tube a couple of inches to a new spot. The sand and rocks spewed out the top of the tube and splashed back into the water. If there were coins or any other lightweight treasure mixed in with the ballast, eventually they'd come up too.

I gave Jules the tube, and I anchored and then rigged a towel awning for Otis while she vacuumed. We traded off every few minutes when our arms got numb, not talking much because of the motor noise and also because if I'd opened my mouth the only thing that would have come out was:

Please, please, please, please, please!

Or maybe:

Come on, come on, come on, come on, come on!

Or possibly:

Now, now, now, now, now!

The motor got louder. At first I thought maybe the air-lift was overheating, but then I realized the new sound wasn't coming from our boat. It was coming from another boat about forty feet away and headed straight for us.

"Whatever happens—" I said.

"We *don't* stop vacuuming," Jules said, handing me the tube.

I squinted in the glare of the sun. The other boat was the *Windfall*'s massive dinghy, a gleaming speedboat with Fitz and some minions aboard. Images of great white sharks flashed before my eyes.

Fitz raised a bullhorn over his head and blared it three times—*HONK! HONK! HONK!*—and then, "Attention,

Mako! Attention, Mako!" *HONK! HONK! HONK!* "Mako! Clear the area!" *HONK! HONK! HONK!*

By now Fitz was close enough for us to see his navy polo shirt, his Pimientos cap, and the big gold medallion that gleamed around his neck. Nearness didn't stop him from using the bullhorn, though.

HONK! "I repeat, clear the area. *Now!*"

"Jules..."

She shot me a look. "Stand our ground, remember?"

I thought about that awful night at Harbor Burger and channeled my inner Otis, the one who deflected an entire restaurant of people through the force of his determination.

"You're right." I straightened my spine and imagined flashes of electric power sizzling out the top of my head. "We haven't come this far to get bullied by a stuck-up blockhead with a dumb hat."

Jules grinned. "Exactly."

CHAPTER THIRTY-EIGHT

True Fact: ALMOST. ISN'T. GOOD. ENOUGH.

"Girls! Are you listening to me? I said leave! *NOW.*" Fitz's boat was fifteen feet away, and yet he was still using that stupid bullhorn.

HONK!

"Inside voice, please," Jules said, like Fitz was a first grader horsing around during story time.

Fitz's eyes bulged. I mean, literally actually bulged. The rest of the crew kind of shrank away from him. But then Fitz pulled himself together and smirked.

"I called the Coast Guard and they're on their way."

"Blue," Jules said. "I think it's my turn with the airlift, isn't it?"

"Why, yes, Jules." I passed her the tube. "Yes, it is."

We may have sounded cool, but there were fireflies

zooming between my ears, all wearing little Coast Guard uniforms.

"Go ahead," Fitz said. "Whatever you suck up belongs to me."

"I don't think so, Mr. Fitzgibbons," said a voice I couldn't believe was mine. "We found it; we keep it. Plus, that payroll belonged to my ancestors." Maybe. Or maybe they stole it, but either way it definitely didn't belong to Fitz Fitzgibbons.

"So, actually, anything *you* suck up belongs to *her*," Jules said.

Fitz smiled a new smile. I didn't like this smile. It reminded me of Curtis Chesterman, the kid in third grade who liked to pull wings off moths and light caterpillars on fire.

"Little girls, let me explain the situation so you'll understand. According to our federal government, my two permits mean I'm the finder *and* the keeper."

Which was what Laurie and Marisol and Dad had been saying, but I hadn't understood. Until now.

My heart started a slow crawl south.

"Ignore him," Jules whispered. "He's lying."

"But if he's right, we're doing his work for him!" I whispered back.

The only thing worse than Fitz finding the treasure

was Jules and me finding the treasure and handing it over to him. Fitz would invent a whole new smile for that moment of victory.

A distant hum grew to a roar: another boat, one with an American flag flying from its mast and the words U.S. COAST GUARD emblazoned on its side. A Coast Guard officer wearing mirrored sunglasses like a state trooper (which made her look super cool) stood on the deck. Along with Mom and Dad, who were signaling their worry like beacons.

Mom looked over at Fitz and frowned. Dad looked like he wanted to commit a—what was the word?—a *felony*.

"Are you all right?" Mom yelled across the water.

I nodded. Even though I wasn't.

"The Coast Guard called us," Mom said, answering my unspoken question.

"What took you so long?" Fitz said, not into the bullhorn for once. "These kids have been here forty-five minutes already. What are my tax dollars paying for?"

The Coast Guard woman kept her cool. "I'm Officer Charlotte Dalvito. What seems to be the problem, sir?"

Fitz explained to everybody how Jules and I were trespassing and attempting to steal what was rightfully his, which was apparently something called super-huge grand larceny, and how Officer Dalvito needed to arrest us right this second.

Officer Dalvito pulled a walkie-talkie off a clip on her waistband. "I'm going to need a few minutes to look into this with my commander, sir."

Which was when Ed and Anna chugged up on an old lobster boat they must have borrowed out of desperation. Because it was really important that as many people as possible should see me completely and totally fail.

Jules: holding the airlift, laser eyes aimed at the sludge glug-glugging out the top of the airlift. Me: my heart somewhere near my feet. Otis: dozing under a towel awning. Mom and Dad: gripping the rail of the Coast Guard boat like they wanted to jump it and swim for us. Anna: fresh from a costume change with a big red jellyfish sting on her arm. Ed: purple with fury.

"Jules Buttersby, I need to talk to you *right now!*" Ed pointed at the deck of the lobster boat like he expected Jules to somehow float over the water and appear in front of him so he could yell at her up close, but Jules refused to tear her eyes away from the sludge.

Meanwhile, Officer Dalvito wasn't giving Fitz what he wanted fast enough. Fitz yelled, "Ed, get your kid out of my water *or I'll take her out myself!*"

Ed froze. Then turned to face Fitz, slowly, like a jewelry-box ballerina with the motor running low. *"What did you say?"*

"I said"—Fitz stretched the word "said" so it had three

syllables instead of one—"get your kid out of my water or *I will take her out myself.*"

A whole story played out on Ed's face: first anger, then doubt, then sadness, then horror. For once, I was sure he wasn't acting, because after the story ended, Ed reached both arms out toward Jules and said, "You were right about everything. I never, ever, ever should have signed on to this movie. Can you please forgive me?"

Jules, her hand still on the airlift, started to cry. "Of course, Daddy."

It was like the rest of us had disappeared. The hunt was forgotten; the boats were back on their moorings.

Until my dad broke the spell.

"Fitz Fitzgibbons! *What are you doing with my father's coin around your neck?*"

Dad, who was on the Coast Guard boat, was closer to Fitz than me. I used the binoculars to zoom in on Fitz's medallion. Gold, about the size of a half-dollar with the letters *V-O-C* on it.

Pop Pop's coin!

"Ha!" Fitz sneered. "I bought it from an antique dealer who said you told him some story about how it's been in your family for three hundred years and your father thought it might be part of the *Golden Lion* payroll. When one of my guys found your last name in the ship's log, I had my people analyze the area."

Wait. Fitz only knows about the treasure because Dad sold Pop Pop's coin? I staggered back a step like the news was a bullet to my gut. Across the water, Dad turned pale. We locked eyes. I could see the sorry in his; I don't know what he could see in mine.

Fitz patted his chest. "Best two hundred bucks I ever spent."

I wanted to tear the coin off Fitz's neck and strangle him with the chain. But Dad stayed calm. A scary calm. Still looking at me, he said, "My daughter has a right to be here. My family lives here. I work in Sag Harbor, I pay taxes in Sag Harbor—"

"Oh yeah?" Fitz said. "That's very touching. You can leave now and I won't press charges against your daughter and her little friend."

That did it.

"Now look here, you blowhard, inheritance-stealing, city idiot!" Mom put her hand on Dad's arm, but Dad was just getting started. "You can't waltz in here—"

"Enough!" Ed boomed, and everybody hushed. Years of star power went into that boom. "Fitzgibbons, are you threatening my daughter?"

"Yes!" Fitz smashed his bullhorn on the wheel, where it broke into pieces. "You better believe that's what I'm doing!"

Ed gripped the rail of the lobster boat and leaned

forward as far as he could without going overboard. "Well, think again, because if you don't back off, I'm tanking your movie."

"Ed?" Anna said.

"Dad?" Jules dropped the airlift but I caught it before it hit the deck.

"What do you mean, tanking my movie? And it's your movie too!" Fitz shouted.

"Not anymore." Ed grinned at Jules. "I'm out. And if you don't lay off my kid, I'll make sure it never gets made. I've got a lot of friends in this business. So *back off.*"

Maybe it was my imagination, but the mud glug-glugging through the airlift started glug-glugging a little faster.

Fitz threw what was left of the bullhorn on the deck and roared. He flung everything he could get his hands on into the water, at his crew, at us. "Ram that boat!" he commanded the crew guy at the wheel.

Jules and I shared a look of horror. He meant *our* boat.

"No way!" the crew guy said.

"Then I will!" Fitz pulled the crew guy out of his seat, grabbed the wheel, and shoved the throttle. The dinghy sped toward us like a great white shark, flesh gleaming, mouth gaping. Huger and huger, louder and louder, closer and closer . . .

Mom, Dad, Ed, and Anna were shouting. Officer Dalvito

tried to calm everybody down by waving her arms and yelling things nobody could hear.

Slam! The *Windfall* dinghy smashed into us and the Mako heeled over, hanging half out of the water for endless seconds, teetering on its edge where no boat should ever be.

"We're going to capsize!" Jules yelled.

The Mako was inches away from flipping and trapping us underneath.

"Jules! Otis!" I yelled.

Otis howled from under the towel awning, where he was tangled in rope and cloth. Jules screamed. I screamed.

Slam! The Mako swooped back down.

Miraculously, I still had hold of the airlift, and it was still glug-glugging. *But Fitz was climbing over the side of his boat to board ours.*

"GET AWAY FROM MY DAUGHTER!" Ed shouted.

Officer Dalvito swerved the Coast Guard boat in our direction. Otis thrashed and growled under the towel.

"Jules! Help Otis!" I said.

Fitz climbed over the stern rail of the Mako. Jules fumbled with Otis's towel while he pitched and barked, desperate to be free.

I threw a glance over my shoulder. Mom, Dad, Ed—they were all too far away to protect us.

We're on our own.

I tightened my grip on the airlift pump, bracing myself for Fitz's attack. Jules gave up on untangling Otis and grabbed a boat hook. She waved the long pole in front of her like a Jedi knight and yelled, "Get back!" which would have been much scarier if the boat hook actually had a sharp end. Fitz snatched the boat hook and flung it into the water.

He lunged for Jules.

Which happened to be the exact moment that Otis shook himself free.

In an act of fearsome bravery that was glorious to behold, eighty pounds of fur and fangs flew the length of the Mako—jaws wide, claws out, fur puffed to twice his usual size.

OTIS.

My furious German shepherd landed fully on top of Fitz and tackled him to the deck.

"Call him off!" Fitz begged.

Not a chance. Not for a single *second.*

The airlift tube sent vibrations up my arm.

"Jules," I said. *"Jules."*

"What's wrong?" she said, turning back to me.

"Feel this," I said.

She put her hand next to mine on the airlift tube, where the glug-glugging had turned to click-clacking.

Her eyes went wide. "What the...?"

"Something's coming up," I whispered.

The shouts and growls faded away. There was only the sun on my bare head, the smell of Jules's French sunscreen, the vibration of the tube in our hands.

Click.

Officer Dalvito turned off the motor on the airlift.

"I'm sorry, girls. I really am. I think you deserve to keep searching, but the law is on this—this—" Officer Dalvito jerked a thumb in Fitz's direction. "This *person's* side."

"No!" I shouted. "You don't understand. We just need five more minutes!"

"One more minute!" begged Jules.

Otis released Fitz and came to stand beside me and Jules.

Officer Dalvito shook her head. "I'm sorry."

Jules scrambled for the power button, but Officer Dalvito stopped her. *"No."*

I grabbed Jules's hand, and we squeezed so hard I thought our bones would break.

"This can't be the end," I whispered. "Can it?"

CHAPTER THIRTY-NINE

True Fact: Sometimes being right feels wrong.

"Come on, Belly," Dad said from the Coast Guard boat, which was now alongside the Mako. "Let's go home."

I shook my head. "No."

"Blue, you heard Officer Dalvito. It's over," Mom said.

"She didn't say we have to leave. She just said we had to stop searching," I said, trying to keep the wobble out of my voice. "Right, Officer Dalvito?"

"Right, Blue," she said.

"Then I'm staying." I crossed my arms in front of my chest so no one would see my hands shake. "I want to be here when Fitz Fitzgibbons finds our family's inheritance right where I showed him to look."

"I'm staying too," Jules said. She put on her sunglasses, the ones that hid half her face.

Otis sat on my feet.

And that settled it.

Officer Dalvito accompanied Fitz back to the *Windfall*—Fitz's "Talk to my lawyer!" loud and clear even without his bullhorn—and Mom, Dad, and Ed joined Jules, Otis, and me on our boat (Anna went home to take an oatmeal bath). A few minutes later, Officer Dalvito left on the Coast Guard boat, the *Windfall* moved their search area to ours, and we moved about ten yards out of their way.

It was pretty crowded on the Mako. Jules and I sat side by side in the well with Otis stretched across our laps. Mom and Dad shared the seat at the wheel, and Ed perched on the side of the boat. Nora's letters crinkled in my pockets. She was here too.

Jules and I had been wrong. It didn't take one minute or five minutes for Fitz to find the wreck. It took twelve.

When Fitz's divers sent up the first video image, he and the rest of the crew whooped and high-fived and slapped one another on the backs with joy.

Jules pressed her hands over her ears. I hung my head between my knees and stared at the deck.

"Right under your shot buoy," Mom said.

"Blue put all the clues together." I could hear pride in Dad's voice. "Three centuries of Broens couldn't figure it out, but Blue's the one who found it."

I looked up. "And Jules," I said.

"And Jules," Dad agreed.

"But now Fitz will get all the glory," Jules said, burying her hands in Otis's ruff.

"Not if I can help it," Ed said, coming over to rub Jules's back. "You two did the work that matters, and I'm going to make sure everyone knows."

Maybe that should have made us feel better, but it didn't. My tears weren't the only ones dotting Otis's fur.

I didn't deserve Dad's pride in me. I'd found the treasure for Fitz Fitzgibbons. Not for Pop Pop. Not for Dad. For Fitz.

Sorry and angry twisted into a fiery ball that smoldered in my stomach. Any second now, Fitz was going to find three million florins of gold, silver, and copper.

Hours crawled by while divers dug out the wreck. Every so often we'd hear Fitz announce another find: "A cup!" "Look at that—a hammer!" And once, "Is that a barrel? Bring it up. Let's see what's inside!"

On the Mako, nobody smiled and everybody spoke in near-whispers. It was like being at a funeral reception. Which made sense because it was sort of true—something had died, even if that something was a dream.

Sometime around midday, Ed called one of his assistants and asked them to motor over with lunch. I gave my roast beef sandwich to Otis.

"How about we head back?" Mom suggested again. "You don't have to keep watching this torture."

I looked at Jules. The sun was beating down on us, and our backs were stiff and sore from sitting on the deck for hours. But we didn't even have to say a word to know we agreed.

"We're staying," we said together.

More hours passed, and more finds emerged from the wreck. But the *Windfall* got quieter as the sun headed toward the horizon, and eventually the cheering stopped.

Silence.

And then a scream: *"WHAT???"*

Jules rose up onto her knees. "What's going on?"

Mom, who'd been watching the *Windfall*, lowered the binoculars and smiled. "I don't know for sure, but I believe the *Golden Lion* payroll is officially *not* at the bottom of Gardiner's Bay."

We all gaped at her.

"Ha!" Ed snorted.

"What's so funny?" Dad asked.

"Oh, nothing much," Ed said. "I just happen to know how many—*many*—millions of dollars Fitz spent on his search, that's all."

Everybody was on their feet now, talking, laughing, shaking their heads. Everybody except me and Jules.

Otis snuggled into our laps, and I stroked his shiny black head, listening to the small quiet voice inside me grow louder.

Still out there.

Still out there.

Still out there.

Still out there.

CHAPTER FORTY

True Fact: "Treasure" can mean a lot of different things.

Back home that night I found Dad in the basement, rummaging through a big pile of family castoffs.

"You okay?" I asked.

"Sure, Belly. Just looking for something."

He set aside a bag of Christmas tinsel and dragged away a pair of rusty andirons before pulling out an old cardboard cigar box with ROSE-O-CUBA printed in red ink on the top.

Dad blew off some of the dust. "This is where I kept all my really important stuff when I was growing up. There's something I want to show you." He opened the lid and sifted through the contents. "Here."

He handed me a long brown rock.

I examined it. "What's this?" I asked.

"Treasure," he said with a half smile. "I found it one

day on the boat with Pop Pop when I was a kid. There we were, facedown in shallow water, looking through our view buckets, and all of a sudden I saw something sparkle. It was the sun bouncing off the mica, but we didn't know that until later."

I turned the rock over, shifting it this way and that, trying to catch the light.

"Take my word for it," Dad said. "On a sunny day, you'd swear it was pure gold. And the shape—"

Shiny and flat. "Like a bar," I said.

"So you get why Pop Pop and I were pretty excited. He'd been hunting for gold his whole life, so it was a big deal that he let me be the one to swim down for it. As soon as I grabbed it, I knew."

"You knew it was just a rock?" I said.

Dad shook his head. "The opposite. I knew we'd finally struck gold. I could see it all playing out in my head, like one of those movie montages: Pop Pop and me salvaging the ship with all its cargo still on board, the newspaper headlines: 'Local Father and Son Find Haul of the Century!' I swam back to the boat one-handed, holding the rock over my head, screaming, 'Dad! Dad! Dad!' at the top of my lungs. Pop Pop leaned over the side, and I know it sounds sappy, but his eyes shined brighter than gold ever could. He took the treasure from me so I could climb aboard." Dad stopped and pursed his lips.

"What happened next?" I asked.

He sighed. "By the time I got my legs over, I could read it in his face. Our gold bar was just a rock."

"Oh wow," I said. "You must have been really upset." Poor Dad. To think he'd found the treasure and all that must have meant—fame, fortune, finally being able to spend time with his father on dry land—and then to find out it was just a rock.

"I *should* have been upset, but I wasn't. Before I could get out a word, Pop Pop held it up and said, 'They don't call it fool's gold for nothing,' and we cracked up laughing. After that, we sat in the well, taking turns catching the light with our fool's gold, talking about all the things we'd do when we found the real thing."

Dad took the rock back from me and turned it over in his hand. "I haven't thought about that day in a long time. It was a good day. Maybe our best day."

"Dad?" I said quietly.

"Yeah, Belly?"

"How disappointed are you that we didn't find the treasure today?"

"Not very. I'm very *un*-disappointed that Fitz *didn't* find the treasure." He smiled down at me and sighed. "I'm so proud of you, Belly, that I can't feel disappointed about anything. Pop Pop would be proud of you too."

Dad said "Pop Pop" and "treasure" like nothing weighed

those words down anymore, like saying them made him happy.

"There's a full moon tonight," I said. "Do you think there's enough light outside to make the rock sparkle?"

"We can try," Dad said.

We went upstairs and out to the back deck. The moon hung huge and heavy in the sky. Dad held up the rock, tilted it this way and that, and we waited for an explosion of glitter.

"You see anything?" Dad asked.

I leaned my head on his shoulder and he wrapped an arm around me. "Nope," I said.

"Me neither," Dad said.

Which was fine with both of us.

CHAPTER FORTY-ONE

True Fact: Different can be okay. Sometimes it can
even be good.

A few days later, Jules and Otis waited outside the dressing room at the surf shop while I tried on bathing suits.

"How was dinner with your dad last night?" I asked
through the curtain.

"Good," Jules said. "We went to the seafood place on
the water down the road from you, and he didn't sign a
single autograph the entire time."

Whoa.

"Was Anna there?" I wriggled a red suit up my legs.
Too small.

"They broke up. She told my dad she was 'sick of all
the drama.' "

I could hear the air quotes Jules put around that last

part. "Anna actually said that?" I picked up another suit option off the floor.

"Yup. The drama queen herself." Jules paused. "Blue? He said he was sorry. He said he never should have tried to take over the hunt, and that he knows he can be a total jerk sometimes."

Wow. I struggled to find the right words. "That's—"

"A miracle. I know," Jules said.

I opened the curtain. Jules took in my blue-and-silver-striped bikini, the insulin pump clipped to the waistband, the infusion set with its dangly tube like a small jellyfish on one side of my belly button... and the brand-new continuous glucose monitor sensor like a translucent sand dollar on the other side.

Jules whistled. "Like a cyborg Lara Croft."

"Just letting my diabetes flag fly," I said.

She held up her hands like a picture frame and eyed my devices. "We can bling them with rhinestones if you want."

I swatted her hands. "One step at a time, Jules."

I paid for my new suit, and we headed over to the Long Wharf for ice cream. It took a while because a few people stopped us and asked about the wreck and how we found it and whether we had any idea where the treasure was (for the record, no).

The best part? Not one single person said the words "diabetes" or "Ed Buttersby."

Jules ordered a large waffle cone bowl of salted caramel and chocolate peanut butter with whipped cream and hot fudge. Which was most definitely not fat-free. Otis and I shared some of the sugar-free nut clusters Mrs. Alvarado makes for us.

Jules gave a piece of her bowl to Otis. "I talked to my mom last night. She got a new job."

"That's a good thing, right?" I said. "It means she's feeling better?"

"She's definitely feeling better." Jules licked fudge off her thumb.

"So what's the job?" I asked, taking another bite of nut cluster.

"She's an animator on a new movie about a princess with huge, crazy red hair," Jules said. "My mom's doing the hair."

"That's a thing? Your whole job can be to just draw hair?"

"It's totally a thing. Anyway, my mom was saying all this stuff about my dad. About how no relationship is perfect. And about how there are always compromises and disappointments, and when there's more of the bad stuff than the good stuff, it's better to end it."

I rubbed Otis's head. "So she's not sad about your dad anymore?"

"I guess not as much. But I don't know because then she started going on and on about how she's been going on dates, and I had to tell her to stop because, you know, ew."

"Totally," I agreed.

When I first met Jules, the bad stuff about her definitely seemed to outweigh the good stuff. But then I found out that she was smart and brave and loyal and fun, even if she does think that Prada is just a regular brand like the Gap.

Even diabetes isn't all bad. After all, if I didn't have diabetes, I wouldn't have met Jules.

I got out a bottle from my backpack. "Drink, Magoats?" I tipped the bottle and poured a stream of water into his mouth.

"You share that with him, don't you?" Jules said. "I mean, right now he's licking the top, and later, when you get thirsty, you're going to put your mouth right where he had his dog-germy tongue."

"Yup," I said, with zero shame whatsoever.

"That's—"

"What?" I said, trying not to smile.

Jules didn't answer. Instead, she held out her hand for the bottle, raised it to her mouth, and drank every drop that was left.

"I read recently that dog mouths have less germs than people mouths," she said.

"True Fact," I said. I already had that one in my journal.

Jules gave me back the bottle. "Listen. I want you to know it's totally okay if you keep looking for the treasure without me when I go back to California."

"Not a chance," I said, without thinking it over for even a second. Because I didn't need to.

"I *mean* it," Jules said.

I counted on my fingers: "One: I'm too busy with my science project. Two: I don't even know where to look. And three: Even if I did know where to look and had tons of free time, no way would I look without you."

"Fine." Now Jules was trying not to smile. "But you can change your mind anytime you want."

"Besides," I said, "the important thing is that we found the wreck. Right?"

"Right," Jules said. "Absolutely. Finding the wreck is the important thing."

We looked out at the harbor in silence. At the houses along the coast, the gulls swooping over the water, the waves flowing through the channel.

"Do you really believe that?" I asked, staring straight ahead.

"Nope," Jules said.

I sighed. "Me neither."

315

CHAPTER FORTY-TWO

True Fact: Before there was Otis, there was Nora.

Dear Nora,

I hope you're "on a ten" while the crew practices a scene shift or focuses the lights or whatever else it is that crew people do that I haven't been able to find on the Internet, because this is going to be one looooong letter.

There's so much that's been going on—huge, major things involving crimes (mine), evilness (not mine), and acts of bravery (mine again).

Before I get into any of that, though, I need you to know that I'm looking at a cloud right now, and it looks like a dragon cresting a tidal wave. I wonder, can you see it from where you are too?

CHAPTER FORTY-THREE

True Fact: Sometimes the tiniest, no-big-deal of a thing can turn out to be humongous.

July was almost over, which meant Jules had to go back to California so she could be with her mom for August. Also, I really did have to get started on my science project. I'd thought that maybe I could get away with not doing it after everything that had happened, but Mom said I thought wrong.

On Jules's last night, we had a sleepover at my house.

"Look at it this way," I said while we cooked chicken on the grill for dinner. "At least the ladies from the Historical Society are happy."

The wreck didn't have the *Golden Lion* payroll on it, but it did have a lot of cool artifacts that they were going to put on display. Ed said Jules could fly in for the opening of the exhibition next winter, so at least we'd get to see each other again soon. I kept trying to imagine Jules and Nora in the same room. It's possible their combined energy would set off some kind of nuclear reaction.

We played scent games with Otis and didn't talk about the treasure. We watched a documentary about exploding stars and didn't talk about the treasure. We helped Mom make flower arrangements and didn't talk about the treasure.

And then we went up to my room and talked about the treasure nonstop until we fell asleep.

I woke up at three thirty out of habit. Now that I had Otis *and* a CGM, I didn't have to test in the middle of the night anymore. My blood sugar was a steady 115. All good.

In the short time I'd been wearing the CGM, I'd learned that Otis often alerts at least twenty minutes before the CGM. And Otis will alert when I'm in the shower or swimming, where I can't see the CGM meter app on my phone. And sometimes the CGM will report a false low if I smoosh it while I sleep, but Otis reports just fine no matter how much I smoosh him, asleep or awake.

True Fact: Otis is way better than a CGM and always will be. And even when he can't be my service dog anymore, he will still be my favorite person in the world.

The iPad glowed from the floor next to my bed. I hung my head over the side.

"How come you're still awake?" I asked Jules.

"Because it's a thousand degrees in here and there's a thousand-pound fur rug on me."

My air conditioner had broken again.

"What are you looking at?"

"I found cool stuff," Jules said. "Come see."

I took my pillow and lay down next to her and Otis on the floor. Jules swiped the screen and tilted it in my direction.

"These are all pictures from a museum in Amsterdam. Check out this woman and her husband. They were painted in 1656, the same time period as your ancestors."

They wore big white stiff collars that looked like stacks of coffee filters and dark, heavy clothes. "They look so hot and itchy," I said. "No wonder Abraham and Petra came here."

Jules swiped to the next picture. It showed a whole bunch of ships in a harbor. Big waves and clouds of smoke—a sea battle. In the center, the sun cast light on the biggest ship, her sails heavy-bellied with wind, her flag—blue, white, and orange stripes—flying. Her transom painted gold and carved with a gold—

I grabbed the iPad and sat up. "Is that...?" I said.

"Uh-huh." Jules sat up too. "Look at the title."

Golden Lion.

"WHOA."

"I know!" Jules said.

"What else?"

"You'll like this one. It's really cool. It's not a painting, though." Jules took the iPad back and swiped a few times. "These are the exact kind of trunks the VOC used for their payroll. The museum has a bunch in their collection."

The photograph showed two rows of wooden trunks arranged on a platform. Some a little bigger, some a little smaller. The wood was grainy and medium brown, and the trunks were wrapped in black straps.

Even with a thousand-pound fur rug in thousand-degree heat, I got chills.

"Let me see that." I snatched the iPad out of Jules's hands. Enlarged the description. *Payroll trunks, VOC, wood and iron.*

The straps were made of metal.

Metal straps on wood trunks.

Wood and iron.

Radio static buzzed in my stomach. Otis, sensing my shift from sleepy to hyper, perked up.

"What's going on?" Jules said.

"I don't know," I said. "Maybe nothing. But we have to go to the basement to find out."

We crept downstairs without making a sound. Even

Otis managed not to thwack his wagging tail on the banister.

"Oh wow," Jules said when I pulled the string on the basement light. "You weren't kidding."

"This way," I said. "Be careful of, well, pretty much everything."

I led Jules to the creepy cobwebby crawl space. When Otis saw where I was heading, he hung back. I kneeled and cupped his cheeks.

"You're the one who found this place, Otis. You need to be with us now. Don't worry—I threw away all the mousetraps."

Otis licked my nose, which was his way of saying he'd try.

I shined my phone flashlight into the crawl space, which was just big enough for two or three people to sit but not stand in. Smooth wood and black metal straps lined the walls, floor, and ceiling.

Jules leaned inside. "What the—?"

"You see it, right?" I peeked over Jules's head. "I'm not imagining things? This wood and these black metal straps look *exactly* like the kind of wood and metal the trunks in the Dutch museum were made of."

"You're not imagining things," Jules said. "Come closer. I need more light."

Kneeling on the floor, Jules and I leaned shoulder to shoulder into the entrance to the crawl space while Otis guarded our rear against flying mousetraps. We looked in every corner. Empty.

"Let's check the boards one by one," Jules said.

I set my phone on the floor with the light pointed up. Jules took one wall, I took another, and together we pressed each board, felt every seam, our fingertips turning gray with dust. Our arms made long, wavy shadow puppets on the walls that looked like sails, luffing in a light sea wind. When we finished the walls, we moved to the ceiling.

Nothing.

We left the floor for last. Slowly, silently, we started from opposite sides and moved inward, board by board.

Until I felt something shift under my fingers.

"I think this one's loose," I whispered.

I pressed it again. It wiggled. Jules pressed the one next to it.

"This one, too," she said.

And the one next to that and the one next to that.

Four loose boards in the middle of a seventeenth-century crawl space.

The hairs on the back of my neck tickled.

I tried to pry up one of the boards with my fingers, but even though the boards were wiggly they fit so closely that I couldn't lift it.

"Hang on." I shimmied out of the crawl space and ran to the main room, where I remembered seeing a set of kebab skewers, grabbed a few, and ran back.

But before trying again, I hesitated, standing behind Jules and Otis. "We could stop right now and we'd never know for sure."

Jules yanked her head out of the crawl space and twisted around to look at me. "Are you *insane*? Why would you want to stop?"

"Because..."

I kneeled and stroked Otis's long back. Every minute of every hour of every day since Pop Pop died had led me to this moment, here, in the darkest, dampest, seventeenth-century corner of my basement. The space was full of ghosts—I could feel them trailing their feathery fingers up my arms, murmuring their secrets in my ears—and one of those ghosts was Pop Pop. We'd found Petra and Abraham's ship; now, maybe, we'd found their cargo. What would happen to all the ghosts—*to Pop Pop*—when there was nothing else left to find?

"I'm just saying that it would keep the mystery alive forever," I said. "Maybe that's not a bad thing?"

Jules held back and didn't say any of the things I know she was dying to say.

Otis nudged my shoulder. He was on Jules's side on this one. And I knew that Pop Pop would be too. I could hear his voice—his real one, from before he got sick—telling me that no matter what I found underneath these boards, the adventure we had shared would be ours forever.

Finish it for us, BB. And then go find some new mysteries of your own.

"Okay," I said. "Let's do it."

Jules looked up at the ceiling. "Thank you, Lara Croft!"

She put her hand on mine. We wedged a kebab skewer between two of the boards.

"On three," I said.

We counted together: "One...two...three!"

We pushed.

Nothing happened except the skewer started to bend.

"Use another one," Jules said.

I grabbed a second skewer and wedged it under the other side of the board.

"One—"

Crack.

The short end of the board popped up. Just a little. Just enough for me to claw my fingernails in and lever it up half an inch. Jules wriggled her hand underneath and together we pried the board out.

There was a long rectangular hole in the floor of the ancient crawl space. A wet black nose leaned in and gave it a sniff.

"Anybody in there?" I asked Otis.

Otis sneezed.

"C'mon, let's take off the other ones," Jules said.

The three other loose boards came up easily now that the first one was out. I pointed the flashlight.

We peered into a shallow hidey-hole lined with more VOC wood and metal. Inside was a sack made of raw canvas and, next to the sack, a book made of old, cracked leather. Its twin was upstairs in my living room, filled with the names of every member of my family for the last 350 years.

I reached out, my hand hovering over the sack and then the book, not sure which to take first.

"Go with your gut," Jules said.

My gut told me I'd find more questions than answers no matter what I chose. I knew what Nora would tell me to do.

I went with my heart.

CHAPTER FORTY-FOUR

True Fact: Even the oldest family secrets have a way of coming out.

I lifted the sack with two hands, careful not to jostle whatever was inside. It was heavy and half-full.

We backed out of the crawl space, and Jules and I sat on the floor knee to knee with our legs crisscrossed and the sack in my lap. Otis sniffed the sack.

I gazed around the room. Centuries of cast-off stuff made mountains around us. My family's life stories were in those mountains, those old sleds and gardening tools, picnic baskets and baseball bats and quilts and dented mixing bowls and wallpaper leftovers. Every single thing down here was chosen and used by someone related to me. Day after day, year after year, century after century.

Even now.

I took a deep breath and—

"Wait," Jules said, like I was about to touch a hot stove.

"What?" I pulled back my hand.

"What you said before, about preserving the mystery."

"Jules—" Now that I'd decided to look inside the sack, it was calling to me. Waiting felt like lying naked on top of an anthill.

"Just hear me out. Because right now there's a very real chance that what's in that bag is part of the *Golden Lion* payroll, but there's also a very real chance that what's in the bag is a bunch of seashells. What if it *is* seashells? Are you going to be okay?"

I thought about it, worrying the rough cloth between my fingers. How would I feel if I didn't find the treasure?

Rubbing the cloth made a soft scratching noise that was the only sound in the basement other than Otis's heavy breathing next to my ear and the low hum of something electric or boiler-ish. Jules was completely still, watching me, giving me time to figure out how I was going to feel if I didn't find what I was looking for.

My stomach growled, and I did an automatic body scan. No signs of low blood sugar, not from my body or from Otis or the CGM. And that's when I knew:

I had already found what I was looking for.

I hadn't thought about diabetes once since I'd woken up to find Jules looking at the museum pictures. It's not that I was ignoring it; it was that I had so many other things to think about. Interesting, exciting, important things that mattered to me. It's what—and who—I care about, I realized, that makes me who I am.

Diabetes is something I have to live with, not something I have to be.

I looked at Jules. At her hair, which currently resembled a haystack, or a mouse nest, or maybe a mouse nest on top of a haystack. Then I looked at her pajamas, which were a pair of plaid boxer shorts and a plain stretched-out gray T-shirt, and I decided that maybe she'd found what she was looking for too.

"Let's do it," I said.

"Are you *absolutely*, positively sure?" Jules asked.

"One hundred percent." Which was 99 percent true.

Jules grinned. "I was hoping you'd say that."

I untied the drawstring on the sack, carefully, gently, like it was made of cobwebs instead of twisted yarn. I could feel Otis and Jules on either side of me, feel their unblinking eyes and shallow breaths. And then our circle widened, and it was like I could feel Nora and Mom and Dad and Pop Pop and all the Greats with us too.

I reached inside...

...and found a bunch of objects, all different sizes and shapes, each wrapped in soft fabric. My hand closed around one at random, and I pulled out something about the size of a blackboard eraser, covered in black cloth. Set it on the floor between us.

"No licking," I told Otis.

He gave me his *Who, me?* look and then hunkered down with his nose as close as it could possibly get to the thing without touching.

"Ready?" I said, locking eyes with Jules.

"*Dying,*" she said.

The cloth was rolled around whatever was inside it. I unfolded the corners. Unrolled once. Twice. Three times. I could feel the thing itself now through the cloth. It was hard. And rectangular.

I unrolled it again.

And again, one last time.

CHAPTER FORTY-FIVE

True Fact: 350 years ago, my family sailed to Sag Harbor
on a ship of gold. (TF supplied by Pop Pop.)

Sleek, solid gold winked at us in the naked-bulb basement light.

VOC

1663

There in front of us was a bar from the *Golden Lion*
payroll.

It had been buried under my very own house all this
time.

Which, when you think about it, is hilarious.

Which was why Jules and I laughed. We started out
with nervous *Really, are you sure?* giggles, then morphed into
Oh wow, I can't believe it chuckles, then picked up steam
with full-on tears-streaming, *Please make it stop, it hurts*
laughter.

Finally, we pulled ourselves together enough to notice Otis, who was baptizing the gold bar with gentle licks. Jules rescued it and dried it off with her shirt. "It's *warm*." She pressed the bar to her cheek.

"Let me feel." I took it and pressed it to my face. Jules was right. All those years snuggled up in mounds of fabric—or maybe just Otis's breath—had kept the bar warm.

"Let's see what else is in here," Jules said as she dug around in the sack. She hiccuped, still out of breath from laughing. "Maybe we'll find Dorothy's ruby slippers or the Ark of the Covenant or Amelia Earhart's airplane." She pulled out more bundles.

"Or socks from the dryer," I said. And we cracked up again.

All together there were six gold bars, two copper ones, and a small pouch of silver coins. We spread them out on the black cloths.

"Does this make us pirates?" I asked, wiping my eyes.

"It makes you the descendant of pirates," Jules said with a mock bow.

True Fact: Being the descendant of pirates is the best fun fact ever. Nora was going to love it. What would Dad say when he found out? And Mom?

The silver coins reminded me of another coin. Gold,

with the letters *V-O-C* on it. Hanging from a big ugly chain. "Jules, I think I may be a bad person," I said.

"Because your ancestors were criminals or because you're excited about picturing Fitz when he hears you found the treasure?"

I laughed again. "How did you know?"

"Duh," Jules said.

"His face will turn purple," I said.

"He'll vomit," Jules said.

"His eyes will bulge out of his head the way they did when you told him to use his inside voice," I said, trying—unsuccessfully—to bulge my own.

"He might cry." Jules fake-swooned with joy.

"Think about the headlines!" I held up my hands. " 'Fitz Fails!' "

"I can see it now," Jules said, rising up on her knees. "Fitz picks up his morning newspaper and chokes on his nasty enzyme drink when he reads about how we completely and totally schooled him."

Jules and I took a moment to revel in our fantasy before I said, "Okay. Time to go back to being good people again."

We wrapped up all the pieces and put them back in the sack to keep them from getting scratched.

I ran my hand over one of the walls of the crawl space.

"Abraham must have used the wood from the trunks to make the paneling," Jules said.

"He was a carpenter," I said. "A good one. See how cleanly each board fits against the next? My dad says you can judge a craftsperson by their attention to details."

We admired Abraham's workmanship together. Jules brushed her fingers along the crawl space floor, stopping at the hole where the four loose boards used to be.

"Let's look in the book," she said.

I lifted the book out of the secret cubby like it was made of bird bones, which, after 350 years, it may as well have been. The cover crackled when I opened it.

> A full telling of how Bram and I came to
> be in possession of the East India Company
> Payrolle would fyll this Ledger and more.
> Know, all who read these Pages, that We dyd
> not seek these Funds, but We dyd convaye
> them here to the Village of Sagg Harbor and
> have tryde to make good vse of them synce. The
> Crew of our Ship numbered fourteen Souls
> when We left East India. (The presyse
> Locacyon of our beloved Island shall remayne
> a Secret We guard with our very Lyves,
> lest more Harm come to those few who remayne

there.) At the ende of our Journey—plagued as We were by Illness and violent Weather, pursued as We were by Enemees known and vnknown—only five remayned: Happy Jan, Jeronimo Lobo, Louis Cheval, Bram, and myself. Some Days later, Bram, Happy Jan, and Lobo retrieved our moste precious Cargo from the remaynes of our Ship, which was sunk before a houndish Rock near Mister Gardiner's Island. We called the rock Sorrowwe for the Friends We lost. We shared the Payroll amongst vs fairly and without Rancor. What follows is an Accounting of our Household's Porcyon.

Petra De Winter Broen,
Sagg Harbor, January 1669

She called him Bram.

I don't know why that was the first thing that popped into my head after I read my great-times-twelve-grandmother's story. Maybe because it made them seem like real people who had adventures and got married and gave each other nicknames, instead of old-timey people in coffee-filter collars.

So many unknowns. Petra's story was like something only Nora could have imagined. Who were these violent enemies and where was this mysterious island? Who were the friends that Petra and Bram lost? Jeronimo Lobo and Happy Jan were in the *Golden Lion* ship's log, but Petra wasn't, and I didn't remember seeing Louis Cheval's name either. I'd thought that if I found the lost payroll of the *Golden Lion*, then all my questions would be answered. Instead, I found new questions. My family stories didn't lead me where I thought they would; they led me somewhere surprising, somewhere new.

Suddenly, all the things I didn't know started to feel like possibilities instead of roadblocks. Pop Pop was right again. What's important isn't preserving mysteries; it's seeking out new ones.

I traced the page with my fingertips. Petra's writing was even and careful—nothing like mine. Some of the letters were weird shapes—her *S*s looked like *F*s—and, based on her spelling, I'm pretty sure dictionaries hadn't been invented back then. A splotch of brown showed where her pen had leaked.

Petra touched this same page I'm touching now.

"Can I see?" Jules asked, reaching out her hands.

I gave her the book, even though a selfish part of me hated letting go of it.

"Oh wow," Jules whispered as she ran her fingers along the spine. "Do you realize Petra started this book a hundred years before Thomas Jefferson wrote the Declaration of Independence?" Very gently, Jules turned the page. "The Salem witch trials hadn't even happened yet."

"What else does it say?" I asked, scooching next to her.

"It's like she said. It's a ledger."

I leaned over Jules's shoulder. The pages were lined with neat rows and columns with names, dates, amounts, and descriptions. A list of every person who'd used part of the payroll, when they used it, how much they spent, what they spent it on.

Abraham Broen, April 1666, One Gold Barre, Lumber to Bilde a House

At first the names were only Abraham or Petra. Then, as the years went on, Albertina, and then Jan. More years, more names. Never more than one or two entries during the same time period.

Josef Broen, March 1694, Ten Silver Coynes, Plough Oxen

Cornelia Broen, September 1742, Sixteen
Ounces of Copper, Linens for a Dowry

Isaac Broen, January 1781, One Gold
Piece, One Good Rifle

I could see them, my family, building and growing, dipping into the secret rainy-day funds buried under the house when they needed to buy something important or special.

Until the last entry:

Sara Broen, February 6, 1820, Two
Silver Pieces, Medicine for Fever

The rest of the pages were blank.

"What do you think happened?" Jules said. "There's more treasure here. Why didn't anybody spend it?"

"I don't know. Maybe...maybe..." I couldn't think of a reason. But there was one last place to check for information. "I'll be right back. Otis, stay with Jules."

I ran upstairs and tiptoed through the living room to retrieve the family bible. After all these years, its worn, brown cover still reminded me of the backs of Pop Pop's hands. Down in the basement, I set the bible next to the ledger. Holding these books was the closest I could get to reaching my hands through time to hold Petra's and Bram's.

I flipped through the centuries, one page at a time, careful not to tear the fragile paper.

"What's with all the Lucretias?" Jules asked in the early 1800s.

"Beats me," I said. "We can go visit them in the graveyard across the street, if you want."

We found Sara Broen on the next page, along with her husband, Peter, and their three sons. Except for the youngest son, Henry, who was born in 1816, the whole family died of fever in February 1820.

"Sara and Peter died before they could tell Henry about the treasure," Jules said.

"So Henry never knew it was here. And because Bram was such a good carpenter, nobody else in my family found it for almost two hundred years."

"Until now," she said.

We sat in silence, absorbing the whoa-ness of it all, until we heard footsteps overhead.

"What time is it?" I asked.

Jules checked my phone. "Almost seven. How is it morning already?"

The basement door opened and Dad called down, "Blue? Jules?"

"We're here!" I said.

"What are you doing down there?" Mom called.

I grinned at Jules, who grinned back. "Making history! Come and see!"

Otis woofed.

ACKNOWLEDGMENTS

A gazillion thank-yous to: Ginger Knowlton, fierce champion of Blue and Otis (and me!); Lisa Yoskowitz and Hannah Milton, editors extraordinaire; Marc Acito, we both know what you did and I'll never forget it; early readers Eliza Basch, Joy Goodwin, Emma Dryden, and Katherine Weber; and seafarers Jonathan Teller, Bruce Tait, and (pirate) Jack Nicolls. Bridget, Caroline, Ellie, and Muggsy Kahle; Sam Stern; Dorrie, Luke, and Jedi Nuttall; Frank and Quin Wisneski; and Annie Dycus: Thank you for sharing some of what it's like to live with diabetes and diabetic-alert dogs. Nick, Joe, and Maya: There'd be no Blue without you.

Jennifer Yohalem, in forty years I've never once heard you complain about diabetes, but you did bring me the milkshakes you couldn't have, back in the old days when people thought "diabetics" couldn't eat sugar, and you tested my blood sugar because I thought it was fun, and answered all my questions, and taught me everything I know about diabetes without making me feel bad about how much I didn't know. This book is for you.

ABOUT THE AUTHOR

Nicholas Polsky

Eve Yohalem is the author of *Cast Off: The Strange Adventures of Petra De Winter and Bram Broen, Escape Under the Forever Sky,* and *The Truth According to Blue.* She lives in New York City.